The
LIBRARY
MURDERS

BOOKS BY MERRYN ALLINGHAM

The
LIBRARY
MURDERS

Merryn Allingham

bookouture

Published by Bookouture in 2024

An imprint of Storyfire Ltd.
Carmelite House
50 Victoria Embankment
London EC4Y 0DZ

www.bookouture.com

ISBN: 978-1-83790-846-2
eBook ISBN: 978-1-83790-845-5

1

ABBEYMEAD, SUSSEX, JULY 1958

'I'm really proud of the design.'

Flora Steele stepped back to study the banner she'd worked on for days. She loved the corner roses in particular, their delicate tendrils floating downwards to highlight the name of her bookshop, the All's Well, beautifully clear in large black italics against a cream background.

The Abbeymead crime conference, taking place over the next few days, was an important event for the village and she'd wanted to make sure her bookstall looked the best she could make it. Basil Webb, President of the Dirk and Dagger Society and the inspiration behind the conference, had provided her with a large trestle in the school foyer, an eye-catching position. Everyone making for a seat in the hall would have to pass her table.

'What do you think, Jack?' she asked her companion. 'I'm wondering... maybe it should move slightly to the left.'

'I've just shifted it to the right,' Jack Carrington protested, 'and my arms are saying no more. I might be marrying you, Flora, but there's a limit to my devotion.'

'Just a *little* to the left? I need it to look perfectly even.'

He gave the banner the smallest tweak and, before Flora could say more, hammered in the fixing pins.

'The stall looks splendid with or without the banner.' He waved a hand at the serried rows of new books that had been delivered to Abbeymead school the previous evening.

'It does,' she agreed, 'though I do have fingers tightly crossed. I've ordered loads and I'm desperate for the Dirk and Dagger Society to bring their purses. If I don't sell, I can't return the books and when Basil showed me the delegate list, it looked a bit thin.'

Jack smoothed back the flop of hair that never sat flat. The list *was* thin and it worried him, too. 'Basil hasn't had the over-whelming response he expected.' He flexed his shoulders, trying to lose their stiffness. 'But I always thought he was too confi-dent. I've been wishing for the last few weeks that I'd never tele-phoned him after he left that message with Alice. Helping him has been hard work and completely disrupted the writing. Life would have been much easier if neither of us had got involved.'

She wrapped her arms around him, giving him a quick hug. 'Well, we did get involved, and it would have been difficult for you not to. You couldn't easily have refused – a crime confer-ence held in Abbeymead and you a crime writer living in the village.'

'It's the village that's the problem. It's too out-of-the way to attract large numbers and accommodation isn't exactly plenti-ful. Webb would have been better to have gone for a venue in south London. Somewhere in his own neck of the woods.'

'Did he say why he didn't?'

Jack gave a dismissive grunt. 'He thought it would be too suburban, too dull. He works in insurance, a fairly mundane job, it seems, and I get the sense that crime fiction gives him the adventure he craves. He's fixed on the idea that a village setting is ideal for a murder plot – shades of Christie, I imagine – so perfect for a crime conference. Abbeymead school ticked all the boxes, too. Vacant during the summer holidays, with a good-sized stage and space for plenty of seating.'

'Half a dozen local schools could have provided the same.' Flora tidied the small pile of flyers she'd had printed advertising her bookshop and looked around for the sheet she'd brought to cover the stall overnight.

'It was his sister.' Jack gave a small sigh. 'She lives in Sussex, Basil told me, and listed several villages for him, Abbeymead among them. And we were the ones to win the jackpot! Let's hope he's right. The chap is banking on this conference to revive membership of his society. Over the last few years, the Dirk and Dagger has been losing out to a more dynamic group – would you believe, the Red Herrings? Webb seems to be hoping for some kind of renaissance.'

Flora pulled a face. 'It's looking doubtful, but we're both committed now whether we like it or not – you to help organise the event and me to sell as many books as I can.'

She was trying to be practical, but if she were honest, had never felt more than lukewarm about the proposal to run any conference in Abbeymead. The project seemed fraught with difficulties, not least because of the small size of the village and its distance from any train service. Brighton or Worthing stations were the nearest and what did people do from there? Taxis were expensive and the local bus service was, well, local. But Basil Webb had needed her co-operation as the village bookseller, and she'd wanted to support Jack.

He had found himself landed in the thick of things – not so much coerced into helping, but certainly heavily persuaded. Flora knew how much it had eaten into his writing time, a cause of frustration and some worry. His agent, Arthur Bellaby, was an understanding man but a contract had been signed and there was a deadline to meet. A conference in July had meant, too, that they'd had to postpone their plans to marry. There'd simply been too much to organise – speakers, accommodation, catering – to manage a wedding as well. After that beautiful evening by the Seine when, unexpectedly, Flora had encouraged him to propose, Jack had been hugely disappointed and only brightened when she'd suggested they marry on or near his birthday in October. But how did *she* feel? Very slightly relieved at the postponement, perhaps? Then very guilty at the thought.

'We've Maud out there as an extra resource,' she said cheerfully, looking towards the school entrance and the playground beyond. 'Having the mobile library on site sends the right message – that books are for everyone. Maud will be sure to prompt people into using their local branch.'

'That's another thing. I can't for the life of me see why Basil wanted a library parked in the playground.' She had been trying to lighten his mood but Jack, it seemed, refused to be encouraged.

'Not everyone can afford new books, I get that, and it's true that authors get some payment from libraries, but Maud Frobisher runs a service for Sussex. How is that going to help someone from... I don't know... Oxfordshire?'

'It might persuade them to think libraries? Maud seems to be generating interest already. Just listen!'

An excited buzz emerging from the playground had drifted through the open door.

Jack walked over to the doorway and peered out. 'Basil must be back with his speakers. He was determined to take them for a meal at the Cross Keys, though I warned him the food was inedible. I wonder what's going on out there?'

'Something sensational,' a voice answered and a young woman slipped past him and into the reception area, her hair so dark it was almost black and caught in a long plait that hung halfway down her back. The floral dress she wore was simple, but expertly tailored.

'Rose!' Flora exclaimed. 'Of course, you're here for the opening session.'

'I am,' she answered sunnily. 'A bit early, but I was too eager to stay home and I want to make the most of my ticket. I've always been a fan of crime fiction, but I can only make two of the talks – today's and the one on Wednesday afternoon when the All's Well is closed.'

Rose Lawson, a relative newcomer to Abbeymead, had agreed to take charge of the bookshop while Flora was at the conference. Flora had been a little dubious leaving her beloved All's Well in the hands of someone she barely knew, but Rose had been working for some time at the post office under the eagle eye of Dilys Fuller, and she had decided that was good enough.

'Felix Wingrave is here!' Rose went on, her dark brown eyes alive. 'Just fancy, actually here in Abbeymead!' She turned to Jack, studying him thoughtfully. 'And I love *your* books, Mr Carrington, but you're not speaking? Not according to my programme.'

'I'm not. I thought I'd stick with the organising. Mr Webb needs a fair amount of help.'

Flora's eyebrows drew together. She knew Jack too well to believe that excuse. He would rather have chewed through his socks than give a speech from the stage.

'Do you know what's going on out there?' she asked. 'It sounds as though the mobile library is creating some excitement.'

'Surely, a first,' Jack put in drily.

'It's exciting, all right. I peeked through the window! Miss Frobisher was showing some of the writers who are speaking at the conference a book she's acquired. A very special book, and they were fascinated. Clive Slattery, you'll have his titles at the

All's Well, Flora, loved the illustrations. I saw him surreptitiously stroking the binding!'

'What's the book?' She was intrigued. 'Did you hear?'

'I did. The van door was open. Apparently, it's an illustrated first edition of *A Christmas Carol* – published way back in 1843, and with an accompanying letter from Dickens himself laid into the book! Everyone thought it must be very valuable, though I wouldn't really know.'

'Gracious. Where did Maud find the book?'

'Believe it or not, a customer donated it. Last week in Storrington when Maud was doing her round. He was a wealthy pensioner who wanted the book to go to a good home. Maud is bubbling. I've known her on and off for years and I've never seen her so delighted.'

'She must be excited. Who wouldn't be? I don't know much about old books,' Flora admitted, 'but a Dickens first edition must be worth a great deal of money.'

'The book will go to auction, Maud said, and whatever it makes will help fund the mobile service. She sounded quite indignant on how it was the poor relation among libraries and deserved a boost.'

Rose picked up her handbag and smoothed down her dress. 'I'd best be off and grab a seat in the hall before too many others arrive. I'm hoping for a really good view of the stage – the speakers already here will be introducing themselves, along with their latest books. It's bound to be interesting. But I'll be at the shop tomorrow morning, Flora, well before nine.'

'Thank you. And thank you for stepping in so willingly.'

Flora waited until her new employee had disappeared from view, before she said, 'I feel guilty about Rose. I'm sure she'll do a good job at the All's Well but I can only offer her work for this one week. The shop doesn't make enough money to employ a permanent assistant.'

'She works elsewhere in the village, doesn't she? I've seen her in the post office.'

'She has done the last month or so, but it's only until Maggie Unwin gets back. Once Maggie's arm is out of plaster, Rose will be out of a job, I imagine. And I know she needs the money. Not to mention the company – she seems quite a lonely woman.'

'Dilys Fuller might keep her on.'

'Not a chance.' Human kindness didn't fill too much of the postmistress's heart, and certainly not where her post office was concerned.

Casting a glance around the display table, Jack nodded to himself. 'I think we've done enough, don't you? You're not opening until tomorrow, and Basil has this first session under control. So, time to call it a day?'

Idly, he reached over and picked up a fat volume, sitting at the rear of the bookstall. '*The Sphinx Murders*, Wingrave's latest book. I bet Felix will be interested in Maud's find.' He pulled a face. 'He's into rare books, particularly Victoriana, and he's wealthy enough to fund his passion. Has them on display, I've heard, in the mansion he owns – which is naturally in the most expensive part of Surrey.'

Jack's grey eyes had clouded and Flora knew what that meant. 'You don't like him?'

'You don't get to like Felix. You worship him. He's far above everyone's touch, including mine. He won't be here to sell – he doesn't need to – but to soak up the adulation.'

'That's really harsh.'

'But deserved, I think. Whenever I've met Wingrave, I've found him arrogant and dismissive of other writers' work, but he has an enormous following and is regularly a best seller. He's made a fortune with his writing which, apart from this latest book, hasn't been at all good. But perhaps I'm simply envious of the man's success.'

Jack could be jealous, Flora knew. He'd reacted badly to

Richard, a former boyfriend, intruding into her life once more. But envious? On reflection, Wingrave probably deserved Jack's contempt.

'I sell quite a few of Wingrave's books,' she admitted. 'But I wouldn't say any more than yours. Jack Carrington is very popular with my customers. Is the man that famous?'

Jack gave an impatient shrug. 'Basil reckons Wingrave will be his top attraction at the conference. He's convinced he'll be the one that punters sign up to see, which rather puts me in my place. I'm actually reading this,' he said, giving the book a casual tap. 'And it's pretty good. Better than the usual Wingrave fare. He really does "churn them out", as my father would have it.'

Ralph Carrington's view of his son's literary output had rankled with Jack from the moment he'd spoken those unfortunate words, and it evidently still did.

'When you see him, you can tell Wingrave how much you're enjoying the read and make him even more arrogant!' she said laughingly. 'But you're right – we've done enough.' She readjusted her headband, pulling the waves of red-brown hair into some kind of shape. 'Let's go home and eat the steak pie I mentioned.'

'Cooked by Alice?' he asked eagerly.

'That's the one. Delivered to my door this very morning, straight from the Priory kitchen. And after Alice left, I tramped to the bottom of the garden – I hope you're suitably grateful – and salvaged a handful of carrots and a solitary cauliflower. My vegetable patch is looking a trifle poorly these days.'

'You should have asked me!' Jack teased, earning himself a small slap on the hand. Since he'd begun to take an interest in his garden at Overlay House, the competition between their vegetable patches had become intense. 'But what a brick Alice has been. Even though she's been run off her feet at the hotel, she did something I thought was impossible – persuaded half a dozen of the villagers to open their homes for bed and breakfast.

And rescued Basil from the stew he was in. There were a fair few attendees who didn't want to stay at the pub and couldn't afford the Priory.'

Alice Jenner, the best cook in Abbeymead and head chef at the Priory Hotel, owned by her niece, Sally, was a dear friend to Flora and over the last two years had become a favourite with Jack as well.

'Alice is always a brick,' Flora said stoutly.

2

Flora left her cottage earlier than usual the next morning, wheeling a reluctant Betty from her shelter. Betty did not like early mornings or appreciate a change to her routine; her pedals felt heavy and the few gears she possessed deliberately sticky as she made her way along Greenway Lane. Ignoring the bicycle's lack of enthusiasm, Flora cycled on.

Yesterday, she and Jack had left Abbeymead school well before the first speaker had finished their talk and she hadn't seen Rose Lawson again. Even though Rose lacked bookshop experience, she would be professional and efficient, Flora felt sure. She'd been heartened by the woman's promise to be at the shop well before opening time, following in Violet Steele's footsteps – Flora's aunt had always insisted the shop must be ready for business the minute the Victorian station clock, hanging from the one free wall, struck nine o'clock.

Nevertheless, an itch she couldn't explain meant Flora had decided, as she'd fallen asleep last night, to pay the All's Well a visit before she opened the conference bookstall. The bookshop, inherited from Violet several years ago, was precious. Not simply as a very old building whose beauty must be conserved, or as the means by which Flora earned her living, but as a visceral part of her very self. Everything about the All's Well – its smell – wood and vanilla – its rows of shining spines, the bright splash of book jackets, even its bookish quiet, was in her blood.

Turning off the lane into the high street, she was surprised to see Rose cycling towards her from the opposite direction and at breakneck speed. Their two bicycles arrived at the bookshop's white-painted door more or less simultaneously.

'I'm sorry I'm late, Flora.' Rose was struggling to regain her breath, the sweep of dark hair escaping from the loose bun that she'd adopted today, and falling slant-wise across her face. 'I can't believe it, but I had a puncture as I was leaving the house and had to change a tyre.'

It happened, Flora knew to her cost, but which house had Rose been leaving? She'd heard from Kate, her friend who ran the village café, that Rose Lawson had been reduced to begging a bed wherever she could, and she'd understood that at the moment it was Larkspur Cottage where Maggie Unwin also resided. But the cottage was behind Flora, lying in a completely different direction.

Shrugging the puzzle aside, she said warmly, 'It's such a nuisance when that happens, but well done for managing it so quickly.' Inwardly, she crossed virtual fingers that her new recruit would prove as reliable as she'd hoped. She was abandoning the All's Well for only a short while, but still... the bookshop was a treasure.

'I won't come in,' she said, hoping to reassure her protégée. 'I just wanted to check everything was OK with you before I went to the conference for the day.'

Rose's welcome didn't quite reach her eyes. 'Everything's fine, Flora.' Without saying more, she turned to wheel her bicycle into the cobbled courtyard behind the shop.

Flora felt dismissed, unsure whether she should feel pleased at Rose's assumption of authority or slightly affronted.

No time to feel either, she counselled herself. She had a present to deliver before opening her stall, tucked away in Betty's basket, one she'd been keeping until this moment. Maud Frobisher was due to retire at the end of the month, in time, she'd told Flora, to enjoy the rest of the summer. Attending the conference was her last big event before a whole new world opened for her, and Flora had wanted to mark the occasion.

Maud had been a good friend of Aunt Violet's, the best of friends, in fact, sharing a passion for books and a delight in auctions, and in Betty's basket there nestled a beautiful art nouveau rosewood and brass casket. The two women had competed for it at an auction they'd attended before the war and, though Violet had triumphed, she had good naturedly offered it to her friend. Maud had been shocked, Flora remembered, insisting that Violet had won the prize fair and square. Now, the jewellery box would find a new home, the one Violet had wanted it to have all those years ago.

It took only five minutes more of energetic pedalling – Betty had begun to forget her sulk – to swing right off Fern Hill and into a long tree-lined street that eventually led to the new school, built on an outlying field. Though it was hardly new, she thought drolly, since the original Victorian building had closed at least six years earlier. For many of the villagers, however, it would always be the 'new' place and thoroughly disliked.

The mobile library van was exactly where it had been parked yesterday, but the blinds were down against the early morning sun and there was no sign of Maud. That was surprising – as much as Violet had been, Maud Frobisher was a stickler for time and the first Monday session of the conference was scheduled to begin in less than half an hour. Small groups of attendees were already drifting towards the school entrance, one or two individuals wandering disconsolately away from the library having, it seemed, relinquished the idea of a visit.

And sure enough, when Flora walked across to the van, present in hand, the door was closed. Again, unusual. She knew for a fact that in summer the van could become very hot and on a day such as today, one filled with sunshine and not a cloud in the sky, Maud would leave the door open.

Gently, Flora tapped at the small square of glass set high in the door, hoping not to scare her friend if, by any chance, she'd fallen into a doze. For a woman of her age, Maud appeared always fit and healthy, but the job she did could be a challenge for someone far younger: packing and unpacking heavy cartons of books – the van's selection of reading changed regularly – and every day driving miles around a widespread county such as Sussex.

When Flora tapped again and still received no response, she tried the door handle. Another surprise! The van door swung open. Of course, she remembered, Maud had an assistant in training, a young man Flora had still to meet, and he must have arrived early, perhaps to allow his mentor a more leisurely start to her day. He would have unlocked the van in preparation for the day ahead.

'I was sixty in March,' Maud had said when Flora bumped into her in the high street a few months previously. 'More than time to leave the job. I'll be enjoying a few more auctions soon – and baking a few more cakes! But I've agreed to stay on until the end of July. It gives me a few months to train my successor.'

'I hope whoever it is will prove as hardworking!'

'Me, too.' There'd been caution in Maud's voice. 'He seems a nice enough lad. I didn't have any say in his appointment, mind, that was the council.' She grimaced. For local people, the council was the source of all things troublesome.

'A young man? That will be quite a change.' Maud had

been driving the mobile library since Flora was a child and a female librarian seemed synonymous with the service.

'He's not from Sussex either. From Bath of all places, though he's been settled here a while. He'll be OK, I guess, once I put him through his paces.'

Flora had smiled to herself. She could imagine the paces that young man was being put through.

But this morning she must be quick – by now, her bookstall in the school entrance should be open. It would be an ideal time to sell to people before they took their seats for the first speaker. She would leave the present on Maud's desk with a note, and check later that her friend had found it.

Climbing the van steps, Flora was met with emptiness. There was no assistant and no Maud. Instead, the crowded shelves lining opposite walls of the van mounted a silent guard. Finding a niche on the desk where the jewellery box would be safe, she grabbed a spare pen and Maud's notepad and bent her head to write a short message. It was as her pen began to trace the first D of 'Dear Maud' that she saw it. Saw her. Maud. Sprawled yards away, towards the back of the van, and sandwiched between the walls of bookcases.

Instantly, she dropped the pen and rushed up the aisle to reach the fallen woman. Her first thought was that Maud must have fainted but, kneeling to give what help she could, she saw a trickle of blood oozing from the librarian's head. As she'd fallen, the poor woman must have hit the outer edge of a wooden shelf. Flora jumped to her feet, her throat dry. She must get help. Immediately. The telephone, she thought wildly. There would be a telephone in the school office. She would run there and ring for an ambulance. Then ring Jack and hope to find him at home still.

But as she wheeled around to make for the door, she heard a noise. A shuffling, an uncertain footstep coming from the very rear of the van. Horrified, she watched as a figure emerged from the shadows. The figure of a man. With her nerves taut to breaking point, Flora's immediate impulse was to flee, but then common sense reasserted itself. This must be Maud's assistant, she thought confusedly. But why was he here? Why had he not rung for help?

Her frantic gaze fixed on the man's hand. He was carrying something – a book? Flora's heart tumbled. Not just a book, but one that was large and heavy and very bloodstained.

As her eyes lifted, the man raised his spare hand in greeting, then tugged furiously at blond locks, already in a state of disarray.

'Hello, Flora,' he said. 'I didn't expect to see you here.'

3

———

Lowell Gracey? It couldn't be. Flora's hands were shaking and, try as she might, she could not still them. Five years ago – the last time she'd seen him. A frantic waving of college scarves as her train to Sussex had pulled out of the station. Gracey had been a fellow student in Bath, had shared a room with Richard Frant, the boyfriend who had let Flora down so badly. She had known Lowell almost as well as she'd known Richard, a man consigned now to the margins of her life, the three of them spending many of their winter evenings together in or around the student bar.

Lowell Gracey? her frazzled mind repeated and kept repeating. It couldn't be him. But, amazingly, it was.

'She's dead, you know,' Gracey said, his voice almost truculent.

Flora gulped. She didn't know. Or rather, hadn't wanted to know, expecting, hoping, that Maud would recover consciousness and be saved.

'I felt for a pulse as soon as I saw her,' Lowell went on. 'No chance. She must have hit her head against a bookcase as she went down.'

Flora stared blankly at him, still unable to process what she was seeing. 'What are you doing here?' she said at last. 'And with that?' She gestured limply at the horrid object in Lowell's hand, not wanting to look too closely.

'I found it.' Again, the truculence in his voice was marked. 'It was beside Maud. Someone... someone used it to... kill her.'

Someone, or Gracey himself? 'But why are you here, Lowell?'

'I'm Maud's assistant. I was supposed to take her job when she retired.'

That made no sense. Gracey was a chemist, not a librarian. None of this made sense. And what was she doing exchanging pleasantries with a possible murderer? She needed to leave, needed to make telephone calls. To the police, to Jack.

She turned once more to make for the door but before she could reach it, Gracey had stepped around Maud's body and was facing her. 'I found the book,' he repeated, as though he suspected he would not be believed. 'Found it lying beside her.' He hung his head and for the first time Flora saw eyes that held doubt and some sadness.

Backing away, she asked, 'Why was Maud alone? If you're her assistant, why weren't you with her?'

'I went for a walk,' he muttered. Once more the sullenness was back. 'And while I was gone, someone paid Maud a visit. They must have come to steal and she got in the way.'

'Steal what?'

He walked past her to the final bookcase and bent to the lowest shelf. 'Look. It's gone.'

Flora had visited the mobile library numerous times over the years but had never realised there was a safe, half-concealed by a crowded row of books. Now, she saw it plainly – its door yawned wide.

'The rare book,' he went on. 'The Dickens that Maud was going to sell. It's gone. I told her she shouldn't keep it in the van.

Told her she should store it at County Hall until it went for auction, but she always knew best. "If I don't leave it here, I'll take it home." That's what she said. "Those blighters at County Hall are philistines. They won't know its value and won't look after it properly."' He shook his head. 'I told her that leaving it in the van was an invitation to steal. She just wouldn't listen.'

Was it an invitation? Flora wondered. How many people had known the book was in the safe, how many knew its likely value? Her mind, still partly in shock, began to drift and it wasn't until voices sounded outside that she snapped out of a dangerous vagueness. She couldn't waste another minute. Maud might be past help but Inspector Ridley, Jack's valued contact in the Brighton police, would have to be told.

'Flora? Are you in there?' It was Jack and he sounded amused. 'You're missing out on sales, you know. Basil tells me there's a small queue at your table waiting to buy.'

Walking to the open doorway, she looked down at Jack's smiling face.

'That's right.' It was Basil Webb who had appeared at Jack's shoulder, his bald head shining in the early morning sun. The two of them began to mount the steps into the van. 'Looks like you're doing...' Basil tailed off. 'Oh, my lord,' he said.

'Good grief!' Jack exclaimed, following hard behind. He wheeled around, his gaze searching her face. 'This is terrible. Are you OK, Flora?'

'Yes,' she said, in a voice that lacked strength. 'But there's been a... a...'

'A murder,' Lowell finished for her.

Jack's arms went round her, hugging her close, while Basil, an appalled expression on his plump face, backed away towards the door, without once taking his eyes off Lowell Gracey. A rabbit in the headlights. 'In that case,' he stuttered, 'I think I'd better—'

'Call the police,' Jack finished for him. 'Meanwhile, should you be carrying that?' He'd turned to Lowell and was pointing to the bloodied book, still clutched in the young man's hand, as though permanently glued. 'Perhaps I should take it.' He fished a handkerchief from his pocket and reached out. Silently, Gracey handed him the heavy volume.

'Someone has stolen the Dickens,' Flora managed to say, though a sudden coldness had taken over her body. Realisation was beginning to hit. Maud Frobisher, one of her aunt's dearest friends, was lying dead a few feet away, bludgeoned by a Tolkien trilogy.

Still holding the murder weapon, Jack strolled to the open safe, bending his tall frame almost double to peer into it. 'Stolen by someone who knew the combination,' he said. 'There's no evidence it's been broken into. But we need to leave things just as they are for the police to investigate. Do you have a key to the van, Flora?'

She nodded. 'Maud and I exchanged keys – I gave her a spare one to the school door. It was in case anything... anything happened to stop us opening the library or looking after the bookstall. Then we'd help each other out.'

'And you, Mr...?'

'Gracey.'

'Mr Gracey?'

Lowell shook his head. 'I lost mine and wasn't trusted with another,' he said, an edge to his voice.

'Then I suggest until the police arrive, we lock the van and leave.'

Lowell Gracey gave an impatient shrug and made for the door. Flora, her hands still shaking slightly, felt in her handbag for the van's key and handed it to Jack. Before he locked the door behind them, he was careful to lay the bloodstained book, together with his handkerchief, on Maud's desk.

'You need coffee,' he said to Flora, once they were outside.

'A double coffee,' he decided, giving her a gentle kiss on the cheek.

'I'll find a cup, don't worry. You must go. Aren't you supposed to be starting the day's events? It's already late.'

'The opening presentation will have to be delayed,' he said firmly. 'It's Slattery's, I think, and Basil will have to talk to him. Explain what's happened. Neither of them will be happy, but until Alan Ridley confirms it's OK to go ahead, we're stuck.'

Taking her hand, he walked with her into the school, passing the bookstall on the way. Whoever had been eager to buy had given up trying.

'Was it him, do you think?' Jack asked. 'Gracey?'

'I can't believe it was. But then I can't believe he was Maud's assistant either.'

He looked quizzical.

'I know him, Jack. And it was such a shock seeing him. He was a student in Bath when I was there – Richard's roommate, in fact.' She mumbled the last few words, knowing how Jack hated to hear Richard's name. 'Lowell was a chemist, so what is he doing taking over Maud's job in a mobile library? And more to the point, what was he doing, standing over a dead body and holding a bloodstained *Lord of the Rings*?'

'I've rung the police.' The plump, squarish figure of Basil Webb, his cheeks a dangerous-looking red, trotted up to them. 'An Inspector Ridley is coming.' Jack nodded. 'He'll be here shortly with his team, but they're on their way from Brighton and we're not permitted to open the conference until they give the go-ahead.' He sounded fractious.

'How about refreshments? Are they ready to go?'

'Yes, yes. Coffee, though God knows what that will taste like, but tea as well. And biscuits. I'll make an announcement – get everybody eating and drinking. A couple of the school's kitchen staff have agreed to serve refreshments earlier than scheduled. They've set up a trestle table at the back of the hall.'

Jack squeezed her hand. 'Come on. Let's find you a seat.'

Flora allowed herself to be towed into the hall and sat firmly down on a chair. Trying to put this morning's awful discovery out of her mind, if only temporarily, she forced herself to take in her surroundings. Dark red curtains framed a stage that was empty except for a wooden lectern and a small table holding an extravagantly large jug of water and a posy of fresh flowers. Rows of upright wooden chairs filled the body of the hall, a wide aisle down the middle dividing them into two distinct sections. At intervals, along each side wall, a line of cardboard stands had been erected, wobbling slightly from a breeze that came from the open windows, each stand displaying an enlarged photograph of one of the contributors to the conference, followed by a list of their published works. You couldn't call the venue smart, Flora thought, but Basil Webb had managed to make it look as professional as he could. Only the lingering smell of school jumpers and gym shoes said otherwise.

In a few minutes, Jack had returned with two paper cups. 'It's coffee. It might help to soothe your nerves though I wouldn't guarantee it.' He waited until she'd taken a few sips, before saying, 'Are you up to answering questions?'

'I'll try,' she said in a low voice.

'Why did you go to the mobile library this morning?'

'To give Maud a present. A retirement present – she leaves her job... was due to leave... at the end of this month.' Flora could feel the tears mounting. 'It's awful, Jack,' she burst out. 'Quite awful. She was such a good friend to Violet. And has worked so hard all her life. And never hurt a soul.'

'And when you got to the van?' he persisted.

Flora swallowed hard. 'She wasn't there but the door was unlocked. So I went in, put the present on the desk – now I remember, I've left it there, darn it – and then I saw her. Saw Maud. I thought she'd fainted but when I bent down...'

'And this character, Gracey?'

'He was in the van. At the back. At first, I didn't see him but I heard a noise and there he was, appearing out of the shadows.' Flora gave up trying to drink the coffee.

'With the murder weapon in his hand?'

'Yes. That's true. But... I can't believe he killed Maud.'

'Why not?'

'Why would he, is the question. Why would he kill an elderly lady he's been working with for months? Maud was his mentor. He was taking over from her at the end of July. What possible motive could he have?'

Jack took their cups and returned them to the buffet table. When he came back, he said, 'There's a stolen book to consider. Theft has to have been the motive. There's no other reason why a sixty-year-old librarian would meet her death that I can see.'

'But Lowell didn't have *A Christmas Carol*, did he? He had another book, one that could incriminate him.'

'He might have hidden the Dickens.'

'Escaped with the book and hidden it, then walked back into the van carrying the murder weapon? It's not likely.'

'OK. But perhaps he'd stolen the book just as you put in an unwelcome appearance. So he hid it in the van to collect later.'

'In that case, he would have to be stupid. The police would search the van before he could retrieve it and Lowell must have known that. If the book is there, the inspector will find it. His team will pull the van to pieces.'

'They will. And if I know Alan Ridley, he'll see it as an open and shut case. I accept you know this chap Gracey from old, Flora, but you haven't seen him for years. He might have changed, had things happen to him that you don't know about. On the surface, there's nothing to say he isn't capable of murder. He might not have meant it to turn out that way when he launched the attack, but he was unlucky. And Maud even more unlucky.'

Flora stood up and shook out the printed cotton skirt she'd

chosen that morning. 'It's *too* open and shut. Lowell is an obvious choice but there must be others who want that book. Who might even kill for it.'

'Such as?'

'Those two, for instance.' She nodded towards the two men standing by the buffet table, immersed in deep conversation. 'The one in the corduroy jacket, Clive Slattery, was particularly interested, Rose said, when Maud was showing them the Dickens yesterday. And the other man – is that Wingrave? – collects rare books, doesn't he?'

'That's Felix,' Jack confirmed, 'but I can't see him rousing himself sufficiently to murder.'

As they watched, Felix Wingrave, in a velvet suit of deep green and carelessly tied cravat, bent his head towards Slattery, so close there was not an inch between them, and whispered something into his fellow writer's ear. Slattery himself seemed unable to keep still, all the time fidgeting uneasily at Wingrave's words. Did either of them know about the murder? Flora wondered.

'There were others just as interested,' Jack pointed out. 'Rose Lawson, for instance. She seemed very excited yesterday.'

'Rose? Hardly! She didn't even go inside the van.'

A faint smile crept into Flora's face. It was a bizarre suggestion for Jack to make. Crazy leaps of imagination were usually her province.

But was it so ridiculous? Rose *had* been excited when she'd told them of the rare book. She hadn't entered the van, true, but she'd looked through the window and seen exactly what was going on. And this morning, she'd been late getting to the All's Well despite a faithful promise she would be there before opening time. She had been breathless and dishevelled and arrived from the wrong direction. A puncture, she'd said. Maybe, or maybe not. How much strength would it have taken to hit Maud over the head with a large book? A woman could have done it, and Rose was in need of money.

No, it was just too fanciful – she must stop this train of thought immediately. Switching her attention back to the hall, she became aware of being watched. A man was standing by the buffet table, close to Felix Wingrave, and looking decidedly out of place in a neat three-piece suit. His gaze was intent, and appeared to be fixed on her. She turned her head, thinking perhaps that it was someone sitting to one side of her that was holding his interest, but there was no one.

'That man... do you know—' she began to ask Jack.

'Sorry, Flora, I have to go. I've just seen a police car arrive in the playground and I want to speak to Alan.'

4

_____

'I might have known you'd be involved, Jack.' Alan Ridley and his men had arrived, complete with a white-suited forensic team. 'As soon as I heard the word Abbeymead, I knew Jack Carrington would be in the thick of it.'

The inspector's seeming reproof was belied by a friendly slap on the shoulder. 'But good to see you, old chap. Now... since you *are* in the thick of it, tell me what you can.'

Jack chose to ignore the suggestion that he brought trouble to Ridley's door and said peaceably, 'Very little, I'm afraid. It was Flora who found the body and Flora who knew the victim, Maud Frobisher.'

He hadn't wanted to land the girl he loved with a host of questions, particularly after she'd suffered such an appalling shock, but he'd come late onto the murder scene and he couldn't see he was going to be much help.

Flora had followed him out of the school and now stood beside him, her eyes fixed on the inspector and her slim figure frighteningly stiff. Anything to do with the aunt she'd loved so dearly had that effect, Jack had noticed. And Maud belonged with Violet Steele in a past that Flora had lost.

'I'll try to help,' she told Ridley, 'but I can't tell you much either.' Jack was relieved to hear her voice had regained its steadiness.

'It was you who discovered the body, though?' The inspector's forehead was ridged deeply. 'Talk me through that.'

'I went to the van to speak to Maud. She didn't respond to my knock but, when I tried the door, it was open and I went in. I couldn't see her, at least not at first. Then—'

'You saw this chap, Gracey, with a bloodstained book in his hand.'

'Yes, but I don't think he—'

'It's best you let us do the thinking, Miss Steele. In this particular case, at least. Mr Gracey is a friend of yours, I believe, and we wouldn't want any conflict of interest, would we?'

Flora anchored her long waves fiercely behind her ears. 'Lowell Gracey hasn't been a friend for many years. After college I lost touch with him completely. But, in any case, I think I'm objective enough not to be swayed by old associations.'

'Ah, that's what you say.' The inspector wagged a finger. 'It's what everyone says, but when it comes down to it, we can all be influenced by our feelings.'

'Even you, I imagine.' Flora glared at him.

'Gracey made no attempt to escape, Alan.' Jack was quick to intervene, seeing Ridley's tightened lips. 'And no attempt to conceal what I'm presuming was the murder weapon. That's hardly the action of a guilty man.'

'We'll see, won't we?' The inspector's expression was bland. 'Let us get on with the forensics and you can get back to your conference. I've told that bald-headed chap, who seems to be in charge, that he can carry on. I'll let you know if I need anything else from either of you.'

'Well!' Flora exploded as Ridley strode away to join his team. 'One minute he wants our help and the next I'm an irrational female who allows her judgement to be clouded by, by... a friendship that died years ago.'

Jack muttered an indeterminate *mmm*, but couldn't stop himself thinking that Ridley had good reasons for suspecting Lowell Gracey. Flora's instincts were usually razor sharp but in this case they might not be quite as acute. Looking back on her previous life, as she must be doing, a maelstrom of feelings would be involved: her enjoyment of college life and its friendships, the excitement of her first love affair, Richard Frant's subsequent betrayal and, most compelling of all, the pain of his leaving her to care for her aunt, to cope alone with the heartache of Violet's last illness. True, she hadn't seen Lowell Gracey for years, but she wouldn't want him guilty of such a dreadful crime, particularly if he represented the sunshine she'd known before the sudden darkness that had flooded her life.

Walking with her into the school, Jack's mind was busy, deciding it was better at the moment to say nothing more, but to wait until Ridley had considered the evidence his team would gather.

'Are you joining us in the hall?' he asked. 'Clive Slattery will be halfway through his presentation by now.'

'Thanks, but I think I'll stay with my books.' She slid behind the display table and took a seat. 'You never know, the queue might be back after Slattery's talk and I want to be ready.' She was trying for a cheerfulness she surely couldn't feel. 'But you go, Jack. You might learn a secret or two from a fellow scribe!'

'As long as the audience does, that's all that matters. It's been a difficult start to the conference.'

'They'll be fine – just don't let them look out of the window and see Ridley and his men scouring the van and... by the look of it, the playground, too.'

. . .

Clive Slattery brought his presentation to an end some quarter of an hour later and received an enthusiastic round of applause. Jack saw Basil beaming from the wings, barely hidden behind the stage curtain. The day had begun badly and Webb must be worried. As far as Jack knew, no one had yet asked for their money back and Basil would be calculating that, with luck, the situation would continue and he'd manage to break even.

Jack certainly hoped so, if only to make the venture worthwhile. Against his better judgement, he'd been pulled into acting as Basil Webb's local contact. Coming, as it had, after a hectic stay abroad, he hadn't needed the additional stress or the disruption to his work but Basil had been so enthusiastic, so persuasive, that he'd agreed, if reluctantly. His agent, Arthur Bellaby, had played a heroic part, responding to Jack's anguished call and contacting a dozen or so writers on Jack's behalf, some of whom would be speaking during the next four days.

A crowded refreshment table and a loud buzz over cups of coffee and tea had Jack decide to find fresh air. Passing Flora's bookstall in the school foyer, he saw she was fully occupied, selling, it seemed, a fair number of Clive Slattery's books. That was good. Concentrating on work would stop her mind wandering into hurtful places, for the moment at least.

In the playground he found Alan Ridley, a lit cigarette between his lips. That came as a surprise since Jack had never before seen him smoke. It might explain the inspector's unusually high colour. Unless, today, he was feeling unwell.

'Filthy habit!' Ridley greeted him cheerfully, putting paid to any idea of illness. 'I've tried to quit – lasted a couple of years, would you believe – but it helps me think and I gave in. Here – take one.'

He somehow found the strength to decline the offer of a Player's Medium but the smell of tobacco sent a longing singing through him.

'How's it going?' he asked, trying to distract his senses.

'Good. It's going well. The team will be packing up in half an hour. I wish all my cases were this simple.'

Jack raised his eyebrows.

'It's pretty clear what happened,' Ridley said, grinding the cigarette butt beneath his heel. 'This book that Miss Frobisher was keeping in the safe was worth a lot of money, I'm told. A temptation if ever there was. Leaving such a valuable item in a van!' He shook his head at the folly.

'The book was locked in the safe.'

'It was, and who knew the combination apart from the poor lady who died? That's what I mean about being simple. It was the same person Miss Steele found standing by the body with what I'm pretty sure the pathologist will decide was the murder weapon.'

'But with no sign of the Dickens?'

'Eh?'

'The rare book.'

'Gracey must have concealed it, but we'll get that out of him once we have him at the station.'

'Concealed it where, though? If he'd hidden it in the van, your men would have found it by now.'

'Then he hid it elsewhere,' the inspector said confidently. 'I've ordered a fingertip search of the entire school grounds. That book will be somewhere around, you can be sure.'

Jack thrust his hands in his pockets and looked directly into his companion's face. 'Let me get this straight, Alan. You're saying that Lowell Gracey opened the safe, helped himself to *A Christmas Carol* before hiding the book somewhere in the school grounds, then went back to the van and killed Maud. It makes no sense.'

Ridley looked annoyed, plainly ruffled at being challenged. 'He could have stolen the book before she ever arrived at the van, then when he returned after hiding it, Miss Frobisher was there, distraught that her precious item had gone. She could have accused him of theft – that would have made him panic maybe and he could have taken a swipe at her.' The inspector's voice was cold and clear.

When Jack said nothing, he went on in a slightly warmer tone. 'The chap probably never meant to kill her. It could have been sudden rage at being accused, but she fell awkwardly and hit her head on the bookcase. The pathologist will tell me more when I get his report.'

'It's still a huge supposition,' Jack dared to say.

'Not for me it isn't, but then you don't have all the information, Jack. The caretaker tells me that he was doing his rounds early this morning and heard shouting coming from the van. Someone was in a temper. He heard a woman's voice and he thinks a man's. That was our friend, Gracey, I'm pretty sure.'

Ridley sounded smug and Jack couldn't resist asking, 'Why would Miss Frobisher accuse him before anyone else? He was her assistant and presumably she trusted him.'

'Think about it. She arrives at the van to start work, finds the safe wide open and the book gone. How could that have happened? Lowell Gracey is the only other person to know the combination.'

'You don't know that for sure.' Jack dug a toe into the playground tarmac. He was on delicate ground, he knew. 'Someone else could have learned it,' he suggested, 'and disposed of Maud before emptying the safe. Or that person was already in the van when she arrived. How many people have keys to the mobile library? If there's a master key at County Hall, I don't imagine it would be difficult to get a duplicate cut.'

Why was he playing devil's advocate? Jack asked himself. If Gracey was the only person apart from Maud to know the combination, it was pretty clear he'd opened the safe. And now the safe was empty. But Flora wouldn't agree. She would be battling on Lowell Gracey's side – he knew that as instinctively as he knew her determination to get to the truth. Inwardly, he gave a small sigh. That, of course, was why he was playing devil's advocate.

'I'm as sure as can be,' Ridley said stubbornly, 'that there's nobody else in the frame.'

Jack wasn't looking forward to recounting the inspector's conclusions. Flora would be deeply unhappy and in fighting mode. 'Where do you go from here?' he asked, hoping to stall for a few days while the investigation continued.

'Gone there already, old chap. At this very moment, Gracey is on his way to the station. Arrested for murder.'

5

The first day of the conference had come to an end. Wearily, Flora draped as much of the bookstall as she could with the linen sheet she'd brought from home, hoping to keep the dust at bay until she reopened in the morning. They had been long and busy hours, with frequent bursts of queuing customers between each speaker, then an hour or so spent replenishing her table until the next break and the next burst.

Jack, meanwhile, was busy checking windows and doors before locking the hall and pocketing the heavy ring of keys.

'Anything to take away?' he asked, turning to help her.

'Only empty boxes – but quite a stack, I'm glad to say. Sales have been brisk.'

Gathering the pile of boxes in his arms, Jack strode to the waiting Austin and tipped them into the boot. 'I'll drop them at the All's Well tomorrow,' he promised. 'But right now, it's home.'

It was less than ten minutes later that they drew up outside Flora's cottage. 'Are you coming in for tea?' she asked. 'I'm sorry I can't offer you a meal. I'm too tired to cook. And actually too depressed.'

Flora had taken the news of Lowell Gracey's arrest in silence, but Jack felt sure that would very soon change. 'Don't say you're resorting to sandwiches!'

'I think I might,' she confessed. 'I've some excellent strong cheddar and a bowl of tomatoes I picked over the weekend.'

'Then as chief sandwich maker, I'll do the honours.'

'We'll share maybe?'

'OK. We'll share.' And companionably, they set to work, Jack with the bread knife and butter dish and Flora slicing tomatoes and grating cheese.

But once they were seated at the kitchen table, she appeared to lose interest in the plate of sandwiches sitting fresh and inviting inches away.

'Eat up,' Jack urged. 'You've been working all day. You can't starve because of what's happened.' He bit into his own sandwich in the hope it would encourage her. 'Are you wishing we could turn the clock back and say no to the conference?'

After all the planning, all the hustle and bustle to get this event off the ground, it had been a dismal beginning. Even more dismal that they had agreed to postpone their wedding for it.

'And be getting married instead of dealing with a murder? Possibly.' Flora took a first bite but eating seemed to take her an inordinate amount of effort. 'Still.' She brightened. 'October weather can be good – sometimes – and if we marry on your birthday, it will be extra special.'

His hand found hers across the table. 'It's that already. But we made the decision to postpone, or rather I did, and I guess we have to live with it.'

'Alice is finding it difficult to live with.' Flora smiled faintly. 'She's desperate to "get stuff done".'

Jack nodded and poured them both cups of tea, then helped himself to another sandwich. 'She stopped me in the high street the other day, insisting I choose between platters of cold meat or baked salmon!'

'That's nothing. When we met last Friday for supper, I had at least three different menus dangled at me. By this week I'm supposed to have decided on one.'

Friday evening was her regular meeting with Kate and Alice. It was the friends' time to eat together, to exchange news and discuss whatever local gossip was making the rounds.

'And then a few days ago,' Flora went on, 'the dressmaker who sewed my maid of honour frock sent over samples, and now Kate in her gentle way is badgering me, too. I have to plump for a pattern and material as soon as possible.'

'Why bother with a new dress? Why not wear the one you wore at Kate's wedding? It's a stunner and you looked absolutely beautiful.'

'I'd love to – I felt a princess wearing it – but Abbeymead would disapprove. The village would decide that it wasn't a proper wedding dress. There would be mutters for sure and Alice would be scandalised.'

'She's been scandalised since we ditched our wedding for the conference and once she learns about Maud Frobisher—'

'She'll know already. The whole village will know.'

'—she'll be horrified. She was always suspicious of the conference and I gather Maud was an old friend.'

'He's got the wrong man, you know.' Flora put down her sandwich. The effort of eating had proved too great. 'The inspector. He's made a grab at Lowell because he's easy prey.'

'Because he's also the most obvious,' he countered. 'The evidence is there, Flora, and I've learned more since we talked. The school caretaker heard angry words coming from the van first thing this morning – a male and a female voice.'

'So? It was likely to have been Maud but it doesn't follow the other voice was Lowell's.'

'Maybe, but there's other stuff, too. A valuable book has gone missing from the safe and Gracey knew the combination.'

'What if Maud's death isn't about the book?'

'What else could it be?' Jack got up to refill the teapot. 'Like I said, there's no obvious motive other than theft.'

'At the moment, I've no idea, but we don't usually jump to conclusions so quickly. Neither does Inspector Ridley. I thought when I saw him that he didn't look at all well. Maybe he just wants to get the case done and dusted as soon as possible and Lowell is useful as the culprit.'

Jack paused, kettle in hand. 'In all the time I've known Alan Ridley, he has never been unprofessional. And that would be highly unprofessional. If the inspector is ill, and can't do his job, he would have handed over to someone who could.'

He finished topping up the Brown Betty and brought the full pot back to the table. 'Gracey was in the van, standing by Maud Frobisher's body and holding the murder weapon. The safe door was wide open and the rare book nowhere to be seen. What other story could there be?'

For a moment, Flora appeared stumped, but not for long. 'Even if we go with the book theory, there are other people eager to own it. People more eager than Lowell, I imagine. Perhaps so eager, they'd kill for it. Clive Slattery and Felix Wingrave, for instance. Both of them admired the book hugely and Wingrave collects rare books. One of them could have decided not to wait for the auction. They might have watched Maud closely when she opened the safe yesterday. It wouldn't be difficult to take note of the combination – it's a small space and there seems to have been a lot of people crowded into the van. This morning, one of them might have decided to help himself, only to be surprised by Maud's arrival on the scene.'

'In that case, how did they get through a locked door?' Jack asked, pushing from his mind his suggestion to Ridley of a duplicate key. 'You're complicating matters unnecessarily.' There was a pause before he added, 'It's because you don't want to believe Lowell Gracey is guilty.'

'You're right, I don't want to. And that's because I don't believe he is. The boy I knew simply can't be a killer.'

'He's not the boy you knew, though, is he? He's a grown man and you have no idea what his life has been since you saw him, how long ago? Four, five years? You were amazed to find he was working in the mobile library service. When you last saw him, he had a future in chemistry. What happened in between?'

'I don't know what his life has been,' she acknowledged. 'I don't know why he was quarrelling with Maud this morning either, if it *was* him. And I don't know where a valuable book went to. These are things we should be trying to find out, not making easy assumptions about one man's guilt.'

'I have a conference to help run,' he reminded her. 'I really don't have the time to start poking around in a murder that, as Ridley says and I have to agree, looks an open and shut case.'

'Helping at the conference wouldn't stop you investigating if you really wanted to. The truth is...' She jumped up suddenly, banging her knee on the table. 'The truth is...'

He looked up expectantly. 'Well?'

'You don't want to help Lowell because he was a friend of Richard's. And you're still jealous. Jealous about a man who no longer has any part in my life.'

It was Jack's turn to jump up, his hand ruffling through his hair and sending it into complete disorder.

'That's utter rubbish!' He felt his face warm with anger. 'Do you really think I'd be that petty? I don't care a fig about Richard. I accept I acted stupidly where he was concerned, but that was an age ago. You're marrying me, not him. Why should I care?'

'I don't know, but I think you do. And whether you help me or not, I'm going to find out just what went on this morning.'

6

Flora stayed up late that night reading Felix Wingrave's Egyptian book. She had to admit it was exciting and unexpectedly well-written, but all the time she was reading, Jack had been there, his presence hovering over each page. It made for an uncomfortable experience and, inevitably, a restless night to follow. Flora was deeply unhappy that she and Jack had parted so badly. She shouldn't have spoken the thought that was in her mind but, as so often in the past, she'd allowed emotion to overwhelm a wiser approach.

She'd been angry, that was the truth, angry that Lowell had been arrested, to her mind on superficial evidence, and angry that Jack had meekly accepted Alan Ridley's decision. She was certain a residual jealousy of Richard Frant was prompting at least some of Jack's attitude, but she shouldn't have said it aloud.

When, as she rolled back the bookstall's linen covering the next morning and began to dust the ranks of paperbacks, she heard her name called, her heart lifted slightly. It was Jack and he sounded cheerful, unperturbed it seemed by their spat the previous evening. Anxiously, she scanned his face, ready to plunge into an apology, but before the first words could leave her tongue, she realised he was not alone. Shoulder to shoulder with Jack was a small but solidly built middle-aged man who, even at this early hour, looked bandbox fresh.

'Flora, I'd like you to meet Arthur Bellaby.' Jack gestured to his companion.

'I'd love to meet Arthur Bellaby,' she said, dropping the linen cover and walking towards them, her hand outstretched. Jack had spoken of his agent so often that it felt to Flora as though she knew him already. 'It's you who provides Jack with wonderful coffee. And smoked salmon. And—'

'Caviar and wine,' Jack finished for her.

'And *he* provides me with wonderful stories.' Arthur clasped her hand in a firm grip. 'A fair exchange, I'd say.'

Arthur was exactly as Flora had imagined him: grey haired, kindly faced and wearing a floral waistcoat that suggested an artistic bent without ever quarrelling with otherwise formal attire. It was satisfying for once to have her preconceptions confirmed.

'It's very good of you to come all the way from London to see us,' she said.

'Have to support my writers, you know. And to be honest, Bella wouldn't have agreed to host a talk this morning unless I drove her here.'

Bella Angelo was the only female crime writer Arthur had persuaded into contributing, and Flora could see now the lengths he'd had to go. But judging by the awed hush emanating from the hall, it had been worth it. The fact that Bella was female and a writer of unusually gritty crime appeared sufficient to quieten even the most fidgety of the gathering.

She nodded towards the closed door of the hall. 'The audience seem rapt. And they'll be delighted to see *you* when we break. A London literary agent in person! You will be staying to meet some of them?'

'I have to drive Bella home and feed her lunch on the way,

but I'll be here for a while.' He turned towards the stall. 'It's good you have her books and an excellent display. She'll like that.'

Flora suppressed a grimace. Bella Angelo favoured the gorier end of crime and her book jackets made that obvious.

'Jack tells me you've had a dreadful beginning to the week.' Arthur's face was grave. 'A real-life murder committed yards away. Tragic, but somewhat ironic for a crime conference?'

Flora's fingers twisted into a knot. 'Yes, she was someone I knew very well.' It was difficult to talk of Maud in this way. 'The inspector in charge thinks it's a case of a theft gone wrong.'

'A rare book,' Jack put in. 'An illustrated first edition of *A Christmas Carol*, including a letter from Dickens himself.'

'That is rare. Very rare. I did hear of one sold at auction a couple of years ago – it went for almost three hundred pounds, I think. What was the book doing in a mobile library?'

'It's a long story, but Maud – the lady who died – wanted to show it off before it went to auction. Some of the writers speaking this week were interested.'

'Felix Wingrave is here, isn't he?'

'Why do you ask?'

'Only that he collects first editions, I believe.' The agent frowned. 'There was something about rare books and Wingrave... My memory! I can't for the life of me recall what it was precisely.' He straightened his shoulders, seeming to brace himself. 'Hopefully, the sad beginning you've had won't ruin the event. The conference deserves to be successful – it's enabled me to meet you at last, Miss Steele! I know how important you've become to Jack.'

Jack looked blandly across at her and she gave a tentative smile, neither of them saying what was truly in their minds.

'But I wonder,' Arthur continued, 'would you excuse us for a few minutes? I need to grab this man and talk shop. I hope you don't mind.'

Arthur was a charming man, she decided, watching him walk into the playground, already talking earnestly to Jack who, she hoped, had truly put last night's quarrel behind them. Feeling considerably brighter than she had an hour ago, she began the task of restocking the stall from the additional boxes she'd had delivered. She had sold very well yesterday and there were several gaps that needed filling. It was when she had almost finished the task that Felix Wingrave sauntered out of the hall and walked over to speak to her. Listening to female crime writers was evidently not for him.

'A good show you have here,' he said lazily, his eyes wandering across the ranks of colourful paperbacks.

Flora looked up from the box she was unpacking. He was wearing the green velvet suit again, this time with a lighter green shirt and a new cravat, a multi-coloured square of silk, tied as artfully as before. The slightly stale smell of a smoked cheroot hung about him and mixed incongruously with the aroma of lavender water.

'Thank you,' she said, without stopping what she was doing.

'I would say one thing, though. Give you a little hint, you know. Punters will want to see much more of *The Sphinx Murders*. The book is hardly obvious at the moment. You seem to have accorded it the graveyard slot at the rear. A mistake, in my view.'

'Your book will be right at the front of the stall, Mr Wingrave – at the time your talk is happening. We're showcasing every writer in turn. That's fair, wouldn't you say?'

'Fair? Hardly. Not every writer sells as I do,' he drawled. 'But then if you're uninterested in profit...'

'No shopkeeper can afford to be uninterested. But the conference is a shared event and your fellow writers deserve space.' Flora tried to sound measured, but inwardly bristled.

'Do they? I doubt it. To be frank, I hardly recognised a name on the programme when it was sent to me. But there, why would I, if it was organised by that clown Webb? And Carrington, of course. One mustn't forget Jack Carrington. He's had a hand in it. One's a writer hardly selling at my level and the other a desperate hanger-on.'

Flora bunched her fists. She would have liked to have beaten them into this wretched man's chest. Instead, she forced herself to clamp her lips tight. It wouldn't help Jack to start a quarrel with what was probably the conference's star turn, but he was right. Felix Wingrave was a deeply unpleasant man and she wished him away. A few hundred miles, if possible.

He didn't appear to be in any hurry to go, however, and since he was in a self-congratulatory mood – perhaps that was a constant – she fell to considering how best to use the opportunity.

'I'm sorry the programme isn't to your liking,' she said calmly. 'Perhaps what we needed was a writer like Dickens – not into crime but a great actor. If he took to the stage, there'd be real excitement. Unfortunately, we can't have him.' She gave an audible sigh. 'And even his book has gone missing.'

Flora was keen to hear what this collector of rare volumes had to say. 'I think I saw you in the library van on Sunday? You must have enjoyed examining that first edition. The one of *A Christmas Carol*.'

'That was a bloody shame,' Wingrave muttered. 'It was a beautiful item. Would have looked a treat in my collection – I'd have bought the book in a trice. What was the silly woman doing keeping it in a van of all places?'

Flora bit back a retort. She wanted Wingrave to talk. 'Maud thought it would be safe and was keen to share her find. She very much wanted writers to see the book, I know – felt they would appreciate the opportunity.'

He sniffed. 'I would have done if she'd given me the chance to have a really good look. I think I managed a five minute flick through the pages.'

'More than that, surely. Unless you weren't as fortunate as Mr Slattery. I heard he was hardly able to let the book go.'

Wingrave's head jerked up. 'You think old Clive had something to do with its disappearance?'

'Do you?'

He thought about it for a while, then shook his head. 'The chap would like the book, no question, but he wouldn't have the nerve to steal it. And from what the grapevine has been telling me, actually murder the old girl for it.'

You would, though, Flora thought. You might even assume it was your right to own the book. Where were you early yesterday morning? You didn't appear in public until the police arrived.

'Hopefully, the book will soon be found,' she said, finishing her restocking. 'It can be sent to auction and you and Mr Slattery and plenty of others, I imagine, can bid for it.'

'No chance, dear lady. It's likely to fetch a bomb. I'm a successful writer, without a doubt, but that kind of money... I wouldn't have a chance. My collection will have to do without that particular copy of Mr Dickens.'

Perhaps, or perhaps not. It could have been your voice the caretaker heard quarrelling with Maud. Maybe trying to persuade her to sell the book to you at a lower price than it would reach at auction. And when you didn't persuade, could you have lost your temper and stolen it anyway?

As Flora had anticipated, Arthur was swamped once the rumour spread among the audience spilling out into the foyer that a London literary agent had arrived. She noticed Derek Easterhouse in particular had latched onto the man and seemed unable to walk away. Derek was Basil's brother-in-law and Flora had been introduced to him during one of the many conference breaks. This morning, Easterhouse looked even more scrawny than yesterday, his clothes fitting more baggily and his thinning hair subjected to an unnervingly straight parting and watered flat.

Jack was frowning when he brought her a welcome cup of tea. 'Sorry, I can't stop to chat. I need to rescue Arthur.' He sounded harassed. 'That chap won't let him go.'

Watching from a distance as Jack attempted to intervene, it seemed to Flora that he was out of luck. Easterhouse clung resolutely to Arthur's side and it wasn't until Basil Webb rang the bell to signal that a new session was about to begin that the audience began to drift back into the hall, taking Derek with them.

'He was a tad insistent, wasn't he?' Flora asked, when Arthur shook himself free of people and made for her stall again.

'The chap's got a bee in his bonnet about some book he's written. I couldn't make head or tail of it, to be honest. Couldn't hear much of what he was saying with so many others chirping away. But he just kept going. Which reminds me, I'd better get going. Bella is certain to be waiting for me by the car, drumming manicured fingernails on my new paintwork – and they're very sharp.'

'It's a pity you can't stay longer.'

'It's better he doesn't.' Jack had walked up to them, having seen the new session under way. 'He'd be eaten alive by lunchtime.'

Arthur shook hands with her again and followed Jack into the playground where he'd parked a brand new and very smart Riley saloon. Flora admired it from the open doorway. Obviously writing paid, if not for writers.

7

'I won't be staying for the afternoon.'

It was Elsie Flowers, a battered straw hat pulled low over her forehead. Tucking her admission ticket into a leather hand-bag, its myriad creases suggesting a minor eruption, she said, 'Got my niece coming and she'll expect to be fed, but I'll take a couple of Bella Angelo's books with me. I heard her speak and she was good.' Miss Flowers, with a passion for crime, was one of Flora's best customers in the village.

'You'll have quite a choice. Miss Angelo is prolific.'

Elsie spent some minutes turning over the array of books that Flora had been about to relegate to the rear of the stall. 'This looks good,' she said, 'but so does this one. And this. Not sure I can afford all three, though.'

She looked hopefully at Flora but, knowing Elsie's desire for what she called a bargain, Flora maintained a shrewd silence.

'I liked what she had to say, that Bella,' Elsie muttered, giving up on the free book. 'But this bloke speaking now. A bit wet, I think. And I've got to get to the post office before Dilys bangs down the shutters. You know what she's like. Closes five minutes, ten minutes sometimes, before she should. Depends on how hungry she is.'

Flora did know what Dilys Fuller, their postmistress, was like. She had frequently arrived at the counter as the grille had slammed shut way before the official closing time.

'Here, I'll have these.' The woman handed her two books, their covers splashed with red. Typical Elsie fare, graphic and gory, Flora thought, though grateful for the sale.

'She's right grumpy, too, at the moment. I mean worse than usual.' Elsie must still be speaking about Dilys, she realised. 'She's having to work harder now that Maggie Unwin is off sick. Not that she ever stops moaning about the girl when she's there.'

'Maggie will soon be back at the post office. It doesn't take too long for a broken arm to mend.'

Elsie gave a sniff that somehow turned into a snort. 'If you ask me, it's better for the village if she never came back. I know what my mother would say, and everyone else's, about that girl's goings-on.'

'She made a mistake, that's all.' Flora loved Abbeymead with all her heart, but at times village opinion could be jarring and memories long and unforgiving. 'We all make mistakes, don't we?

'Anyways, glad to see you're not going the same way. Getting married, I hear.'

Flora let out a small gasp. 'Mr Carrington is a single man, or have you forgotten?' Maggie's heinous crime had been to fall in love with someone already married, someone the village knew well – the locum who'd run the surgery for Dr Hanson on his sabbatical.

'I haven't forgotten, but still, marriage is there for a purpose.'

Since Elsie herself had never married, the comment jarred more strongly still. Flora wrapped the Bella Angelo books in a brown paper bag and almost pushed them at the older woman.

'Mind you,' Elsie continued, wholly unaware of the offence she'd caused, 'I like that Rose, the girl who's helping Dilys – and you, I hear – even though she's divorced. Divorced! I ask you. The world's going to the dogs, but Rose Lawson is a good woman. I reckon she's the wronged one there. I mean why leave a nice house and a perfectly good business unless you've been forced out?'

'Rose ran a business?' That was something her new helper hadn't mentioned.

'Didn't you know?' Elsie wore a smug look. She had known something that Flora didn't. 'A bookshop, that was her business. I thought that's why you'd asked her to run the All's Well this week.'

'Not really.' Flora forced herself to look unconcerned. 'Rose very kindly volunteered. She was looking for extra work apart from the few days she does for Dilys and I suggested she help out at the All's Well.'

'You be careful or she'll be taking over.' Elsie gave a cackle. 'Ran this big bookshop with her husband. Owned it, I heard.'

Watching her customer's squat figure perambulate through the open doorway and trot slowly to the school gates, Flora fell into deep thought. Until her divorce, Rose Lawson, it appeared, had owned a bookshop herself. Now, why hadn't the woman mentioned it? Perhaps she'd felt awkward, felt that Flora might sense she was taking over, as Elsie had suggested. Or perhaps she had wanted to keep a low profile at this particular time. But why? Flora's suspicions were reignited.

What, if anything, had Rose Lawson to do with what had happened here? What to do with Maud Frobisher? Of course! The realisation was sudden. Running her own bookshop was how Rose knew the mobile library. *Maud is bubbling*, she'd said. *I've known her on and off for years and I've never seen her so delighted.* At the time, the remark had set up a vague question in Flora's mind of how they knew each other, but she'd never pursued it. Here was the answer: they had been part of the same book community. Had they also shared a knowledge of the Dickens first edition? Rose had said she'd come no closer to the book than looking at it through the van window, but then Rose had said a lot of things that were turning out to be untrue.

Wednesday afternoon would be an ideal time to talk to Rose, Flora thought halfway through the next day. To discover, if she could, what exactly the woman had been doing early on Monday morning before she'd arrived breathless at the All's Well's door. Once she closed the bookshop at lunchtime today, she'd be coming to the conference for the afternoon talk. The programme listed the session as Basil Webb's review of Golden Age crime and was unlikely, in Flora's estimation, to offer much opportunity for selling the contemporary novels that filled her book table. A perfect time, then, to question Rose. Except that a quiet Wednesday afternoon was also the chance for Flora to close her bookstall and do what she'd planned to do ever since Lowell Gracey was arrested.

Conflicting priorities fought a battle in Flora's mind, the visit to Lowell eventually winning the war and, as soon as the conference closed for lunch, she covered her trestle and walked out into the playground to collect Betty from the cycle rack. With luck, she would make the early afternoon bus to Brighton.

'Miss Steele?'

It was the man in the suit. The man who had been watching her from the buffet table on the opening day. Flora was sure she hadn't seen him at the conference yesterday – he was, in any case, an unlikely attendee – and the earlier incident had slipped from her mind.

'Yes?' she said uncertainly.

'Allow me to introduce myself.' He reached into his breast pocket and extracted a business card, handing it to her with a polite nod.

She relaxed a little. Scanning the small white rectangle between her fingers, she read, *Mulholland and Mulholland, solicitors.*

'James Mulholland.' He shot out a hand and she took it, feeling disconcerted by his appearance at a writing conference. Perhaps when he wasn't buried in legal papers, he was an aspiring author.

'I'd hoped to speak to you on Monday,' he said pleasantly, 'but it wasn't possible to see you alone and I felt it inappropriate to follow you home.'

'Just a little,' she said dazedly.

'And yesterday, I had unfortunately business to complete in London. But let me explain.'

'Please. I'd be grateful.'

'You won't remember, Miss Steele – you would have been a young child at the time – but my father, Jonathan Mulholland, was your family's solicitor.'

Confusion turned to anxiety. Was she about to learn another secret from her past? This time something she didn't want to hear. Last summer, she'd found her parents' graves at last, buried miles from home in a Provençal cemetery. It had proved a healing experience, but now Flora was fearful that all the good it had wrought might be undone.

'My father looked after the sale of the Steele family home,' James went on, 'after the terrible accident your parents suffered.'

'Ah!' The mist lifted a little. 'I never knew what happened to the house I lived in as a young child.' Her aunt Violet had seemed not to know either, had had no involvement in her dead brother's affairs.

'Ah, indeed. The house in Hampstead was sold – eventually. My father obtained the best price he could but I'm afraid much of the money went to pay creditors.'

'My father had debts?'

James Mulholland looked uncomfortable. 'Considerable debts, Miss Steele. It took my father many months to find a purchaser for the house, then trace all of Mr Steele's creditors and repay them. By the time he'd accomplished his task as an executor of your father's will, there was only a modest sum left.'

'However modest, shouldn't it have gone to my aunt Violet? She was my father's sister and took care of me.'

'It should have gone to Miss Violet Steele,' he agreed, 'in trust for you until you attained the age of twenty-one. But, sadly, your aunt had moved from the address we had in Highgate and left no forwarding directions. I believe she rented the flat she called home but, when my father questioned the landlord, he was unable to provide us with any details of her whereabouts. Merely to say that she had left months previously.'

'Violet inherited money from her godfather,' she told him. 'It must have been around that time. She used her inheritance to buy a bookshop in the village and the cottage I live in today.'

'This I have discovered, but at the time my father was unable to find her, despite employing a private investigator. The money is still with us, Miss Steele, now greatly enhanced by careful investment, and this is why I am here. I am the bearer of good news.'

Flora frowned, puzzling over his words. Something didn't make sense and, for a moment, her trust in James Mulholland faltered. Was he telling her a bag of moonshine?

'If you've found me now, why couldn't you have found me earlier? Why couldn't the private investigator?'

'He tried for at least six months after we hired him but all the leads he uncovered came to nothing. I think your aunt must have wanted to make a complete break from her life in London. The school she taught at could tell us nothing, local shop-keepers had been paid but were ignorant that she was no longer their customer. Even her neighbours hadn't realised she had left her flat.'

'But you're here,' Flora said stubbornly. 'You did find me.'

'Luck, Miss Steele, pure luck. My regular newspaper published a short article recently, on its books page, about a writer called Felix Wingrave. The article mentioned that Mr Wingrave was extremely popular but had agreed to appear at a crime conference in a small Sussex village. The journalist seemed particularly struck by the location, seeing it as both strange yet endearing. To illustrate the piece, there was a photo-graph of the writer and another of the village bookshop with the owner standing by its door – I'm unsure how the newspaper obtained it – but the name of the bookshop was clear and its proprietor, Flora Steele, was mentioned. The name Steele had me recall that a small child had been involved in the case, one who would be around the age of the young woman in the photo-graph. It set me wondering if possibly we might have found a member of the Steele family and prompted me to show the article to my father.'

'Your father still works as a solicitor?'

'No, no. He retired some years ago – heart trouble made working difficult – but I knew he'd always felt discomfort that we had been unable to repay the money owed to your family. As we talked it over, my father recalled that at the time he'd had the unpleasant task of telling your aunt there would be little money from the sale of the family home and then not for some consid-erable time, she confided to him that she'd always wanted to leave teaching and run a bookshop. Left with a child to care for and with finances so precarious, it was unlikely now, she said, ever to happen. The newspaper article, however, suggested that quite possibly it had happened.'

'And this prompted you to come to Abbeymead?'

'It was enough,' he said simply. 'I took a room at the Cross Keys and bought a conference ticket from Mr...'

'Webb.'

'Mr Webb, on the first day. I wanted to approach you then. You were in the hall, drinking tea with a companion and I waited, hoping to see you alone. But immediately you finished, you disappeared. I'm not sure where but you were not at your bookstall.'

She had been with Jack, she remembered, talking to Inspector Ridley in a far corner of the playground.

'Unfortunately,' he went on, 'I had to leave to drive back to London for an important meeting that evening and the business took much longer to complete than I'd expected. I've not been able to return to the village until this morning.'

Flora's head was in a muddle. James Mulholland seemed perfectly genuine, his business card looked the real thing, but the tale he'd told was hardly believable. And yet... when Flora thought back to those long past days, she could just about remember how hastily she and her aunt had left London. She'd been whisked out of school one day and the next found herself in Abbeymead. Violet had never explained why, simply telling her that country life was better for children and she would soon learn to love the village. She would have her own bedroom in the cottage and she could help her aunt when she wasn't at school to set up the new bookshop. Since she'd been a child whose head was rarely out of a book, it had seemed a delightful treat, one not to be refused. And maybe she'd been left too numb to ask questions, after the shock of being told she would never see her parents again. The sudden move to rural Sussex was simply one more inexplicable change in her life.

'Miss Steele?'

Flora was recalled to the present. She was in the playground of Abbeymead school and clutching the handlebars of her bicycle.

'Sorry,' she said, flustered.

'I will need to see your birth certificate, of course.' He sounded apologetic. 'But that shouldn't be a problem? And anything else that might substantiate your claim. Photographs, letters, that kind of thing.'

'My claim? You came to me, Mr Mulholland.'

'A legal term, that's all. The claim will be against your parents' estate. If we can arrange for a copy to be made of everything you have – for our files, you know – we should be able to settle the business in a matter of days.'

'I'll bring what I can find to the Cross Keys,' she said, trying hard to think straight, 'but not today. I've something I must do.'

'We must delay a little then. I have to leave for London again this evening, but I'm happy to come back. Shall we say next week, Wednesday lunchtime? I would offer you a meal, but I've found the food at the inn execrable.'

'I'll be there,' she promised. 'And you could try Katie's Nook. You'll find meals at the café are very good.'

He nodded, picking up the small briefcase he'd slotted between his feet, and walked to his waiting car. Flora was left fazed, wondering whether or not to abandon her plans for the afternoon. How, she asked herself, was she to get her head straight enough to question Lowell when all the while she was absorbing the news that James Mulholland had brought?

Violet had never mentioned her brother's will or the family home and, if Flora had thought of either as she'd been growing up, it was to presume her aunt was too upset to talk of her brother's death. Now, she was beginning to wonder if there had been a very different reason for Violet's silence: the trouble into which Christopher Steele had fallen. The fact that at the time of his death, he had left his child unprovided for, not to mention her unborn sibling.

And what of the money that was coming to Flora? Mulholland hadn't mentioned a precise sum, but might it be enough to change her life once more? Enough to affect Jack and their future together?

8

As soon as the conference broke for lunch that Wednesday, Jack went in search of Flora but, delayed by one person after another with questions he'd already answered or requests to discuss the conference in general, she was nowhere to be seen by the time he reached the foyer. Her bookstall was neatly covered with the linen cloth, and her handbag and light cotton jacket had gone. He wondered if she'd ridden Betty to the All's Well. It was half-day closing and she might have wanted to see Rose before her helper shut up shop. Rose wouldn't be tardy – she had a ticket for the conference and would want to use it on her free afternoon.

Unless... Flora was striking out alone. That was more than likely. Maud Frobisher deserved her time and her loyalty, that was how Flora would see it. Deserved to have the truth revealed however long it might take. Jack had wanted to forget their earlier disagreement, push it aside as unimportant, but he shouldn't have. Flora's last words that evening had been to insist she would continue the investigation – if necessary, alone.

He'd been certain in his own mind that Alan Ridley had

good grounds to arrest Gracey and been angered by Flora's assumption that a latent jealousy of her former sweetheart was influencing him. Afterwards, when he'd had time to cool down, he accepted there was some truth in Flora's accusation. He'd succeeded fairly easily in dismissing Richard from his mind, partly he suspected because the man was an idiot, but Lowell? This was the second person from Flora's past with whom Jack had had to contend and this time he wasn't minded to give him the benefit of the doubt, which meant prejudice was at work. At the same time, though, all the evidence pointed to the young man being guilty, just as the inspector claimed.

Whatever Flora was doing, she hadn't wanted to confide in him, and he couldn't blame her. There could be a wait before he found out – until she was back at the school tomorrow and reopening the bookstall. But... he might just catch her in the playground if she, too, had been delayed.

Making a sudden dash to the door, he was just in time to see Betty's rear wheel disappearing out of the school entrance and a man in a three-piece suit wiping the windscreen of an extremely smart car. Jack had seen him before, he was sure. His was a figure you wouldn't forget, a figure definitely out of place at this conference. A professional man, by the look of it, but hardly a writer. Had he seen him with Flora earlier this week? Was that it? There was some connection, he thought.

Unable to recall exactly what, Jack was about to wander back into the hall, to a buffet table currently being plundered for sandwiches and sausage rolls, when Kate Mitchell, no Kate Farraday – he still hadn't quite got used to the idea that Kate had married again – walked into the foyer. She was carrying a heavy tray, full to the brim with small cakes, and was followed by a strapping Charlie Teague, with an even larger tray of sandwiches. It seemed that Charlie was once more earning money in his school holidays, this time at the Nook.

'We're a bit late with these.' Kate was puffing while her helper stood nonchalantly to one side. 'We've been so busy in the café and Tony has only just found time to drive us here.'

'Is Tony around?'

'No, he had to go straight back to the Nook. We can't afford to close for long, but I needed to bring these. Mr Webb has ordered an extra tray of cakes and one of sandwiches for each day.'

'You should have asked me to pick them up. The Austin is parked outside and I can always make a dash to the village. Tomorrow I'll come by the café before lunch and collect the trays for what will be our last day. Charlie, you'll give me a hand?'

'Course I will, Mr C,' he said gruffly. Charlie's voice had begun to break. 'It will be better'n washin' up. I'll take these in, shall I?' Somehow, the boy managed to carry both trays through the hall doors and leave them, intact, on the buffet table.

'Thank you, Jack,' Kate said. 'That would be really helpful. But where's Flora?' She glanced back at the covered bookstall. 'I was hoping to see her.'

'That's a question I can't answer. I suspect she's off on one of her missions.'

'Not walking into danger again, is she?' Kate looked worried, causing him to wonder if he, too, should be concerned.

'Let's hope not,' he said lightly. 'Can I give you a lift to the Nook?'

Charlie, who had just returned from the hall, looked hopeful. 'There's no need,' Kate said, disappointing her young helper. 'We've nothing to carry on our way back and I imagine you'd be best to stay around.'

'I should be here to introduce the afternoon session,' he confessed. 'If only to give Basil a break from his duties. But I'll tell Flora she missed you.'

'I'll see her on Friday evening, in any case.' Kate's pale blue eyes sparkled. 'It's our usual meet-up and Alice will be cooking!'

Resigned to walking back to the village, Charlie gave a casual wave of his hand and made for the door. Kate, however, didn't follow immediately. There was something she needed to say, Jack sensed, but didn't want to. Sure enough, fumbling in her handbag, she drew out a white foolscap envelope.

'Could you give this to Mr Webb?' she said quietly. 'I don't want to disturb him while he's busy, but it's... important.'

Jack looked at the envelope. 'A bill?'

She flushed slightly. 'It is. We've supplied sandwiches and snacks for the last three days.'

'And you haven't been paid for any of it?'

Kate shook her head. 'I'd hoped for something on account. The café tends to run on a shoestring.'

'I'll make sure he gets it,' Jack assured her, at the same time feeling a deep misgiving. If Basil had so far paid nothing for the copious amounts of food Kate and her café had supplied, it suggested he was running this conference not just on a shoe-string, but on fresh air. And that was worrying.

Tucking the envelope into his pocket, he walked back into the hall to find Basil Webb surrounded by an eager group of readers, all wanting, it seemed, to discuss the conference or share their ideas for future events. He would have to bide his time before he tackled him over the bill.

One of those who hadn't joined the circle was Derek Easter-house. Like Flora, Jack had been introduced to him earlier in the week as Basil's brother-in-law. He'd thought him a nice enough chap, though a bit of a bore. The man wanted to write more than anything in the world and was not shy in letting you know. As Jack watched, his skinny figure, trousers seeming to hang from his frame, walked across the hall to Felix Wingrave who, sandwich in hand, was eyeing the rest of the buffet.

In seconds, Easterhouse had pounced and proceeded to talk

at the writer, his hands emphasising the points he was making. Jack saw Wingrave's face at first stiffen then darken into something approaching a scowl. Despite that, the man kept talking, but Felix had turned away and was making a business of asking for another coffee. It seemed he, too, considered Derek a bit of a bore. When Easterhouse dared to touch the green velvet sleeve to gain attention, Wingrave irritably twitched his elbow. Literally, shaking the man off.

Defeated, Easterhouse made for the hall door, passing Jack on the way, his face wearing thunder and his lips compressed.

'That was a trifle brutal,' Jack said, as Wingrave sauntered up to him.

'The hanger-on, you mean?' Felix fingered a chain that hung from his neck. A monocle? Given his interest in Victoriana, perhaps it was. 'Have to be brutal with a man like that, old chap, otherwise I'd never be left in peace.'

The whole point of the conference, Jack thought, was for readers to meet and talk to writers of their favourite genre. Evidently Wingrave had no intention of playing the game, so why was he even here? A big fish in a small pond seemed the likeliest explanation.

'The man did a writing course with me, way back,' Felix went on, 'when I was still grubbing around for money, and he's been pestering me ever since. Wants me to read his work, tell him what's what, grab him a publisher. Some hope!'

'Is his work any good?' Jack asked innocently.

'The usual amateur stuff. Nothing to set the pulses racing. Mostly waste paper, I'd say. Anyway.' He put down his empty cup. 'Don't think I'll hang around for the afternoon. It's that fool, Webb, giving a session. Couldn't endure an hour listening to him!'

Jack, however, did listen to 'that fool Webb' and thought he did creditably. The subject of Golden Age crime was a much trodden field and Basil had little more to add than Jack already knew, but he spoke fluently and illustrated his talk with a number of lesser known novel extracts that worked well. The audience listened politely and managed several intelligent questions at the end.

By the time the conference finished for the day, there was still no sign of Flora and Jack's concern had grown. Debating whether to call at her cottage on the way home, he decided in the end that it might be wiser to wait. She was sure to be back at her bookstall tomorrow.

'What did you think?' It was Basil, his pudgy cheeks shining.

'About your talk?'

'Yes, the talk.'

'Very good,' Jack said obediently. 'The audience enjoyed it.'

'I think they did.' Basil's relief was heartfelt. 'I think they've enjoyed the whole conference, despite the unfortunate start. I wanted to offer readers the chance to talk crime with each other and with their favourite authors and I think I've done that. So... one more day wrapped up and just tomorrow to go. To be honest, I won't be sorry. It's been quite a responsibility. I probably didn't appreciate how much hard work it would involve. Mind you,' he said generously, 'you've been a great help, Jack.'

Jack gave a faint smile and felt in his pocket for Kate's envelope. 'One more job for you,' he said lightly. 'Kate Farraday's bill for the refreshments.'

Basil took the envelope with evident reluctance. 'Ah, yes. Thought that would be coming.'

'The Nook has provided food for the last three days,' Jack reminded him. 'And it's only a small business.'

'Quite, quite. I'll see to it immediately.' He tapped the envelope against his fingers. 'Just a bit difficult at the moment,' he said in a low voice, 'but I'll make sure Mrs Farraday gets paid.'

'Difficult?'

'This conference hasn't brought the money in that I hoped

it would. In fact, I've a nasty feeling there could be quite a shortfall. Definitely not what I needed.'

Jack hesitated. It was a delicate subject and he was unsure whether he should press the matter, but the conference was in part his responsibility. 'Are you in trouble, Basil?' he asked after a long pause.

'A little,' the man confessed. 'I'm not too flush. Not at the moment. And my sister... she's depending on me.'

'Your sister? She's here at the conference?'

'Thelma? Lord, no. It's romance she likes. I've tried for years to get her interested in the Dirk and Dagger – actually introduced her to Derek – but it's been hopeless. Romantic fiction is all Thelma reads.'

'If that's so, how is the conference important to her?'

'She and Derek are in a spot of bother.' When Jack looked puzzled, he added, 'Struggling – money, you know. Thelma was always at home but now she's working all the hours she can, bless her, but a shop job is never going to pay a king's ransom, is it? I had hoped... well, I was counting on it really... but there, plans don't always go right, do they? Leastwise, mine don't.' There was a sour note to Basil's voice.

Leaving Webb to do the final lock-up, Jack walked back to the Austin, his mind filled with a similar sourness. Their conversation had been disturbing – Basil's voice had held an uncomfortable desperation. Money was scarce for him but, by the sound of it, even more so for his sister. Had the man really expected this conference to make things right for him and his family? It looked very much as though he had. And looked, too, as though he would be badly disappointed.

From the very start of the conference, Jack sensed, there had been things happening that he couldn't quite grasp, under-currents that weren't obvious, involving not only Basil, his sister and brother-in-law, but Rose Lawson, too, and of course Gracey. When he paused to think about it, these were all people who, in different ways, could benefit from the missing Dickens. The conversation he'd just had might have held a clue and he wished Flora had been with him. Her antennae were sharp, sharper than his. She might well have picked up hints, implications, niceties, that could have led them to the right questions and so the right answers.

9

Flora pedalled hard along the narrow road to reach the high street where she left Betty in the All's Well's courtyard and, with minutes to spare, was in time to catch the early afternoon bus into Brighton. She had said nothing to Jack of this visit to Lowell – since their disastrous sandwich supper, she had seen him only fleetingly – and, although their disagreement had seemingly been forgotten in yesterday's welcome to Arthur Bellaby, she didn't want to put it to the test by mentioning Gracey's name, nor the raw instinct that told her Lowell was innocent.

If the police allowed her to see her former friend, she would make sure she found out just why he'd quarrelled with Maud if, in fact, it had been his voice the caretaker had heard. And whether or not Lowell had seen anyone, anything, out of the ordinary early that Monday morning. Hearing his side of the story was crucial, particularly as uncertainties had begun to surface: Rose Lawson, for instance, had been meagre with the truth, if not telling an outright lie.

It was a long, slow journey to Brighton and, whereas ordinarily Flora would have sat back and enjoyed pottering through the Sussex countryside, its pastureland spread wide and the long snake of the river Adur winding far into the distance, she sat fidgeting on the edge of her seat, impatient to get to her destination. Fidgeting, too, because she felt uneasy. There was now something else she wasn't sure she could discuss with Jack – James Mulholland's sudden appearance in her life, along with a possible inheritance. Only possible because she couldn't count on it. That would be foolish. There had been too many mistakes in the past, too much bad timing. It would be sensible, wouldn't it, to keep silent until she knew whether or not she really did have good news to tell?

The first houses appearing on the Shoreham Road had her sit straighter, and then it was on to Portslade, to Hove and, finally, to the Brighton seafront. The bus stopped outside the Ship Hotel, the oldest hostelry in town, frequently chosen by the Prince Regent for his guests after he'd built his mad palace by the sea. All those Regency romances she'd read as a young girl brought to life!

From here it was only a few steps to the Town Hall, the neo-classical building's once honey-coloured stone now faded to an indeterminate grey. Brighton police headquarters was situated in the basement and Flora made her way around the building to the entrance she recalled from her visit with Jack last spring.

At the bottom of the stairs, the cavernous interior that she'd all but forgotten echoed to her footsteps and, hearing them, the sergeant behind the large reception desk stopped biting the end of his pencil and looked up.

'Good afternoon, miss. Lost your way? Shouldn't you be on the seafront enjoying the sun?'

But when she asked after Lowell Gracey, his face took on a serious expression. 'A friend of yours, is he?'

Did he sound accommodating? Flora wondered. Was she going to be lucky?

'He was for many years,' she answered. 'A very good friend. I wonder... Can I see him? I really want him to know he's not facing his problem alone.'

'Quite a problem!' The policeman gave a hoarse laugh. 'Murder's a serious business. His solicitor can visit the chap, of course, but I'm not sure the inspector will be happy for—'

'I'll be only a few minutes,' Flora said desperately. 'Just enough time to tell Mr Gracey that he's not forgotten.' She pinned on what she hoped was her most winning smile.

The policeman gave his sparse moustache a small tug while he thought about it. 'I s'pose it will be all right. A little biddy strip of a girl like you isn't going to do much harm. Let's see.' He turned to take down an enormous key from the board behind his head. 'I'll have to lock you in with him, mind. You know that?'

Being locked in didn't feel too wonderful and being called a little biddy girl even less so, but Flora was on a quest and she was going to see it through.

'I don't mind at all. Lowell isn't a violent man.'

The sergeant cocked a sceptical eyebrow. His prisoner, after all, was a potential killer. 'I'll keep an eye out, in any case,' he promised.

She was led along a brightly lit passageway, the ceiling arches reminding her she was in a cellar and the series of locked wooden doors that she was in a prison.

Lowell Gracey was seated on a wooden chair beneath the semicircle of a barred window, high in the wall. The room was bare of other furniture except for a wooden slatted bed pushed tight against one wall and, against another, a rudimentary wash-bowl with a slop bucket beneath. A very small amount of light penetrated the cell and Lowell, his eyes close to the page, was trying to read from the book he held in his hands.

'Flora!' Suddenly aware of his visitor, he sprang from his chair and sent his book skittering across the cold tiles.

'Steady on!' The sergeant jangled the cell key in his hand as a warning.

Lowell subsided onto his chair and the policeman, sending a final hard look in his direction, locked the door behind him.

'You'd better sit on the bed, Flora,' Lowell said wretchedly. 'It's not exactly home from home here.'

'I can see that. But how are you?' A foolish question. Lowell's pallid face and a body that had grown suddenly gaunt, weighed on her heart.

'In a word, bewildered. I don't understand why I'm here.'

She leaned forward, searching his face intently. 'You must know why, Lowell. Maud is dead and you were there, by her body, with what the pathologist has confirmed was the murder weapon.'

Lowell spread his hands. A gesture of resignation? Or despair, Flora thought. 'I told that inspector chap how it was.' His voice cracked and he swallowed hard. 'I came back to the van and found Maud lying by the bookcase. I felt for her pulse and it was clear she was dead. That damned book, the trilogy, was beside her and I picked it up. I wish to God I never had, but I was shocked, trying to make sense of what had happened. Then you turned up.'

'You'd seen Maud before? Earlier that morning?'

'Yes.' He hung his head.

'And did you quarrel with her? I should tell you that the caretaker heard angry voices coming from the van.'

'Yes,' he admitted, his head sinking lower.

'Was the Dickens book the reason for the quarrel?'

'The Dickens?' He looked confused. 'No. Why would it be?'

Flora shifted to one side, trying to make a more comfortable nest for herself on what she guessed was a horsehair mattress. 'As far as you know then,' she pursued, 'the safe was still locked and the book secure at the time you were having words with Maud?'

'Well, yes,' he said uncertainly. 'Though I don't know it for a fact – I never checked the safe. But why would I?'

'If it wasn't the first edition you were quarrelling over, what was it?'

Lowell took a long time to answer, his feet jiggling on the tiles. 'Maud told me she wouldn't be retiring,' he said at last.

It was Flora's turn to look confused. 'Not retiring? But why not? She was ready to enjoy a different life and looking forward to it. She told me so only a few weeks ago.'

'*I* was looking forward to a new life, too,' he said glumly. 'It was the money, that's why she wasn't retiring. But isn't it always? The old girl had lost money on her investments, she told me, and couldn't afford to give up work after all. She was very sorry but I'd have to carry on as her assistant for a while.' Lowell's voice had turned bitter. 'How long, I asked her. She didn't know. Some indeterminate date in the future. Meanwhile, I was to keep working on the pittance the council pays a library assistant.'

He got up from his chair and walked to the window, looking upwards to the small source of light. 'I lost my temper then, I admit. I needed her job, needed the money it pays.'

Lowell turned to her, his head making small jerky movements, as though the admission was being wrung out of him. 'I can barely afford to live off the money I earn, let alone pay my debts.'

'You have debts? How much?' she asked gently.

He looked down at the scratched floor tiles. 'A huge amount.'

'But how, Lowell? We graduated the same year and you must have been working for most of the last four or five.'

'Work was the problem.'

He crossed his arms across his chest, holding himself in a

tight grip. For a while, he sat rigid, unable, it seemed, to speak. But then his arms relaxed and the confession began. 'I took a laboratory job in no-man's land. A research lab, all very secret, tucked away miles from anywhere or anybody. There was nothing to do, nothing to see, nobody to socialise with except a bunch of exceptionally tedious scientists. It's no wonder I went off the rails.'

When she looked questioningly at him, he mumbled, 'Gambling. Horses.'

'How did you manage that if you were miles from anywhere?'

'Oh, I was a clever chap. I set up an account with a bookie in the nearest town and listened to race meetings on my radio. Even took *Sporting Life* so that I could study form and get the latest tips. It was about the only joy I got from life. I hated the job. Hated the people. Hated the place.'

'So, why didn't you leave? There must have been plenty of other science posts you could have applied for.'

'Inertia, I expect. Or perhaps it was addiction, like I was hooked into the life I'd fallen into and couldn't find the will to get out. It had a kind of comforting rhythm, I suppose. All week bent over test tubes in the lab, then every weekend glued to the radio in between dashes to the telephone to place my bets.'

Flora couldn't stop her face expressing the shock she felt. 'I did win,' Lowell protested, reading her feelings correctly. 'Sometimes.'

'But evidently not often enough.'

'No, not often enough.'

She said nothing for a while, wondering how best to get Lowell to understand how crucial his gambling might prove for Ridley's investigation. At the moment, her friend appeared oblivious to the danger he was in.

'When Maud told you early on Monday morning that she

wasn't retiring after all,' Flora began, 'you lost your temper, you said.'

'Wouldn't you? I'd been her assistant for six months. Training, they called it. Being bullied and bossed about was more like it. I only stuck it because I'd been promised her job when she went. I could see a way forward at last – the salary would be enough for me to start paying some of the money I owed. You have no idea of the kind of people I owe it to, Flora. Loan sharks. They're not exactly gentlemen. Then what do I hear? Maud tells me she's sorry but it's not going to work that way. She's spoken to the library bigwig at County Hall and it's been decided that she'll stay on for the moment, and I'll need to wait my turn.'

'When she told you that, what did you do?' Flora asked the question with her heart in her mouth.

'I didn't grab Tolkien and bash her over the head, if that's what you think,' he said belligerently. 'I went for a long walk around the playing fields, trying to cool off. I had to go on working with her after all. Then, when I got back to the van, I found her... dead.' His voice was flat.

'And the safe was wide open,' Flora added.

'I didn't realise it at first, but yes the door was open and *A Christmas Carol* had gone.'

'Do you have any idea who might have taken the book?'

He shook his head. 'It was valuable. Very valuable, according to Maud. It was a natural target for thieves, what with the van parked out in the open and no security. Like I said, I warned her of the problem. But she was getting forgetful. She could have taken the book herself, worried there were too many people who knew about it. Taken it home with her on Sunday evening, perhaps.'

'I'm sure the police will have searched Maud's home thoroughly, yet the book is still missing.'

His shoulders slumped. 'Then it was stolen. But I've absolutely no idea who could have taken it. Or who killed Maud to get hold of it.'

There was another long silence while Flora fidgeted from side to side trying to get comfortable on the lumpy mattress and Lowell stared moodily at the floor.

She was the one to speak first. 'You never said how you came to be working in a mobile library. It's one of the last places I would have expected. You're a trained chemist, Lowell.'

'Got thrown out of the job, didn't I?'

'Your bosses found out about the gambling?' It was a guess but she saw from Lowell's face that she had guessed right.

'Of course they did. And there was no mercy. "You're out of here at the end of the month and there won't be a reference." That was the attitude. After that, there was no way I'd be taken on by another firm. One of the more chatty fellows at the lab told me I should try for a council job. They're ten a penny, he said, and because the pay is so rotten they're always recruiting. I took that to mean I might not need a reference or I could invent one and no one would ask questions.'

Flora's eyebrows had done a lot of work this afternoon, but now they rose almost vertical.

'You wrote your own reference!'

'It was easy. You should try it if you're ever stuck. I'd moved down to Sussex by then, found a sofa in an old pal's flat and saw the library job advertised in the local paper. And Bob's your uncle.'

'He may well be, but you haven't exactly enjoyed the experience, have you?'

'To be honest, it's not been bad,' he admitted. 'The old girl could be a trial, but I wish she was still here.'

Flora got up to go, shaken by what she'd heard. She would need time to make sense of an avalanche of thoughts, but already it felt as though this afternoon had wrought a serious change in her thinking.

She was at the cell door and about to knock to be let out when Lowell asked, 'Ever see Richie, these days?'

Flora swivelled round. 'Last September, in fact. Richard is in Paris, did you know? Working as a freelance journalist.'

'We haven't kept in touch,' he said simply. 'Still carrying a torch for him, are you?'

'No,' she said with emphasis. 'Not for a moment.'

'Just as well. He was stupid. Brainless, I'd say. He should have hung on to you. You were always a chippy girl, but you were pure gold.'

10

Flora was glad of the long bus journey back from Brighton. It gave her time to think – and there was a lot to think about. By the time she'd alighted in Abbeymead's main street, she had made at least one definite decision, to say nothing to Jack of Mr Mulholland's visit and the possibility of an inheritance. Not until she was sure exactly how much money was involved and seen it safely stowed in her bank. It was premature to speculate on the kind of change it might bring to their lives. In a few months, they would be married – an enormous leap for them both – and certainly enough change for the moment.

Dismissing Mr Mulholland from her mind, the journey had given her time to ponder all that Lowell Gracey had said. There was no doubt now as to whose voices the caretaker had heard – Lowell admitted to the quarrel – but was insisting that Maud had been alive when, furious, he'd stormed out of the van meaning to walk off his anger. Had he perhaps stormed out, not from anger, but from an urgent need to hide the valuable book he'd just thieved? In his absence, Lowell was suggesting, someone else had paid the library a visit, murdered Maud and stolen the Dickens. But how was that even possible? Who could have been watching the van that morning and taken their chance when Lowell slammed out? Who else could have known the safe combination? An inkling that perhaps Jack was right, that Inspector Ridley had arrested a guilty man, had slowly crept into her mind, though she fought against believing it.

Waving the bus driver goodbye in the high street, she ignored the siren call of the All's Well, deliberately walking past the shop door and turning into the courtyard to collect Betty from her shelter. Once in Greenway Lane, she cycled on past her own cottage to arrive at the door of Overlay House as Jack was parking the small red Austin in the lane.

'There you are,' he said, clambering from the driver's seat. She was surprised that he sounded relieved. What had he thought she'd been doing?

'Come on in and I'll make some tea. Or maybe something stronger?' he suggested, when he saw the strain in her face. He opened the car boot and pointed. 'See – a case of red wine, just arrived at the post office. Arthur calls it mellow. It should be good.'

'It's not even supper time,' she protested. 'You're leading me astray.'

'Probably, but you look as if you need to stray a little.'

He led the way into the house and, bottle in hand, crossed the black-and-white-tiled hall to the sitting room and the corner cupboard that Flora knew stored an odd selection of glasses. She flopped down on the lumpy sofa and stretched her legs.

'I think you might be right,' she admitted. 'About Lowell. Mind you, only might. But I'm sorry I snapped at you the other night.'

He looked up from pouring wine into two mismatched glasses. 'You weren't that far out,' he admitted. 'I was hasty.'

'Lowell Gracey,' she went on. 'I went to see him this afternoon.'

'That's where you were! You went to Brighton, to the police cells?'

'I took a bus to the seafront and found my way from there. As a special favour to Lowell's friend, the desk sergeant allowed me to see him.'

'And?' Jack brought their glasses to the table.

'And it was definitely Lowell who quarrelled with Maud, though he swears he left her alive and well.'

'You believe him?'

'I want to. I did believe him. But now... he has motive, Jack. The strongest you can imagine.'

He sat down beside her, clinking his glass with hers. 'Tell me.'

'Maud was supposed to retire at the end of this month and Lowell take her place.'

'So I heard.'

'But she decided not to. That came as a shock to me. She couldn't afford retirement after all, it seems – much of the money she'd invested had disappeared, she told Lowell – and she would need to work a few more years.'

'That was sufficient motive to kill her?'

Flora took a sip of wine, then another. 'This tastes wonderful. So... so...'

'Mellow?'

She grinned. 'Arthur certainly knows how to live!' Flora gave a small puff of a sigh. 'The motive could be sufficient in Lowell's case. He confessed that betting on horses has left him deep in debt. He was desperate to earn Maud's salary even to begin paying back what he owed. I gathered he's borrowed money from people who aren't too particular how they collect it.'

'Phew. That *is* a motive.'

'A double motive, in fact,' she said unhappily. 'We don't know when the Dickens was stolen. There's a presumption it was on Monday morning and Maud was unlucky enough to meet the thief. But what if it was stolen the evening or night before? Lowell knows the combination of the safe and he had a key to the library van – he told us that he'd lost his key, but what if he hadn't? What if the book had disappeared when Maud walked into the van on Monday morning? Might she have accused Lowell of taking it, as the only other person who had access? And if she did, would he feel he had to get rid of her?'

'The book would fetch a good deal of money, even sold illegally,' Jack said thoughtfully. 'It could probably clear the man's debts in one swoop. But you're still reluctant to believe him guilty?'

'It's so out of character. I accept all that stuff about not knowing him for years, but people don't change that radically and Lowell Gracey was always gentle, a mild man who never picked fights. If there was ever trouble, it was Richard who led the charge.'

Jack's changeable grey eyes darkened. It was clear he wasn't to be easily convinced. 'If someone is desperate enough...'

'I have my doubts about Rose Lawson,' she said abruptly.

Jack gave his wine a swirl. 'They're probably justified. I've always thought she might be in debt.'

'Maybe not in debt, but she needs money. She owned a bookshop with her husband, that's something I've learned, and something she never thought to tell me. So, why didn't she? Wouldn't it be the most natural thing in the world to mention the fact, when I asked her if she could look after the All's Well this week? But she said nothing.'

'It hardly makes her guilty.' Jack put his empty glass down. 'Another?'

She shook her head. 'Better not. If Rose worked in the book trade, she might have the contacts, or her ex-husband might, to sell a valuable book like the Dickens to the right collector. One who didn't have too many scruples about where it had come from. And there's something else.' She looked down at her feet, uncomfortable with the thoughts that had been building. 'Rose was late getting to the shop on Monday morning, despite promising me she'd be there before time. She arrived in a pelter, bang on nine o'clock, and from the wrong direction.'

'Did she say why?'

'She'd had a puncture.'

'That's reasonable. And as for not coming from home – she might have had to borrow a puncture kit elsewhere.'

'It's all reasonable, isn't it? Lowell in a fury at Maud's news and going for a walk to cool off. Rose, flustered and dishevelled, because she'd suffered a puncture. Or was it because she'd called in at the school before she ever got to the All's Well?'

Jack moved closer, as though to protect her from her own words.

'She knew about the Dickens. That's clear from what she said on Sunday evening.'

'She knew about it and grasped that something exciting was going on, but she only saw the book through the window,' he countered. 'She might not have appreciated just how valuable it was.'

'We've only her word that she didn't examine it closely. Maud could have invited her into the van – they knew each other – and given her a special viewing before the others arrived. She could have watched Maud open the safe and decided to return the following morning and steal the book. The money she'd gain from selling it would solve all her problems, too.'

'But would she have been able to overpower Maud?'

'I don't see why not. If she turned up at the library early on Monday, Maud would be unsuspicious. Rose could have cobbled together some excuse for being there. Miss Frobisher was an older woman and not particularly strong and Rose would have been physically capable of hitting her with a heavy book. Perhaps when her back was turned and maybe in a moment of madness. Maybe she meant only to stun Maud, but instead she killed her.'

'We keep coming back to money – it seems to be at the bottom of this murder. Most people need money but we have characters here who could be described as desperate. Money would rescue them from some very bad situations. It's not too dramatic to say that it would change their entire lives: Lowell Gracey, Rose Lawson – and Basil Webb.

'Are you sure about the wine?' When she shook her head, he poured himself a second glass. 'Webb is someone we shouldn't forget. It seems to me that he's organised this conference on a wing and a prayer, and he's clearly very worried there'll be no money at the end of it. On the contrary, a loss. Worried for himself maybe, but even more worried for his sister. *He* was at the school very early on Monday. He made a point of telling me he'd be there and that I needn't arrive until later. Webb knew about the Dickens, too – he was the one who suggested to Maud that several of the writers already on site might like to take a look.'

'And what about the writers themselves?' Flora added gloomily. 'I can't ditch the image of Clive Slattery actually stroking the book. And Wingrave, too. He didn't hesitate to tell me that he'd love to add the Dickens to his collection, but that if it went to auction, he wouldn't be able to afford the price.'

Jack sat back on the sofa and pulled her close. 'It looks very much as though we're into another investigation. Not a dangerous one this time, let's hope. But I wish we could just get married.'

Flora laid her head on his shoulder. 'So do I,' she said, a little surprised to find herself saying it.

11

The weather had been sultry of late, the sky too often a dull pinkish grey with barely a splash of blue, the heat of the sun felt rather than seen. But today, the last of the conference, hedgerows were splashed bright with sunlight and the sky above, a cloudless blue orb. The refreshing coolness of early morning, though soon to disappear, for the moment held fast.

Jack decided to walk to the conference, leaving the Austin parked in the lane outside Overlay House. He'd begun to feel as though he'd spent a lifetime locked between four walls when, in fact, it was just four days. But they'd been long hours and spent for the most part in the hall or the school office, lent to Basil for the week. The need to feel air on his face and earth beneath his feet had him take the path through Church Spinney to the top of the high street.

The trees, this far into the summer, wore their leaves a little wearily, their tips edged with dust, an earlier vigour long gone. But it was a pleasant walk, the path bumping its way over tree roots and winding round bushes that had grown thick from the July warmth. He had almost reached the end of the track, fields opening to one side and the glimpse of a road ahead, when he stumbled slightly. A tree root, he thought, one he hadn't noticed. But it was a large sheet of paper, a tattered poster by the look of it, that had wrapped itself around his foot and caused him to trip.

Leaning against a tree trunk, he tore the chunk of paper from the sole of his shoe and began to crumple it into a ball, ready to dispose of once he reached the school, but the black and red lettering had him pause and he spread the poster wide. Battered and dirty it might be, but its message was clear enough.

Want excitement? it blared in a red that flamed. **Then come to the Abbeymead Crime Conference. You'll find we don't just talk about murder.**

There'll be bodies galore! And blood will be spilt!

Then in smaller black letters:

Buy a ticket for the day – You might get a surprise!

What the hell did that mean? What did any of it mean? Jack looked around, noticing for the first time the remnants of other posters pasted onto a good many of the trees. How many were there and how long had they been here? He felt his skin tighten. The bloodcurdling message was too close to reality, even in a place such as this where only walkers were likely to have seen it.

But the spinney wouldn't be their only host, he thought, otherwise what would be the point? He'd seen nothing similar anywhere else in Abbeymead, but what of the surrounding villages or the local market town? These same posters could have reached any of them. Whoever had paid for the printing would be keen their provocative message was read by as many as possible. And it *was* provocative. It suggested, didn't it, that blood would flow at the conference, that murder wouldn't be confined between the pages of a book?

The primary question, however, was who was behind it? Who had designed and circulated such an aggressive piece of marketing? As soon as he'd understood what he was looking at, Jack had suspected. Surely, it had to be Basil Webb. The reference to buying a ticket for the day – that had been Basil's idea. Initially, he'd insisted that attendees pay for the entire conference but had soon softened his approach to sending out day tickets, and finally to selling tickets on the door. Anything, in fact, to raise money. And money was what this poster was about. To entice people with the promise of something dramatic.

If it was Webb, he must have had the posters printed weeks ago. Must have arranged their distribution days ago. Could he have known that Maud Frobisher was about to lose her life? Jack recoiled at the thought. It had to be a coincidence, and a tasteless one at that. A publicity stunt that had become a horrible reality.

Yet Basil had almost certainly benefited from that same publicity. Jack had noticed how audience numbers had been growing, how every day there were fewer vacant chairs in the hall. The thin list of delegates had now become a respectable tally. More tickets sold meant that Basil was far less likely to face a shortfall. Far more likely to make a profit, albeit a small one. A profit that would help Thelma, the sister he loved.

Loved her so much that he'd plan a publicity campaign with murder in mind? Jack wondered if Thelma's 'spot of bother' might prove to be more menacing than a simple struggle with money. Basil had been noticeably tight-lipped when he'd talked of her and, to Jack's eyes, the brother-in-law, Derek Easterhouse, was no more forthcoming. For the most part, the man had appeared moody and unhappy. Perhaps the marriage was in difficulty and Basil was trying to protect his sister from her husband. From Derek's anger? Or, if things were really dire, making sure Thelma had the money to escape if she needed to.

Leaving the spinney, Jack veered left into the high street, trying to dismiss suspicions that had begun to gather strength. It was too far-fetched, surely, to believe that Basil could have planned such a heinous crime? But money, the recurring motif of this investigation, had again reared its head. Basil had given little away in their conversation but his need for cash might be as great as Lowell Gracey who owed money to dangerous men or Rose Lawson struggling to build a decent life for herself after a bruising divorce. And Felix Wingrave? Certainly wealthy enough to have no need to murder, except... he was a collector of rare volumes who coveted a book too expensive even for him. And collectors could be unrelenting in pursuit of an object they craved. One of these people, if not guilty themselves, knew something more. But which one?

Flora wasn't sorry to see the last day of the conference arrive. The hubbub of a crowded school, the near constant buzz of conversation, had left her with a headache most evenings. And she'd found herself badly missing the daily routine of the All's Well.

Today, Basil had decreed the programme would start a little later than usual, giving Flora time to call at the post office in search of stamps. She had a birthday card to post to Jessie Bolitho, the housekeeper who had looked after them so brilliantly in Cornwall. A holiday that hadn't, in the end, quite matched that description.

Dilys Fuller was only just pulling up the shutter on the post office counter when Flora walked into the shop.

'You're early.' It was more of an accusation than a comment. 'Got to get to that conference, I expect.' The postmistress tugged at the sleeves of her jumper. It seemed the garment had shrunk.

'Dratted thing,' she muttered. 'These sleeves have never been long enough.'

Not shrunk then, but clearly one of Dilys's creations, its pale pink background scorched by stripes of scarlet zigzagging across an ample bosom.

'So how's it going?'

'The conference?'

'Yes. What else? The wretched thing that's deprived me of my assistant. Been on my own all week, I have.'

Attempting to stifle the lengthy grumble that was threatening, Flora went into soothing mode. 'Rose will be back with you very soon – I'll be taking over at the All's Well the day after tomorrow.'

'Good thing. Not that Rose Lawson is much help when she is here. She can serve in the shop but can't do the counter to save her life. Post office work isn't easy, you know, though folks always think it is. It's not just letters and stamps. My goodness, no. There's postal orders, licences for cars, for radios, for them new-fangled televisions, parcels to take in, telegrams to transcribe. Rose couldn't cope. Neither can that Maggie, at least not well, when or if she decides to come back. I'm the poor soul who has to keep the post office going.'

Dilys was sounding even more cavalier than usual; a chance maybe, Flora thought, to learn something of a woman who didn't always tell the truth.

'How long has Rose worked for you?' she asked hopefully.

The postmistress wrinkled her nose. 'Two, three months. I dunno. Came in here... must have been round about Easter asking if I had any work going.'

'It was good of you to find her some.' Flattery generally worked with Dilys.

'I gave her a day, sometimes two, that's all. But I'd taken on Maggie and I can't afford to employ every rag, tag and bobtail who comes asking.'

'Rose must have been grateful for any work. I did hear that she'd gone through an unpleasant divorce.'

'Messy by all accounts,' Dilys agreed. 'That husband of hers took her to the cleaners. Good and proper. Now, what d'you need?'

'A strip of stamps, please. I've a card to post. They owned a shop together, I believe.'

Dilys bent down to find her folder of stamps, then bobbed up again, slightly out of breath. 'It was the husband who controlled the money. No surprise there.' She nodded sagely. 'And no surprise he wasn't too generous when things went wrong. Employed some flash solicitor to make sure he ended up with the business and the house *and* any savings.'

'Poor Rose.' She dug into her purse for change.

Dilys chewed her lip. 'The girl's trying to rebuild her life, I'll give her that, but it's not easy. She's having to share a room with Maggie at old Mrs Waterford's. Better than sleeping on her friend's sofa over at Wiston, I s'pose. That's where she was before Maggie offered to share, but I dunno what she'll do when there's no job here.'

'She must be entitled to some money if she helped to build the business.'

'You'd think so, but she's got no clout. Should get a third of everything, my sister Rene says, but only if she wasn't at fault. That smart arse solicitor will have hidden what money he could, then made sure he blamed her for the break-up. She won't get her fair share for sure. Nor would any woman, if you ask me.'

'Perhaps better not to divorce?'

'Better not to get married at all.' She peered at Flora through the opening. 'You've changed your tune, I hear. The girl who was so independent!'

'I suppose it's possible their business wasn't too successful,' she said hurriedly. 'It was a bookshop, wasn't it, and bookshops don't make much money.'

Dilys sniffed and put Flora's change into her till. 'It wasn't one like yours. It didn't sell modern stuff.'

'An antiquarian bookshop?'

'That's right. Old stuff. Very expensive and falling to bits.'

'Antiquarian books?' Flora was shocked enough to repeat the question. It was a possibility she hadn't considered.

'That's what I said,' Dilys snapped, clearly irritated.

Flora stuck a stamp on Jessie's card and drifted through the door to the post box outside, forgetting to say goodbye. Her mind was working at full stretch. Not only did Rose Lawson have contacts with the book trade but, plainly, as someone who'd run an antiquarian bookshop she would recognise the value of the missing Dickens. And more importantly, she was likely to know exactly who to go to if she hoped to make an undercover sale. Yet when Rose had first mentioned the book, her words had suggested she had no such knowledge. Why the pretence?

Earlier, Flora had speculated that Maud might have shown Rose the book before she invited the group of writers into the library van. Wouldn't it be natural, she thought, riding out of the post office courtyard without checking for traffic, for Maud to do just that, knowing it was the woman's area of expertise? She might even have asked her what Rose thought the book would make at auction. That sum of money would loom large for a woman forced to move from friend to friend, sofa to sofa, and about to lose the one job she'd managed to acquire.

Flora nodded to herself. Rose was a definite on her list of suspects.

12

The sounds emanating from the school hall suggested to Flora that the early afternoon session had just finished: an awkward screech of microphone, a general scraping of chairs as the audience got to its feet, the rattle of cups and saucers at the refreshment table, and a very few people wandering out into the foyer in the hope of making a last minute purchase from the bookstall.

Her table had done well this week and on this final day she had already sold a satisfying number of paperbacks. Emptying the tin box of her takings, she zipped banknotes and coins into her handbag for safe keeping. In a few hours, the conference would end and she planned to ride to the All's Well to lock the money away until she could pay a visit to her bank in Steyning. Aunt Violet had installed a small safe beneath the shop's desk and over the years it had proved its worth.

For now, though, she could relax a little – maybe find a seat in the hall for the very last talk. Naturally, it was Felix Wingrave who had been given the honour of wrapping up the conference and sending the audience happily on its way. Having made good progress with *The Sphinx Murders*, Flora thought she might enjoy hearing him speak. He was an unpleasant man but, if he talked as engagingly as he wrote, it would make an interesting close to the conference. So far, she'd avoided discussing the book with Jack, knowing how much he disliked Wingrave and remembering, too, the man's contemptuous dismissal of her fiancé and his work.

Throwing the linen cover over the books table, she slipped into the back of the hall alongside Derek Easterhouse and the last few members of the audience to take their place. The numbers for this particular talk meant standing room only, but from here Flora had a good view of the proceedings. The layout of the stage remained as it had for the whole conference, though the vase of fresh flowers that adorned the small side table on opening day now looked decidedly jaded.

Whether he wanted to or not, Jack had been asked to introduce Wingrave, while it would be Basil no doubt who said the final words. At that stage, he would have a large audience, a captive audience, to whom he could extol the delights of joining the Dirk and Dagger Society. Ostensibly, the goal of the conference had been to increase the society's membership, mattering as much as making any kind of profit, and she hoped Basil had managed to fulfil at least one of his aims.

Jack was in the wings, she saw, waiting for the audience to settle before he strode onto the stage. His tall figure was jacketless, the day having turned very warm, and his hair was doing its familiar wild flop, but he was the nicest-looking man in the room, Flora thought proudly. He usually was. Behind Jack, at his left shoulder, the bright colours of a cravat announced that Felix Wingrave's moment of glory had arrived.

Jack was halfway across the stage, making for the microphone, when there was a loud rumble. People began looking around, glancing out of the window or twisting their heads to scan the closed doors of the hall. Someone was pointing and Flora followed their hand. What she saw made her breath catch. She stood rooted, paralysed by fear, her body seizing up, her muscles rigid. There was a warning yell from one of the audience. A roll of asbestos-based material, huge and damagingly heavy – no wonder the safety curtain was referred to as an iron – was plummeting to the stage.

At the very moment she grasped the danger, Jack became aware of his likely fate. With surprising speed, he threw himself to one side, though not quickly enough to prevent the faux red velvet hitting him hard on the shoulder and knocking him to the floor. But saved, nevertheless, from certain death.

The smack of a weighty curtain crashing onto the wooden stage was followed by an eerie hush. Then, suddenly, there were feet running: Basil Webb darted from backstage, Clive Slattery, sitting in the front row, jumped the barrier of lights, even Felix Wingrave managed to emerge from the wings. Seeing Basil bending over Jack's prone body, Flora waited no longer. Heart thundering, she pushed past the members of the audience who had been standing nearby and, reaching the aisle that ran beneath the wall of long windows, made for the end of the hall and the short flight of stairs that gave access to the stage.

Jack's face was very pale but he was conscious. 'How bad is it?' she asked him, crouching beside Basil, a tremor in her voice.

'I don't know what happened,' Basil said before Jack could answer. 'It should never have happened.'

'Obviously not,' she said curtly. 'But it has, and we need to get Mr Carrington to a doctor.'

'Yes, yes. But the next talk, Felix...' he muttered fussily.

'Does any of that matter?'

'Dear lady.' It was Wingrave who stepped forward. 'You cannot be serious. Think for one moment of the situation we are in. My fans' – he flapped a velvet-clad arm at the audience beyond, sitting dumb and shocked into silence – 'my fans have been waiting four days to hear me speak. Four whole days!'

'I'll have to take Mr Carrington, Felix,' Basil said a trifle desperately. 'I've a car outside.'

'No matter, dear chap. You must carry on with whatever. *I* will carry on here.'

Felix beamed, and walked to the front of the stage, picking up the microphone as he did. With his other hand, he gestured for quiet and the audience fell obediently silent.

'My dear readers...' he began.

It was fortunate that Dr Hanson was in his surgery preparing for his evening consultations when Jack hobbled into the waiting room, supported by Basil on one side and Flora on the other.

'Nasty bruises,' the doctor said, once Jack had stripped off his outer clothes. 'And more nasty bruises on the way, I'd say. But you don't appear to have broken anything.'

Leaving Jack to dress himself as well as he could, Dr Hanson came out to speak to Flora. 'I've anointed the wounds with arnica. Regular aspirin for a while... and,' he said to Jack, who had walked back into the waiting room, 'I'd advise you to use a sling for a few days. It should take the pressure off your shoulder. What happened exactly?'

When Flora explained, the doctor shook his head. 'A safety curtain? Highly dangerous. Wasn't it checked beforehand?'

'It was.' Basil was quick to intervene. 'I checked it myself. Checked the mechanical lever and the rope. There was nothing wrong with either.'

'Well, there was this afternoon.' Flora's tone was crisp. 'Perhaps when you get back to the school, you should look again. First, though, can you take us home to Overlay House?'

Slightly cowed, Basil was eager to shuffle them into his car and drive the few hundred yards to Jack's front door.

'Good luck with the end of the conference,' Jack called after him as Basil scurried back to his car. 'Sorry it's proved a damp squib.'

'Not for you, it hasn't,' Flora said severely, helping him over the threshold and into the newest sitting room chair. She didn't want to scold, but she'd been truly frightened seeing that weight of curtain fall headlong onto an unsuspecting Jack. 'There's been too many fireworks. You need to rest.'

'I'm OK. A bit battered, that's all, so no fussing.' He smiled slightly. 'I wouldn't mind a drop of brandy, though. You know where it is?'

Flora did, pouring him a small measure, and feeling huge relief when she saw his face become a little less ashen. She'd felt sick at the thought he might have suffered an injury the doctor hadn't discovered.

'Are you up to talking?' she asked and, when he nodded, sat down in the chair opposite. 'Was it an accident, do you think?'

'I've been wondering.'

'Do you know how the safety curtain operates?'

'I'm not sure on this particular stage. If it's a modern fitting – if the fire curtain has been replaced recently – there should be a lever backstage. Didn't Basil mention one? But it may still need someone to pull a rope – in an emergency. Pulling on the rope causes the curtain to fall rapidly.'

'And cutting the rope?' As she'd waited for Jack at the surgery, Flora had had time to think, and become convinced that this had been no accident.

'Then the curtain would plummet. An emergency option only.'

'We need to look at that curtain. Particularly the rope, if there is one. Or rather I do. If it's been tampered with, it won't be an easy thing to disguise. I've left Betty in the school playground and I'll need to go back to collect her. The building should be nearly empty by now. Most of the audience will have driven off or taken a taxi or walked to the high street to catch the bus. And if Basil Webb *is* still around, I should be able to dodge him.'

Jack put down his glass and sat a little straighter. 'You need to take care,' he warned. 'If it was deliberate... I don't want anything falling on *you*.' He was silent for a moment. 'I should be with you,' he muttered.

'You're staying here – and I'll be careful. I'll make sure no one sees me poking about. But if that curtain was rigged, why was it you that was targeted?'

'I've no idea. I've done nothing to attract attention, welcome or unwelcome. In fact, I've been a singularly uninspiring sleuth this time round.'

Flora jumped up to walk to the window and back. 'Perhaps,' she said, 'it wasn't meant for you. Felix Wingrave was waiting in the wings and about to follow you onto the stage.'

'If they were after Felix, their timing was ropey.' He grinned at the pun.

'Stop teasing. This is serious. Think – who would want to kill Wingrave?'

'Plenty of people,' he said glumly. 'Me, for one.'

'Jack! You're being flippant and a blow to the head is no excuse! We'll talk about it later, but a cup of tea before I go?'

He shook his head. 'I'll make do with the brandy.'

'Don't have too many glasses. Remember, you've stairs to climb tonight. Do you want me to come back?'

'And undress me? No, thanks.' He reached out for her hand. 'I'm keeping that delight for later.'

She smiled down at him and kissed the top of his head. 'Use the sling Dr Hanson gave you. I'll telephone you this evening and, if you're not coping, I'll be back.'

As Flora had surmised, most of the conference attendees had left for home with only a few hardy souls still talking to Basil in the playground. Of Felix Wingrave there was no sign. He had evidently given his talk, blessed his followers, and left for his Surrey mansion.

Basil, she saw, was gamely maintaining his bonhomie, fixing a bright look on his face and trying to sound upbeat. His body, though, was telling a different story. The stooped shoulders, a slightly bowed head and the mechanical gestures as he spoke, signalled dejection. He would have been counting on a rousing end to the conference, one which might have produced a size-able number of new members for his society, and he must be bitterly disappointed with how it had turned out.

Nodding briefly in his direction, Flora walked past the group into the school foyer as though to collect something from her bookstall. She would have to spend much of tomorrow transporting any unsold items to the shelves of the All's Well, but right now the trestle was ignored and, slipping through the hall doors, she made her way to the flight of stairs that led to the stage. It was bare. The lectern and small table had gone, and so had the safety curtain.

She frowned and looked up at the ceiling. The curtain's fittings could not have been repaired so quickly, but the heavy roll of cloth had been fixed back in its place. The caretaker's temporary solution? But a solution that made her task more difficult, if not futile. The curtain was hung so high that the man must have taken a long ladder to the job, the end of the pulling rope now so far above Flora that it was impossible to scrutinise in any useful way.

As she lowered her gaze, however, her eyes picked up what looked like threads of material scattered across the wooden boards. Picking up a small tuft, she brought it closer for inspec-tion, feeling its coarse texture between her fingers. If this wasn't the remains of rope, she would eat spinach for the rest of her life, and she hated spinach. It *was* rope. And it had been severed.

She stood looking out at the empty hall, the chairs still

arranged in their neat rows, the curtains no longer moving in the breeze from windows now closed. An accident had occurred on this stage, but it had been death that had been planned.

Had it been Jack's death? The thought curled her insides. Or someone else's? And why?

13

———

Jack woke early the next morning, an entire side of his body extremely sore, but he knew how lucky he'd been in escaping the full force of the safety curtain relatively unharmed. He was certainly well enough to help Flora dismantle her bookstall and ferry any unsold books to the All's Well. A quick glance at the clock told him he had time for a decent breakfast before setting out.

Flora was still eating her way through a bowl of cornflakes when he arrived at her front door. 'I didn't expect to see you today,' she said, walking back into the kitchen. 'Are you sure you should be here?'

When she'd telephoned last night, he must have sounded more feeble than he'd realised. 'Battered but still on two feet,' he reassured her, following her into the kitchen and helping himself to a cup of tea from the pot on the table. 'And just how were you proposing to move a pile of books without the Austin?'

'Wheelbarrow?' She grinned. 'Actually, I was about to call at the Nook and ask Tony if he and his van had a spare hour, but if you're sure...'

'Ready and waiting. I imagine Rose Lawson will be at the shop to help unpack?'

'She should be. I asked her to do the full week, and said I'd take over from tomorrow morning. Why?'

'It occurred to me that perhaps we should grill her before she leaves the All's Well. About the shop she ran with her husband – find out for sure what kind of market they catered for. Antiquarian books aren't necessarily first editions. In fact, it's likely the shop sold few really valuable books. So... would Rose have the necessary contacts – people who could negotiate a private sale of the Dickens without raising a dust?'

'It only needs a single person,' Flora pointed out, 'and it's likely she or her ex-husband would have one contact they could go to.'

'You're supposing she'd take the ex-husband into her confidence. In the circumstances, that doesn't seem likely.'

'If there was money in it for him, I reckon she'd ask for his help – and get it.'

'I still think it's worth pressing her a little. What about her acquaintance with Maud Frobisher? It would be good to pin her down on just how well she knew Maud. Well enough to be shown the safe, shown the Dickens, asked for an estimate of its value? Even if her answers aren't that helpful, they might add a few more pieces to the puzzle.'

Flora slid her cereal bowl into the sink and picked up her handbag and keys. 'It might be useful, but could *you* talk to her?' she said diffidently.

He was surprised. Flora was usually more than ready to step in, eager to question, determined to burrow into whatever mystery was going.

'I don't want to upset Rose, not at the moment.' She stood by the kitchen doorway, her feet doing a slight shuffle. 'She's clearly a suspect but if she *is* innocent of any wrongdoing... I'm thinking that maybe, at a stretch, I could manage to employ her one or two days a week,' she finished in a rush. 'When she's not working for Dilys.'

Another surprise. Flora was fiercely protective of her bookshop, territorial in fact, and it had taken her a deal of heartsearching, he knew, before she'd agreed to work at the conference and hand the All's Well over to a woman she had only just met.

The hazel eyes when he glanced at her held a challenge. 'I've enjoyed the change in routine,' she said defensively, 'being out of the shop for a while and maybe... maybe I should think of letting go a little.'

Jack said nothing, knowing he was likely to be stepping on eggshells.

'Getting married, I mean,' she said awkwardly. 'It will mean changes so why not at the shop?'

'Why not?' His tone was light, not underestimating for a moment Flora's difficulty in accepting a different way of life. 'Ready to go?'

Once at the school, it took them nearly an hour to load the Austin with the remaining books and find room in what was a small vehicle for the various bits and pieces that Flora had brought with her – a wooden stool, a locked strong box, the linen cloth and book stands – all of them having helped the week to run smoothly.

They worked quickly and without interruption, the school seeming empty but for themselves. The grounds when they arrived had appeared deserted and, when Jack checked the hall before locking up for a final time, it was a thick silence that greeted him. He knew from Flora's telephone call last night what she had found scattered across the boards of the stage: clear evidence that the pulling rope had been severed. Now, as he looked towards the stage, he could see the safety curtain had been hung in its rightful place and at a correct angle, its temporary position amended.

'The caretaker must have been at work very early this morning and managed to get the mechanical lever working. It's lifted the curtain to where it should be,' he said to Flora as she followed him into the hall. 'OK for now, I guess, but that rope will need fixing soon. For safety's sake, you have to have alternative ways of operating a fire curtain.'

'Let's keep clear of it – just in case. It gives me goose pimples. I won't be sorry to say goodbye to this hall.'

'And hello to the All's Well?'

She beamed. 'My treat of the week!'

'Time to go,' he decided, ushering Flora through the main entrance and locking the school door behind them.

Jack glanced through the latticed windows of the All's Well as he pulled into the kerb, catching sight of what seemed a crowded shop. It appeared that some of the conference audience had stayed the night in Abbeymead and, on their walk around the village this morning, had found the bookshop.

'Too many people for any questioning,' he said, climbing from the driver's seat and opening the tiny boot. 'My interrogation will have to wait.'

Rose Lawson glanced up as the doorbell clanged, a flustered expression on her face.

'Ignore us,' Flora told her, as they began carrying boxes into the shop. 'We won't be long. I'll need to find space for these extra books, or leave them with you to sort out later – oh, and lock the conference takings in the safe. But then we'll be off.'

In fact, very little space was needed. Fascinated, Jack watched as several customers who had been wandering aimlessly around the shop, browsing shelves in dilatory fashion, suddenly spotted the cartons of books and made a dive for their contents. Either they'd not been quick enough to buy at the conference or they'd discovered they had more money left than they'd expected. Within a short time, most of the boxes were empty.

Flora waited until Rose had finished serving her last customer before walking across to her.

'If you can come by tomorrow morning, Rose – before lunch – I'll have the week's wages ready,' she said quietly. 'Along with huge thanks for all your very hard work!'

'I've enjoyed it.' Rose pushed her long dark hair back from her face. 'It was good to be working with books again. Any time you want help, Flora, please ask.'

Jack looked at Flora, his grey eyes expressive – the fact that Rose was no longer being coy about her experience with books had been a mutual thought – but she gave a slight shake of the head to his unspoken question. This wasn't the time either to grill Rose or to broach the new plan for the bookshop.

'If I can't ask questions,' he said, as they walked out of the All's Well, 'how about an early lunch? We could eat at the Nook before I drive you home.'

'Good idea. I can see Kate – I haven't spoken to her for an age.'

'It's been four days.'

'It's felt like an age,' Flora retorted.

It was Kate who greeted them with a happy face when they walked through the café door and, hearing their voices, Tony bobbed out from behind the kitchen counter.

'The conference is finished!' Kate said. 'And what a success – or so we've heard.'

'A success for Flora,' Jack agreed. 'I've never seen so many books disappear as quickly.'

'There seems to have been a right to-do yesterday, though,' Tony put in. 'Some accident on the stage. We didn't get all the details but it sounded serious.'

'It wasn't anything to do with either of you, was it?' Kate's pale blue eyes held an anxious expression. From past knowledge, she must suspect their involvement was highly likely.

'No,' Jack said blandly and was echoed by Flora.

Kate looked relieved. 'So what can I get you? We're doing spam fritters today – a special request by some of the regulars – and maybe tomato soup to start with?'

'Perfect,' they said in unison.

Jack deliberately chose a table away from the window, tucked into one of the small alcoves. He had something to show Flora and didn't want their conversation overheard.

'Before the food arrives, what do you think of this?' He passed over the table the dirty and crumpled poster he'd found in the spinney.

She frowned, gingerly spreading the sheet of paper across the blue gingham tablecloth and scanning its message.

'What do I think of it? Tacky.'

'Very. But who would you guess was behind it?'

'First off, tell me where you found it.'

'Stuck to my foot in Church Spinney, would you believe. Copies had been posted on most of the tree trunks.'

'The spinney is a strange place to publicise a conference. I presume that was its aim.'

'And strange that the poster hasn't appeared anywhere else in the village.'

Flora pursed her lips. 'Not that strange. If posters like this had been plastered around Abbeymead, the village would not have been happy. There would have been mutters and more, people probably disowning the conference, perhaps even trying to prevent it happening.'

'If not here, it must have been plastered elsewhere. You don't pay for posters to decorate a spinney. But where? And who?' he asked again.

'Basil Webb? He has most to gain from a big attendance.'

'My thoughts exactly. I reckon it must have been a

desperate attempt to drum up business for the conference when his delegate list began to look sad. And it probably worked – particularly the offer to buy a ticket on the day, with the promise of something nasty to come.'

'If it *was* Webb's idea,' she said, 'he must have had the posters printed earlier. It takes time to produce them.'

'Ordered in advance and used when he saw things getting sticky.'

'We both noticed the audience had grown over the week. Maybe this poster was the reason.' Flora paused.

'The poster *and* Maud Frobisher's death on the first day of the conference,' she said slowly. 'Her murder was reported in the local paper and plenty of people would have read of it. But how gruesome that is!'

'We shouldn't jump to conclusions. All of it might be coincidental: the poster, the murder, the increase in attendance.'

'And it might not.' She tapped impatient fingers on the table. 'There's something else. Something that's just occurred to me. Your accident – could that have been a publicity stunt?'

Jack began to decry the idea, but she pressed on. 'The caretaker checked both the hall and the stage the day before the conference began – he mentioned it to me when I was setting up my stall, pleased that everything looked shipshape for the event. There was nothing wrong with the curtain then. And have you realised? Basil has made no move to report the incident to the police, to the council, to the school. That's odd, don't you think?'

'Maybe... but a publicity stunt?' he protested.

She leaned across the table, her voice low. 'The rope was deliberately cut. We know that. It was only luck that you escaped. Maybe when Basil said "it shouldn't have happened", what he really meant was that it shouldn't have been an accident. If he did cut that rope, he'd be expecting, wanting a death. A juicy article to fill the newspaper columns.'

'Somehow I don't think my name would fill too many columns.'

'Don't be modest, Jack. You're wrong. And, in any case, it might not have been you destined for the chop. I've mentioned it before – it was Felix Wingrave standing in the wings.'

Jack leaned back in his seat. 'Yes, there's a thought. If I'd introduced him seconds earlier... But, no joking, who would really want to hurt him? It's true he's upset a fair number of people – been openly critical of their books, given them rotten reviews – and some of *them* attended the conference. But murder?'

'If it's a grab for publicity, an angry writer won't be the guilty one. It's far more likely to be Basil messing up his timing and almost killing his most celebrated author.' She was silent for several minutes. 'Except the idea doesn't fly, does it?' she said at last. 'The conference was about to end when that curtain came down. There was no need for Basil to drum up more interest.'

'Unless Webb intends to run another conference and piggy-back on the success of this one. Or he means to write a book.'

'Write a book? Basil?' Jack saw the grin she couldn't suppress.

'He's mentioned the possibility. Casually, it's true, and I had the feeling that if he ever got going it would turn out to be more of a booklet than a book. But he has it in mind. He wants, as he said, to "immortalise this brilliant conference through the printed word".'

'How ridiculous.'

'He's scraping around trying to raise money,' Jack said grimly. 'Money was what the conference was about, apart from needing to increase the society's membership. It's what any book or brochure will be about. Money for his sister – the East-erhouses are in trouble, don't ask me why exactly, and Basil is trying to help.'

'By murdering people or attempting to murder them?'

'I agree. It sounds a bit extreme, even for Abbeymead. But—'

Jack had no time to spell out the 'but' before Kate arrived at their table with bowls of home-made tomato soup.

'Here you are,' she said, manoeuvring the bowls into place without mishap. 'And it's on the house!'

'No, really—' Flora started to protest.

'Yes, really. The conference brought the Nook a huge amount of extra trade and you two did much of the hard work. Lunch is to say thank you. Also,' she continued, giving them an unusually severe look, 'it's time for you both to relax – and you can start now. You've October to look forward to, don't forget!' A coy glance and Kate whisked herself away.

Neither commented on this sally, their attention fixed carefully on the food. It wasn't until they were halfway through the soup that Jack dared to ask, '*Are* you looking forward to October?'

Flora looked up, her spoon suspended mid-air, and her smile told him everything.

14

Flora always enjoyed her Friday evenings and the time spent with her closest friends, exchanging news and the occasional gossip over a home-cooked meal. Tonight, though, she felt almost too tired to leave the house. The thought of changing her skirt and blouse for a dress, of choosing jacket and shoes, then walking the length of Greenway Lane to Alice's cottage, seemed overwhelming.

But Alice would have done them proud this evening – she cooked for her friends as beautifully as she did for any Priory guest – and much as Flora longed to curl up on her sofa and finish reading Wingrave's Egyptian mystery, she forced herself to climb the stairs to her bedroom and make herself ready.

This week had been hard work, harder than she'd expected, and it was inevitable, she supposed, that her energy would slump once the conference was over. But there was more to her reluctance, she knew: the end of the conference would bring with it the return of wedding plans in all their exhausting detail. Plans that were bound to resume tonight. From the moment Jack and she had returned from France and announced they were getting married, the wedding had dominated Alice's conversation. Only the advent of a writers' conference in Abbeymead had caused a welcome distraction.

Now, Flora feared, they would be back to endless discussions of which dishes should be served at the wedding breakfast or what size of marquee should be erected on the village green – most of the village was expecting an invitation, as far as she could make out, and she'd long given up any hope of controlling events.

Jack, in a wild moment, had suggested they sneak away this autumn for a long weekend, confide in the vicar that they'd changed their plans and marry somewhere blissfully quiet. A seaside town out of season perhaps, with witnesses plucked off the street. The idea so appealed to Flora that she almost agreed, but she knew it would break Alice's heart and disappoint Kate and Sally hugely – they were to be her bridesmaids. Knew that it would upset village worthies like Dilys at the post office, Mr Houseman the greengrocer, Amy Dunmore the vicar's housekeeper, and a hundred other people. And... she had said no to the suggestion while her heart had said a definite yes. Jack had looked resigned but he'd understood. He may have lived in Abbeymead a mere seven years, but he'd imbibed enough of the unwritten rules of village life to know that any important event must be shared by everyone.

Alice lived a walk away of fifteen minutes or so, along Greenway Lane and across the high street. Her cottage, smaller even than Flora's, was sandwiched between a narrow flint-and-brick house, and a small, incongruously modern office block, a replacement for a house lost during the war. Alice's immediate neighbours had suffered a direct hit from a stray missile – a German bomber making its way back from a raid on London.

Her friend had the door open before Flora had raised her hand to the knocker. 'This is some lovely,' Alice declared. 'All of us here tonight! Sally, too.'

Sally Jenner, Alice's niece, rarely came to their Friday

evenings. Only, Flora thought, when there was more than usual going on in the village or more than usually serious matters to discuss. Her spirits sank a little lower.

But it wasn't until they'd taken spoons to Alice's magnificent lemon chiffon pie that the wedding assumed centre stage. Up until then, the conference had held sway and Flora had begun to believe that she might escape without any mention of October or marquees or wedding fare.

But as she was about to take a second mouthful of lemon pie, Alice said, 'Mr Preece was tellin' me where you can get a small marquee – a large tent really – at a reasonable price.'

'Really? That could be useful,' Flora murmured, intent on her pudding bowl. 'This is utterly delicious.'

'Isn't it?' Kate agreed. 'I found a new recipe in *Woman and Home*. A customer left the magazine behind and Alice said she'd make it for me. I think it might be too elaborate to offer at the Nook but it's a wonderful way to end a meal.'

'We can put it on the Priory menu,' Sally put in. 'What do you think, Auntie?'

'I'm always lookin' for new desserts, it's true. Katie, you know that pattern for your bridesmaid dress...' Alice was not to be distracted.

Flora gave an inner sigh and, for the next few minutes, determinedly lost herself in the utterly delicious pudding.

'... I reckon that niece of Dilys could adapt it to suit both of you. She's a good dressmaker, I've heard, and she comes over from Worthing most weekends to see her aunt. We should ask her to make up the material you bought, Sal. It would give her a few hours' break from Dilys and her complaints. What do you think, Flora?' Alice frowned heavily. 'And what about your own dress?' Flora's dress had almost escaped scrutiny, but not quite.

'She's away with the fairies,' Sally teased. 'Or still at the conference.'

'Oh! I've just remembered.' Kate surprised them. 'That accident yesterday in the school hall.' She turned to Flora. 'You swore it was nothing to do with you or Jack, but that's not what it said in the *Evening Argus*. Tony bought the paper when he picked up our groceries and they had a report on it. It mentioned Jack, said that he was hurt.'

'Jack is fine,' Flora said, hoping to quieten the loud exclamations. 'There was a problem with the safety curtain, that's all. It dropped when it shouldn't have, but Jack managed to dodge.'

'Completely?' Alice asked suspiciously.

'Almost completely. You saw him today, Kate. He was fine, wasn't he? But the paper was quick with its report,' she said thoughtfully. 'Someone must have tipped them off. I wonder who.'

But really, she didn't. Remembering the poster Jack had shown her, Flora could be fairly certain. There hadn't been another death, true, but there could well have been, and the paper would have been eager to make the most of whatever incident had happened. They might have reminded their readers of Maud's death at the very beginning of the conference, an unhappy 'sandwiching' of events, though lucrative for a newspaper looking for sales. And lucrative for Basil Webb if there were to be more crime conferences in the future, not to mention a forthcoming book on the Abbeymead experience.

'Did the article mention the conference by name?' she asked lightly.

There were creases on Kate's forehead as she searched her memory. 'I think it did. It mentioned Basil Webb and how well he'd done to stage a big conference in such a small village.'

'And that he was thinking of running more events like it?'

'How did you know?' Kate looked surprised. 'You must have seen the *Argus*.'

'No, but I got to know Basil a little and he seems to enjoy publicity. Unlike his brother-in-law. Derek was at the conference, too, but keeping a low profile.'

Flora hoped the change of tack wasn't too obvious. She wanted information on the Easterhouse couple, if there was any to be had, but she needed to tread carefully. Alice disapproved heartily of what she saw as 'poking around in business that doesn't concern you'.

'The poor man seemed quite lost during the conference,' she went on. 'He's an aspiring writer, I heard, but so far has had no success. I don't expect working for the county council is terribly conducive to writing.'

'It's not conducive to anythin', in my view,' Alice said decidedly.

'Do you know anyone there – at the council offices?' Flora asked, looking around the table and being met with blank expressions on all three faces. 'Or would Hector, Sally?' It was a gamble. Hector was Sally's relatively new sous chef. 'He worked at County Hall, didn't he?'

'I can ask him, but why do you want to know?' Puzzlement had replaced indifference.

'No real reason. I felt sorry for the man and wondered if there was anything I could do to help him. I sell books, after all, and he interested me.'

Alice stood up to clear their pudding bowls. 'You know where that kind of interest leads,' she warned. 'In any case, Hector worked in the kitchens at County Hall and left months ago. He won't know the chap.'

'What's his name?' Sally asked, ignoring her aunt's dismissal.

'Easterhouse. Derek Easterhouse.'

Alice paused at the door, dishes in hand. 'Easterhouse? That rings a bell. Do you remember the name, Kate?'

'Wasn't he the man who married Thelma Bolding?'

Alice walked back to the table and nodded at Kate. 'You're right! Thelma Bolding. Her mother never expected her to marry – if you ask me, she didn't want her to wed. Thelma was too useful around the house and in the creamery old Mother Bolding ran at the time. That's long gone, of course. But then this chap turned up at their shop. He was stayin' with a friend in the village, and wanted to buy a pot of cream to go with some scones he'd got from the bakery. A way of thanking his friend for the visit, he said. He might have passed on his thank yous, but he left the village with more'n a Sussex cream tea!'

'He must have liked Thelma.' Sally was always ready to enjoy a romance.

'It was more that *she* liked him. She never kind of took, did she, Katie? A bit of a plain lass and too quiet by half.'

'It was nice they found each other,' Kate said happily.

'They didn't stay in Abbeymead then?' Flora had spotted a possibility. Thelma, she remembered, lived somewhere in Sussex and if she could find her and persuade her to talk, they might learn something more of her brother. Something that could prove crucial to their case against Basil.

'No. I think they ended up in that new town – Crawley? But *he* came from over Eastbourne way.' Alice had walked back to the door, still on her way to the kitchen. 'What was that village? The one with the posh restaurant?'

'It's Jevington, Auntie. The restaurant's called The Hungry Monk.'

'The Hungry Monk! Why wouldn't they be hungry? All that prayin' and fastin'. It goes without sayin' they would,' was Alice's riposte before disappearing into the kitchen.

Walking home to her cottage a few hours later, Flora was still tired but a good deal more satisfied. Thelma Easterhouse was someone they could trace, someone they could talk to, and now she had a way in – the woman had been born and bred in the village and Abbeymead still remembered her. Armed with the information, it should be easy enough to concoct a story, unconnected to the conference, to explain why she and Jack were knocking at Thelma's front door.

15

Flora had barely opened the bookshop on Saturday morning before the doorbell clanged and Rose Lawson, her long, dark hair coiled into an elegant bun, was on the threshold. Abandoning her search for the feather duster, Flora walked over to greet her helper.

'Rose, just the person I needed to see! The feather duster?'

'I stored it behind the kitchenette door. In that funny little cupboard on the left. Sorry. Have you been looking for it long?'

'No, don't worry.' Flora gave a shake of her head. 'I've only just begun the morning's chores. But I have had time to sort out your pay. You did a brilliant job keeping the All's Well in business.'

Rose flushed. 'I'm glad the week went smoothly. Sales were pretty good – I hope the conference stall did as well. It certainly looked like it when you called yesterday. All those empty boxes! But it's good to see you back in your bookshop, Flora, though I've loved being here. It was like... like old times.'

'I imagine so.' She slipped the small brown envelope she had just filled into Rose's hand.

'Thank you.' Her visitor held the envelope aloft. 'A life

saver! Maggie has been so good in sharing her room but without this, I would have had to leave Mrs Waterford's.'

The envelope was tucked away in the straw basket Rose carried. It was then that Flora became aware that in the basket was a parcel wrapped in brown paper. A book-shaped parcel.

'Off to the post office?' she asked casually.

'No. Off to London, in fact.'

'Really?'

The remark brought Flora up sharply, her first thought how could Rose afford to travel that far? The journey made no sense. If you had absolutely no money, why would you spend the small amount you *had* managed to earn on a train fare to London?

But aloud, she said, 'You deserve a day out. Shopping or sightseeing? The weather is good for either.' It had been a calm morning, a few clouds, a hint of sun. Peaceful weather.

Rose's flush grew deeper. 'Neither. I'm meeting my husband,' she said awkwardly, then corrected herself, 'My ex-husband.'

Another shock. Flora tried not to look surprised. 'It's good that you're on reasonable terms again,' she ventured, wondering if the village grapevine had got the situation very wrong in thinking the two had parted badly. But Dilys wasn't usually wrong. She was as sharp as Alice in picking up what-ever story lay behind events and, according to the postmistress, the evil husband had taken as much as he could from the marriage and left Rose with nothing. Certainly, the woman's way of living suggested she had come out of the relationship very poorly.

'I wouldn't say reasonable,' Rose said at last, evidently strug-gling to find the right word. 'But, in the end, you have to find some way of going forward.'

'I suppose so.'

If that were the Dickens novel nestling in her basket, did the way forward involve the ex-husband? Would he be asked to transact business for Rose, maybe on the understanding of a substantial cut for himself?

'I'll wish you a good journey then. I hope all goes well.'

'Me, too.' Rose flashed an uncertain smile and, giving Flora a brief wave, was out of the door and on her way to the bus that would take her to Brighton station.

Flora was left troubled. She wanted to offer Rose more permanent employment at the All's Well but, with her suspicions raised once more, she'd held her tongue. There were too many oddities to be comfortable. What had been in that parcel and why go to London when you had very little money? And to meet a man who had treated you so badly? To make up and be friends again? It seemed unlikely. She wanted to trust Rose, wanted to believe in her, but any offer of work at the bookshop would have to wait until she felt a great deal more certain that the woman was innocent of any wrongdoing.

The All's Well closed at lunchtime and much of the remaining weekend was spent by Flora in searching. James Mulholland had asked for her birth certificate and any papers or photographs she could find that would substantiate her identity. The certificate had proved easy enough to locate – in a file she kept in the kitchen drawer along with bank statements and her insurance documents for the bookshop and the cottage. But other papers? Photographs? By Sunday evening, she'd rummaged through every cupboard and emptied every drawer without success until, bowing to the inevitable, she dragged a stepladder from the garden shed and clambered into the small loft. There was a box here, she knew, that contained her aunt's papers, one she'd stored away after Violet's funeral and had not looked at since. She had been too sad.

For some reason – Flora suspected that she'd asked Mr Houseman to hide the box as far from sight as possible – it had been pushed to the very edge of the boarding, where the roof met the loft floor. The limited head space had her bent double, her forehead dotted with sweat and her limbs contorted and aching, before she was able to clear a path to the container she needed. First, several old suitcases had to be dragged to one side, and behind them a nursing chair that had once possessed a beautifully embroidered seat – should she get it repaired? – then a defunct radio, two blackout blinds and several framed pictures.

Grasping the last painting, she collapsed onto the loft floor, for the moment too hot and tired to go on. It was an image of Venice, she made out, such an iconic city that she recognised it immediately. Beneath a wash of rich blue sky, palazzi, with their steep roofs of terracotta tiles, lined either side of the Grand Canal, their façades a harmony of faded pink and grey and white, while at the water's edge, red-and-white-striped poles marked each building's landing stage. Small waves rippled from bank to bank, the waters of the canal disturbed by constant traffic: vaporetti, motor boats, a gondola ferrying a passenger from one side to the other, fruit barges loaded with what looked like oranges and bananas. Every kind of boat for every kind of purpose. In the distance, the beautiful white dome of a church, more a cathedral, stood proud and immense as the canal curved majestically out of sight.

Where was that? she wondered. She had read that the city had a hundred and thirty-nine churches but this one, she felt sure, would be special if you knew Venice. And she would love to know Venice. Suddenly Flora's years-old yearning to travel sprang to life again. She had already visited Paris, she scolded herself, had spent weeks earlier this year in the warmth of Provence. She really shouldn't want more. But somehow she did.

Leaning the picture carefully against the discarded suitcases – she would hang it where she could see it every day, she decided – she shuffled onto her knees and opened the card-board box she had never wanted to see again. A death certificate was the first item she pulled from the box and swiftly put to one side. Ancient bills, long since paid, took up an inordinate amount of space, along with old book catalogues and a list of suppliers.

Eventually, several mementos of Violet's earlier life surfaced, from the time she was teaching in Italy – small square photographs of the Ponte Vecchio in Florence, the Spanish steps in Rome, a menu from a local restaurant, a heavy gold necklace much favoured by Italian women but, as far as Flora could remember, never worn by her aunt. These were followed by more intimate treasures: a lock of baby hair, a pair of small bootees... and, at last, a letter written by her father to his sister, announcing the arrival of a baby daughter. They would be calling her Flora, her father had written, and both he and Sarah were hoping that Violet would stand godmother to the little girl. Surely, here was a letter that would satisfy the most pernickety solicitor.

Feeling relieved but dusty, she tucked the papers into her skirt pocket and the chosen painting under her arm and clambered down the stepladder. She had earned her tea and toast, she reckoned – and earned an evening in which to read her book. The ladder could wait for its return to the shed. Flora had Felix Wingrave's mystery to finish, and she had reached a crucial moment in the plot...

It was a few minutes to eleven before she closed the pages on what had been a very scary ending. An avenue of sphinxes stretching between the Luxor and Karnak temples, that came alive to pursue a hitherto triumphant hero, was not the best image with which to send her to bed. Slightly spooked, she made her way upstairs, trying to dismiss the book and fix her mind elsewhere.

Fix it on tomorrow, she thought. On a Monday morning that would see her first full day back at the All's Well, properly in charge again. A happy prospect. The crime conference had been interesting but unnerving, starting with Maud Frobisher's horrible murder and ending with Jack narrowly escaping death. It wasn't what either of them had expected when they'd agreed to be part of Basil Webb's grand project. Nor had they expected or wanted to be part of another investigation so close to their wedding, and with so many still unanswered questions. Questions that swirled through Flora's mind as she lay, eyes tightly closed, attempting to sleep.

Eventually, she succumbed, but for no more than a few hours. Suddenly, she was awake. A noise that penetrated the countryside calm. The hooting of owls, the rustling of wildlife as it prowled her garden, were familiar sounds. Flora slept through them without stirring, but this was different. Startled, she sat up, her ears straining. A chipping? A rattling? Was it at a downstairs window?

She stumbled out of bed, throwing on her dressing gown, her feet searching for slippers. No fox ever chipped at a window ledge, no badger ever rattled brass fittings. She must have an intruder! Reaching into the drawer of her bedside table, she pulled out a torch and made her way silently down the stairs.

On the ground floor, she could hear more clearly – the noise was definitely coming from the sitting room, directly below her bedroom. Holding her breath, she turned the key in the kitchen door and slipped out into the garden. It was a warm night, and the bed of roses beneath the kitchen window, now in full flower, bathed her in their scent. Pitch black it might be but, knowing every inch of the garden, she had no need of the torch. It had been instinct only that had caused her to grab it.

Gliding around the building, she saw a dark shadow ahead.

A man's figure crouching beneath the sitting room window and working to prise it open. It was proving a surprisingly noisy task. Did he really believe he could break in without waking the inhabitants? Whoever this would-be house burglar was, he wasn't very good at his job. And why was he trying to get into the cottage anyway? She had nothing worth stealing. Her bicycle was probably her most valuable possession and Betty was safely stowed in the garden shed.

There was a decision to make. She could creep back to the house and telephone Constable Tring. That would be the sensible thing to do, though largely pointless. She would be lucky even to wake the policeman, let alone persuade him that she had a burglar. Or she could telephone Jack. He would certainly come, but the arrival of the Austin, the crunch of tyres, would alert the man he had company, and give him time to run. Flora was determined that would *not* happen. Whoever he was, he wouldn't escape. She would know this person who had dared to violate her home, she thought indignantly.

She weighed up her chances. The man had a clear physical advantage, being a great deal taller and heavier. On the other hand, he had his back to her and was unsuspecting, intent on his nefarious work. She hesitated for a few seconds only. She would go for it!

In an instant, she had covered the few yards between them and raised her hand, bringing the unlit torch down onto the man's head. He staggered back, his legs about to crumple but, clutching hold of the window sill, he saved himself from falling. A snarl on his lips, he twisted around and grabbed her in a fierce hold. The torch went flying – too flimsy, she thought, furious with herself. She should have taken the heavy-duty light she kept in the kitchen, not this piffling thing. That way, she could have knocked him unconscious.

Flora was pinioned fast to the man's body, the sickly smell of lavender water making her feel nauseous. She was hurting, too, her limbs crushed between powerful arms. She tried to scream. Not that anyone would hear – her nearest neighbour lived well out of earshot – but her assailant was unlikely to know that, and a scream might cause him to flee.

Her yell, though, was stifled at birth when a large, suffocating hand clamped around her mouth. In a frenzy, she bit into the fleshy palm and now it was his turn to yell. In a sudden movement, he thrust her away, and she fell to her knees – inches from the torch she'd lost. Groping in the dark, she switched the beam full on, training the light upwards and finding his face.

Felix Wingrave!

'What!' she exclaimed.

He seemed not to hear her, too busy inspecting his injured hand. 'You're a vixen, Flora Steele,' he said through his teeth. 'You shouldn't be allowed to roam free.'

'On the contrary, it's you who shouldn't be roaming free.' She had regained her wits along with her breath. Staggering to her feet, she embodied fury. 'How dare you try to break into my home!'

'I wouldn't have done any harm,' he said sulkily, his hand tucked inside his jacket. Like an injured paw, she thought.

'So why break in?'

'I was looking for something. Something that belongs to me.' His tone was grudging. 'I thought you might have it.'

Flora was mystified. 'What could I possibly have of yours? And why not use the front door and ask? I have a knocker.'

'It doesn't matter,' he muttered, pulling down his jacket. Not velvet this time, she noticed in the torchlight, but a serviceable tweed.

'*I* think it matters – a lot. You were damaging my property, engaging in a criminal act, in the middle of the night. You owe me a thorough explanation.'

'And *you* have mortally injured me. I pity Mr Carrington, marrying such a wild cat. See – blood!' He pointed dramatically at a hand that he had bound with a linen handkerchief, now badly stained. 'You owe me an apology.'

Flora gave her head a mental shake. Felix Wingrave appeared utterly dead to his wrongdoing. And why was he still in Abbeymead?

'Shouldn't you have left the village on Thursday evening? Or did you stay behind especially – to do some house-breaking?'

'So many questions,' he complained.

'And no answers. I should report you to the police.'

'But you won't, will you?' A sly look had crept into his face. 'I reckon we're after the same thing, Miss Steele, and neither of us would want the police on our tail.'

Bewildered, she tried and failed to find words before he had turned and walked away, leaving her gaping. In seconds, she heard the front gate clang shut.

What on earth had that been about? Had Felix Wingrave written one too many mysteries and, after a few drinks, begun to re-enact them? Though, thankfully, without the sphinxes. But what could she possibly have that he was after? Something she wanted, too, he'd said. Their only connection was through books. Was that it – they were both looking for the same book?

The Dickens! It struck her in a blinding realisation. Wingrave was after the rare edition of *A Christmas Carol* and suspected she had... stolen it maybe? Or, more charitably, removed it from the murder scene?

One thing was certain. The urbane exterior that Wingrave cultivated was only skin-deep. He was a man capable of breaking the law to get what he wanted, and capable of violence if need be. She rubbed arms that were still burning from his savage grip. And then she thought of Maud.

Her aunt's friend was a good deal stouter than Flora but no taller. Wingrave could easily have attacked her, if he'd wanted the book so badly. And it seemed that he did. If Maud had been alone in the library van early on Monday morning, the safe door open perhaps and the Dickens clear to see, had the temptation for Wingrave been too great? Had he taken his chances and knocked her to the ground?

But, then, a noise outside: Lowell Gracey returning from his angry walk, maybe readying himself to apologise to Maud. In a panic, Wingrave would flee, leaving the rare book behind and, when it was later reported missing, he would assume that someone else had taken it. He'd reason that it couldn't have been Gracey. Gracey had been searched and was in a police cell. The van had been searched, too, along with the playground and playing fields, and nothing discovered. It had, then, to be a third person who had happened on the book and spirited it away.

And she, apparently, was that third person!

16

She would ring Jack, Flora decided the next morning, halfway through dusting a second bookcase. She should have called him first thing, but it wasn't too late – before he chained himself to his typewriter for the day. She had news to tell him, not about Rose, that could wait, but he needed to know of her encounter last night with an unexpectedly violent Felix Wingrave.

'I'd just got to my desk,' Jack panted down the phone, having taken the stairs at double speed. 'You have impeccable timing.'

'Don't be grumpy. It's a beautiful morning and you're back where you like to be.'

'Except right now I'm not. That week away has distracted me and the one thing I'm not wanting to do is sit down at a type-writer and produce words. Can we do something else?'

'Jack—'

'How about finding Thelma Easterhouse?' he interrupted. 'We've decided Basil needs more investigation and I reckon his sister could be a good source. And thanks to Alice and Kate we have the perfect introduction, it seems.'

'I can't just lock up the shop and go. I don't have that luxury.' She thought for a moment. 'We could make it this evening, after closing time?'

Flora heard a long sigh travelling down the wire. 'OK, if it must be. But good when you get the extra help you talked about. Have you seen Rose to ask her?'

'I've seen her,' she admitted, 'but I'm not making a decision at the moment.'

'Why? What's stopping you?'

'I'll tell you later. I rang you about something else. Some*one* else – Felix Wingrave. He tried to break into my cottage last night.'

There was a silence at the end of the phone. Then, 'Say that again.'

'Felix Wingrave tried to break into the cottage last night,' she repeated dutifully. 'He seems convinced that I was the one who took *A Christmas Carol* from the library van. He didn't accuse me of murder, I suppose that's some comfort, but he seemed to be suggesting that after I'd found Maud dead and Lowell was carted off to a police cell, I made away with the book. In his version of events, I must already have stolen it, but when chaos broke out I took the opportunity to smuggle it from the school.'

'But why?' Jack sounded baffled.

'Why would I take it? For the same reason as he came looking. It's a rare object to be possessed, a book I couldn't possibly afford at auction.'

'So... he was going to steal it from you?'

'That was the general idea, I think. I caught him trying to jemmy my sitting room window open. Around midnight.'

'Did he... did he attack you?' Jack asked uncertainly.

'He was rough,' she admitted. 'He grabbed hold of me – I have a trio of bruises on both arms to prove it – and he tried to stop me from yelling with a very large hand on my mouth. But I bit it.'

For a moment, there was another silence and then she heard Jack's laugh ringing down the phone. 'He should have known you better. But seriously, thank God you're safe. I can't bear that he might have hurt you.' He sounded tight with tension. 'And what the hell was Wingrave thinking?'

'I imagine his collector's fervour got the better of him.'

'Pity. I was beginning to soften. I finished his latest book last night and it was good. Now I shall have to hate him all over again.' Jack was making light of the incident, but the edge to his voice betrayed him.

'It wasn't a pleasant experience,' Flora admitted, 'but it does mean we're a little further forward. We know now that he's someone who *doesn't* have the book.'

'We also know he wants it very badly. What a crazy thing to do! It's possible, isn't it, that he murdered Maud trying to get hold of the Dickens but somehow the plan didn't work?'

'It's possible,' she agreed. 'I've been thinking much the same thing. But who on earth has this wretched book? I doubt Thelma Easterhouse will help us with that.'

'She might offer a clue as to why Maud died. We have precious few others. I know we fixed on theft as the motivation, but there's always a chance that we're missing something. I'll look for an address in the telephone directory. The Easterhouses live in Crawley, according to Basil – and Alice, you say – and pick you up from the shop around five? I should have written a complete sentence by then.'

The Easterhouses lived in Willow Walk, a terrace of flat-faced, red-brick houses that sat in the middle of what, in effect, was a massive construction site. Crawley, it seemed, was a town in the process of being built. A tiny, roofed porch and wide symmet-

rical windows presented a uniformity that was saved from dull-
ness by the riot of colour in each square patch of garden. An
abundance of flowers grew beneath ground-floor windows and
lined each side of the concrete paths that led to everyone's front
door. A Silver Cross pram was parked on the next-door neighbour's grass, the covers pulled back and empty of a baby. Flora
wondered if the Easterhouses had children. Basil was unmar-
ried himself and had never mentioned a niece or nephew.

Once they had turned off the Brighton Road, they'd found
their way to Willow Walk by dint of Jack constantly stopping
the car and asking for directions from anyone who appeared a
native of the town. There had been a few wrong turnings, a
roundabout that by all accounts shouldn't have been there, but
by six o'clock he was parking the Austin outside number seven.

'We're here,' he said and sounded pleased.

'Hopefully before Derek arrives back from work.' Flora
peered out of the car window, trying to spot any movement in
the house. 'I've a feeling he won't be too happy having us ask
questions.'

'From the little I've seen of Derek Easterhouse, he's not
happy at all. Come on, let's introduce ourselves to the gorgeous
Thelma before he can intervene.'

If Thelma wasn't exactly gorgeous, she was very
presentable: small and slim and neat, her short brown curls
brushed tightly back from her face and held in place by two
serviceable tortoiseshell clips. A button-through floral dress and
sensible white sandals completed the picture. Flora noticed a
rumpled pinafore in Thelma's right hand; it must have been
hastily untied at the sound of the door knocker.

'Mrs Easterhouse?' Jack asked in his warmest voice.

Thelma's forehead fell into several deep creases and she
twisted her head first right and then left as though to check the
road outside. 'Yes? Is something wrong?'

'Nothing at all,' he assured her. 'My name is Jack

Carrington and this is Flora Steele. We live in Abbeymead – I believe you know the village well.'

That seemed to reassure her though the creases didn't entirely disappear. 'We've been working with your brother this last week,' Jack went on. 'At the Abbeymead crime conference.'

'Oh! You know Basil.' That appeared to be more reassuring.

'It's about your brother that we've come. I wonder if we might have a word.'

'I've just started dinner—'

'So sorry to disrupt your evening,' Flora said quickly, 'but we'll only be a few minutes. We're hoping to help Basil, you see. He's planning to write a book. Did you know?'

Thelma looked astonished, then aghast. 'Really?'

'Yes, really. Jack is a writer himself and I sell books. We'll be acting as Basil's mentors, I suppose, and we both thought it would be useful if we could get a little more information about your brother. About his interest in crime, for instance, before he starts writing.'

Jack gazed in awe at her – how did she come up with this stuff? – but quickly fell into the role allotted to him. 'The book will recount Basil's experience of putting on a writing conference from scratch and I could advise him better if I had some background. Stuff from his family. Stuff that Basil might not think would be useful.'

'Yes, I see.' She sounded doubtful still, but beckoned them across the threshold, leading them into a sitting room on the right of the hallway.

It was a bright airy room but decorated in the varying tones of beige that Flora hated. 'What a beautifully comfortable sofa,' she said, plumping herself down on part of the obligatory three-piece suite. 'You could do with one of these, Jack.'

Inured to her complaints about his knobbly sofa, he said nothing.

'So, what can I tell you?' Thelma asked nervously, perching on a chair opposite.

Jack made a show of extracting a notebook and pencil from his inside pocket. 'I wonder, do you remember when Basil first had the idea of a crime conference?'

'It was... let me see... last year, I think. He came over for Sunday lunch, he often does, and he and Derek – Derek's my husband – were talking about how people were cancelling their subscriptions to the society Basil runs. Derek's a member, you see.'

'Are you?' Flora put in suddenly. 'Was that how you and your husband met?' She already knew the answer but hoped the innocent question would quieten some of Thelma's evident fears.

'Yes, that's how we met. I've never been a member but Basil introduced us.' Thelma didn't look enamoured by the memory. 'Anyway,' their hostess went on, 'afterwards, while we were having a cup of tea, they came up with the idea of running some kind of event. Something that would interest crime readers but be special, too.'

'Do you read crime yourself?' Flora intervened again, sensing that Thelma's lack of any real interest in the Dirk and Dagger might provide a weakness they could probe.

'Goodness, no!' Thelma sounded shocked. 'I'm more of a Barbara Cartland fan myself. But Derek loves crime. He always has and he's a writer, too.' She turned to Jack. 'He's not yet published but—'

'Will be very soon, I'm sure,' he finished gallantly.

'*I'm* not that sure... but I hope so.' She took a deep breath. 'It's become... important.' To Jack, the otherwise innocent word seemed to carry more significance than was warranted.

'And in the meantime?' he hinted.

'They decided that a conference where readers could meet their favourite authors would attract new members and then

Basil suggested it would be a good idea to hold it in Sussex. In a village,' he said. 'A traditional Sussex village, the kind of setting you find in an Agatha Christie.'

'And you came up with Abbeymead?'

'It was where I was born,' she said simply. 'Where I lived until I married Derek. I've never been back, you know. How is the village?' Her voice had softened and for the first time her shoulders lost their tension.

'I expect much the same as when you lived there,' Flora answered. 'Life doesn't change much in the countryside, does it? The conference was a brave idea – something of a gamble with all the costs involved. Is your brother always such a go-getter?'

'He's very determined,' Thelma said thoughtfully. 'And when he sets out to do something, he does it, even if it turns out to be difficult. I suppose he is what you just said, a go-getter.'

Flora beamed and nodded. 'And to hold it in a village that very few people have even heard of!'

Thelma had lost any pink her cheeks had possessed. 'I suggested Abbeymead when he asked me for Sussex names – Basil's not exactly a country boy. He's lived in south London most of his life. Moved in with my uncle and aunt as a toddler when Dad died and never visited the village. Mum... she wasn't easy. She never wanted children, you see. I only got to know Basil properly when we'd both grown up. But I wasn't keen. Not on the village idea. Well, not really keen on the conference. It seemed risky. Asking people to travel a long way and then put up at a country inn. I didn't believe it would attract enough people.'

'It will have attracted sufficient numbers to break even.' Jack was uncertain of his figures but was hoping to reassure her once more. 'It did well for a first attempt. You should be proud of your brother, though I think he's a little disappointed. I know he was hoping to make a profit.'

'Not for himself,' she said quickly. 'He's a good brother.' The words escaped before she could recapture them.

'For you then,' Jack suggested gently.

'Things *have* been a bit difficult,' she conceded.

'You have a lovely home,' Flora said, hoping for more.

And more came. 'At the moment, I have.' Thelma bit her lip. 'But maybe not for much longer. Derek... he's had a few problems.'

'Surely, you can't be moving. It looks a wonderful place to bring up a family.'

'We don't talk about a family,' she said primly. 'Derek is too busy with his writing. But rents here are quite high and we might have to move. To Basil's place, even if it's only temporarily. But his is a small flat and I really hate London.'

And Basil, Flora imagined, would hate sharing his small flat with two grown people. She sounded sympathetic when she spoke and felt it.

'I'm so sorry to hear that. You must be very worried. But... can I ask, what's happened to change things so badly?'

'The council happened, that's what,' Thelma said bitterly. 'They've given Derek the push after fifteen years' solid work in the accounts department.'

'I can't believe it.'

'It's true!' Her voice had risen. 'And for no reason that I can see. He wasn't wanted any more, that's what they said.'

'That's dreadful.' It was, unless there *was* a reason but one that Derek wasn't comfortable sharing with his wife.

'More than dreadful.' Thelma studied the buttons on her dress. 'It's made Derek ...' She seemed unable to finish the sentence. 'And it will destroy the life we have here. I'm trying to get work wherever I can, and do as many hours as possible, but shops, you know, they don't pay much and I'm not what you'd call an educated woman. I left school at fifteen and there was never a chance to do much else. My mother needed me at home, and I've never had anything like a career.'

Thelma Easterhouse and millions of other women, Flora thought.

'I'm sure you're doing everything possible,' she said warmly. 'And your husband is bound to find a new job very soon.'

The woman continued counting her dress buttons, her head bent so low that the rigid white line parting her hair was visible. 'He has tried,' she said. 'But no one's been interested. So far.'

'Basil's book may save the day.' Jack's tone was rousing. 'Particularly now he's planning another conference.'

'Is he?' Thelma looked up from her button counting. 'I didn't know that.'

'Brothers don't always confide, do they?' Flora put in, knowing nothing about brothers but quite a lot about human nature. 'He'll probably tell you when he's arranged everything to his liking. If he's as determined as you say he is.'

'Too determined sometimes,' she murmured. 'But you're probably right. He nearly always gets what he wants.'

'I hope he gets what you *both* want,' was all Flora had time to say before the click of the front door heralded the return of Thelma's husband.

Jack rose to greet him as he walked through the sitting room door and Flora followed suit. 'Mr Easterhouse, how are you?' he said genially, holding out his hand.

'Fine,' he said warily, though he didn't sound it, and his handshake was flabby. Flora decided not to risk it and took cover behind Jack.

'Any luck?' Thelma's voice was subdued.

Derek shook his head and the glare he directed at his wife told her clearly to keep quiet.

'We came to talk about the book your brother-in-law is writing,' Jack explained. 'We're hoping to help him as much as possible.' The lie was now rolling smoothly off his tongue. 'Your wife has been kind enough to give us some background on Basil.' In fact, very little had been said about Basil, and Thelma's forehead – the creases were back again – signalled she had realised it. 'Thank you for seeing us, Mrs Easterhouse, but it's more than time we went.'

'Yes, you were getting supper and we mustn't hold you up a minute longer.' Flora smiled a goodbye and made for the door.

17

Once more back in the Austin, they navigated their way very slowly through a confusion of newly built streets to reach the Brighton road. It was only then that they spoke. Both had been mulling over exactly what they'd learned in what had been a strange meeting.

'You go first,' Jack said, swinging the car onto the south-bound carriageway.

'Derek Easterhouse isn't a happy man,' Flora began. 'He's lost his job for no apparent reason, though it appears serious enough to make it difficult for him to find another job. This at a time when there are hundreds of posts vacant and many of them with the county council.'

'Thelma's "Any luck?" question, I'm presuming, was to ask him how he'd fared today.'

'I think so. And by the look of it, he fared badly – so what *is* stopping him walking into another job? Applying for jobs for which he's not qualified? A difficult attitude when he's inter-viewed? Or maybe he's blotted his copybook in some way and new employers don't want to know.'

'If he has, he hasn't told Thelma. She puts the blame squarely on the council for being arrogant and unfair.'

'Or she does know and isn't telling.'

'The same goes for Basil when I talked to him.' Jack put his foot down on the accelerator. 'He didn't even admit to his brother-in-law losing his job. I was left to assume Derek was still working for the council. If we could discover why the man was dismissed... but Basil. We went to Crawley to learn about *him*.' The Brighton pylons were coming into view and he got ready to take the right-hand turning towards Steyning. 'He loves his sister, that's for sure.'

'Even though they didn't grow up together. I wonder why he feels so strongly about her that he's prepared to risk his own security?'

'Perhaps he doesn't see it that way. He's very determined and gets what he wants, according to Thelma. I can testify to that. He more or less railroaded me into being joint organiser of the conference. And the fact that he ran such an event, miles from anywhere, and persuaded a number of well-known authors to attend, means that he aims high.'

'Maybe impossibly high.' Flora wrinkled her nose. 'Does he really expect to make money on a book written by an unknown who has never picked up a pen before? Or make enough from putting on a second conference which could end up with as little profit as the one that's just finished?'

'Unless...' Jack began.

'Unless he hopes to supplement it in another way? Like selling a rare edition of a book he's stolen.'

'Having murdered Maud Frobisher first,' he finished for her.

He was remembering a conversation he'd had with Webb at the conference. Basil had seemed fixated on the missing book, on how much the Dickens was worth and how much a rare edition would actually make if sold as a stolen item. At the time, his intensity had unnerved Jack.

That book would solve all my problems, Basil had said, seeming to make a joke of it. *Selling the Dickens would make up any shortfall from the conference.*

More importantly, Jack thought, it would ensure his sister kept her home.

Perhaps I should go looking for it, Basil had continued and, when Jack had reminded him that if and when the book was found, it would be library property, Webb had appeared unrepentant.

'There's something else to consider, Jack.' Flora interrupted his thoughts. 'Something that makes the Easterhouse situation more acute and might have prompted Basil to take action.'

'More acute than his sister losing her home?'

Flora shifted in her seat to look at him. 'I don't imagine Basil would welcome the idea of sharing what must be a small flat, but if there's trouble between the Easterhouses... Basil might be fighting to save his sister's marriage as well as her home. He might just be fighting to keep her safe.'

'You really think there's trouble?'

Flora heard Thelma's voice in her head, its tartness, its resentment. Saw the woman's tightened lips and anxious eyes. 'I do,' she said firmly.

Jack drove slowly along Greenway Lane, pulling into the side of the road as they reached Flora's cottage. He was only vaguely aware of a shape hovering to the left of his vision until, hearing Flora's gasp, he pulled on the handbrake and bent his head to squint through the passenger window.

'Who—' he began.

'It's Lowell,' she said uncertainly. 'Lowell Gracey.'

'What the devil does he want?' A variety of emotions took hold of Jack. 'And why isn't he in a police cell?'

'Perhaps if we ask him, we'll find out.' Flora's tone was cool.

'*You* can find out. I'm going home.'

He sensed her swift turn of the head and the look she threw at him. 'Why the huff?' she asked.

'I'm not in a huff. I'm tired. It's been a long day and unless you think Gracey is a danger, I'd like to go home and get my supper. I'll leave it to you to sort him out.'

'Go home then,' she said more sharply. 'Lowell won't hurt me and I might even discover what's going on.'

She was through the garden gate and walking up the brick path to her front door before he called after her, 'I wish you luck!'

Driving off towards Overlay House, he did so without a backward glance. He *was* in a huff, Jack had to admit. The sight of Lowell Gracey, out of police custody and waiting on Flora's doorstep, had infuriated him. He'd get on to Alan first thing in the morning, he decided, discover just why the inspector had let the man go. It wouldn't soften his annoyance – wouldn't explain, for instance, why Gracey as a free man had chosen to go straight to Flora – but it would at least help him feel he was doing something positive. That he was fighting back.

It wasn't a fight, he knew in his heart. Gracey was an old friend of Flora's, nothing more, someone she hadn't seen for years and someone who, until a few minutes ago, was under lock and key for suspected murder. There was nothing to fight about, he told himself. Nevertheless, he spent an agitated night, hours of sleeplessness worrying about Gracey when he could have been turning over in his mind all he'd learned the previous day, details that might help solve the mystery of Maud's murder: Wingrave's bizarre attempt to break in to Flora's cottage and the man's willingness to use violence; the sacking of Derek Easterhouse from an otherwise secure job and Flora's suspicions that the marriage was in trouble; Basil's fierce determination, his refusal in his sister's words to let anything stop him. All potentially crucial information, yet none of it impinged on Jack that night.

Instead, he spent fruitless hours second-guessing Lowell Gracey. Why had he singled out Flora as soon as he was released? What was he plotting? *Was* he plotting or was it he, Jack, who was going slightly mad?

At dawn, he was up and making himself three rounds of toast and two pots of coffee, courtesy of Arthur, while he waited for the moment he could telephone Alan Ridley. His first attempt failed, Ridley not yet having arrived at the Brighton station. Rather than a fourth round of toast, he walked through the French doors into his back garden and did a slow tour, first of the two herbaceous borders and then of his large vegetable patch, deciding as he stood there that he must ask Charlie to come over at the weekend to help him clear a section and sow lettuce and radish for the autumn. He would be giving up the lease of Overlay House but not until late October.

The garden was always calming and planning for the new season a distraction for Jack's harried mind. When he called again, he was able to greet the inspector, newly arrived in his office, with a cheerful hello.

'Good to hear from you, Jack.' Ridley's voice crackled down the phone. 'I was wondering where you'd got to. Been thinking it was time we met up.'

The Cross Keys, Jack thought, groaning inwardly.

'A pint at the Cross Keys? How about lunchtime tomorrow?'

'Sounds good,' he lied. 'I'd welcome a catch-up. But... Lowell Gracey? What happened? He appears to be on the loose.'

'I had to let him go, old chap. Not enough evidence to prosecute.'

'His fingerprints were on the murder weapon,' Jack objected.

'They were, along with a dozen others. But he's never made any secret of the fact that he was holding the weapon. Your... Miss Steele... testified to it. Gracey stands by his story that he came back from a walk around the playing fields and found his boss lying in a pool of blood.'

'And the argument the caretaker heard?'

'He admits he and Miss Frobisher had a bit of a ding-dong. Apparently, he was due to take over her job and then she withdrew her resignation. But he was quite upfront about it.'

'Was he also upfront about the amount of debt he's in? It gives him a very strong motive for getting rid of Maud.'

'Course it does, but like I say, we've no evidence. If I could pin the theft of that dratted book on him, I might have some luck. But so far, zero success. I hope *you've* got something for me.'

'I might, though it's nothing to do with Gracey.'

'Anything, Jack. See you around one o'clock tomorrow – in the bar.'

For the rest of the morning, Jack buried himself in work, but with a mind that was always wandering towards Flora's cottage, speculating on what might be happening there. Had Gracey taken up permanent residence? Had Flora gone to the bookshop despite her new lodger? Should he walk to the shop and apologise for his shortness yesterday? His fingers thrashed the Remington's keys with unnecessary force. He was damned if he would!

Writing today was slow and painful, words refusing to come or, when they did, coming in sentences that he hated. When he heard a loud bang outside, it was gratitude that he felt – whoever it was would save him, at least for a while, from further effort.

It was Charlie Teague, arrived at the front door, his bicycle thrown onto the gravel path with a loud crunch. 'No cricket today?' he asked. Charlie, he knew, was a keen cricketer and this summer holiday had marshalled as many of his former school mates as he could to play on the village green.

'We've played already and I won.'

'Your team won,' Jack corrected him.

'Nah, I won, Mr C. I'm the best!' He made sweeping movements with a phantom bat to demonstrate his prowess.

'And you've come to see me...?'

'Oh, yeah. Mum asked me to bring these.' He produced a carefully wrapped packet of small cakes, dented slightly from the rough treatment it had received.

'A present?'

Charlie nodded. 'Mum's baking day and you sent those tomatoes. Proper good they were.'

'Don't say your mother has got you eating tomatoes at last?'

'If you use loadsa salad cream, they're OK.' He peered round Jack's figure into the kitchen beyond.

'Lemonade?' Jack asked.

'Yeah, please.'

'Actually,' Jack said, leading the way into the kitchen, 'I'm glad you called. I need your help this weekend, but only if it doesn't take you away from helping your mum.'

'I do that plenty,' the boy said confidently. 'And I'm helpin' Mrs Jenner, too, when she asks.'

'At the Priory?' He was surprised.

'I'm learnin' to cook,' Charlie said proudly.

'Well, that is... interesting.' Jack reached up for the bottle of home-made lemonade Kate had given him a few days ago.

'I'm good at it,' Charlie said, gulping down at least half the glass Jack handed him. 'Mrs Jenner's gonna train me. She says I'm good.'

'If Mrs Jenner says so, you must be. But will you have time for my garden this weekend?'

Charlie took another large gulp of his drink. 'I could come on Sunday,' he said benevolently. 'Saturday I'm at the Nook and Friday evenin' is when I deliver books for Miss Steele.'

'A bee that's extremely busy!' Charlie was a prodigious worker.

'I like the food stuff better'n books.' He took another large sip of lemonade, then within a few seconds had drained the rest of his glass.

'Another one?'

'If you're offerin', Mr C. I liked workin' for Mrs Farraday at the caff. She's real nice. Not that Mrs J isn't nice, but she's a whole lot...'

'Stricter?'

'Yeah. No messin' with Mrs Jenner.'

'Do you think you'll work at the café now you've left school?'

'Mebbe, but at the Priory, too. It was good last week deliverin' to the conference. All them writers. It was special. Miss Steele was doin' well on her stall, wasn't she? I'd have looked after the shop for her but I'd already promised the caff.'

'You're in too much demand. Mrs Lawson did the honours instead.'

'She's OK, too.' An uncertain look passed over his face. 'Is Miss Steele all right?'

'Why do you ask?'

'She didn't look happy when I saw her. There was this bloke at the conference. Funny clothes he had on. A suit like he was going up to London. I saw him talkin' to Miss Steele in the playground then he went off in his big car and she was on Betty and goin' somewhere, but she looked kinda shocked. Like he'd told her something she didn't want.'

'Miss Steele is fine, Charlie. Nothing to worry about.'

The words sounded hollow to Jack. What was going on in Flora's life? This must be the man he'd seen drive out of the playground with Flora following after him on Betty, yet she'd made no mention of the encounter.

Feeling Charlie staring at him, he said briskly. 'So Sunday? Around ten?'

18

'Why are you here?' Flora had asked.

Lowell Gracey had followed her into the cottage and stood, feet planted astride the hall mat, wearing dejection like an over-coat. His shoulders were stooped, his head bent and his hands were thrust deep into trouser pockets.

'Sorry, Flora,' he mumbled. 'The thing is... I need a bed.' It was a plea, not a demand.

'The police have let you go?' It was self-evident but Flora was battling bewilderment. The last time she'd seen Lowell, he'd appeared destined to spend weeks in a Brighton police cell.

'They had to,' he said in a low mutter. 'Not enough evidence to keep me locked up. There won't be either, no matter how hard they look. I'm innocent!' His head jerked up and his eyes were suddenly bright.

'Well, that's good,' she said feebly. 'But what now? What are you going to do?'

His head lowered again and he kicked at the cotton rug, sending its fringes into disarray. 'Can you put me up for a while? It won't be for long,' he added swiftly, 'just until this mess is sorted out.'

'I think we need to talk.' Flora's shock was diminishing and practicality taking over. 'Come into the kitchen and I'll make tea.'

Once the pot and teacups were on the table and Lowell installed in a kitchen chair, Flora sat down opposite. 'Where had you been living before you were arrested?'

'I shared a flat in Brighton,' he said briefly.

'So why—'

'I've been chucked out. I missed paying rent this month – how could I, banged up in a cell?' He was suddenly belligerent. 'The blokes I shared with gave my room to someone else. Wouldn't wait a moment. Judge and jury, they were.'

'But you could rent another flat, surely?'

There was no way she would let an old friend down, even though she hadn't seen Lowell for years, but Flora was desperate to see him move on. Jack's reaction if Lowell became her lodger was predictable and not one with which she wanted to cope.

'What am I going to rent with?' he said gloomily. 'I'm suspended from work and the council won't take me back, if ever, until the police investigation is over and I've been proved innocent.'

'The council isn't paying you?' It was beginning to dawn on Flora that she'd been chivvied into a corner.

Lowell shook his head. 'No work, no pay.'

'But if the investigation drags on, you could be without money for months.' It was a dire prospect.

'It's why I need your help, Flora. Please. You won't know I'm here, I promise. I'll do the shopping, do the cooking, anything. I just need a roof over my head until those...' he bit back the description on his tongue, 'until the police decide who they really want to bang up.'

They sat in silence for several minutes, drinking tea while locked in individual worlds.

'I need to find the murderer,' Lowell said at last. 'I don't trust the police to get it right, not after they arrested me without any real evidence. *I'm* the one who needs to find out who killed Maud – they won't. Get my life back on track. The inspector, he was pretty decent actually, seemed to think you and your chap were dab hands at amateur sleuthing. Will you help me?'

Yes, Flora thought, and not just help, but redouble our efforts. She would, at least. She couldn't have Lowell staying at the cottage for long. He would be a constant source of discord between her and Jack, and she wasn't too happy either that she'd be sharing her home with a man she no longer knew well.

'I'll help,' she said, 'and so will Jack.' It was said with more confidence than she felt.

Lowell's face broke into a rare smile. 'It's important we find who did that to Maud. For her, of course, but for my job and the money I owe. The men I need to repay aren't exactly patient types.'

An uncomfortable prickle travelled down Flora's back. Did that mean unsavoury characters would be finding their way to her cottage on their hunt for a man they believed had defaulted? It was one complication she didn't need.

'The police might have let me go,' Lowell went on, 'but I know they're still after me. They won't believe I had nothing to do with Maud's death and they'll keep digging to find stuff against me, when they should be using their time to find the real murderer. Like investigating Basil Webb.'

'Basil?'

There was a fluttery feeling in her stomach. Could Lowell add more to what they'd learned today? A decisive scrap of evidence?

'He quarrelled with Maud, you know.' Her friend spoke with certainty. 'I told the coppers but they weren't interested. No, not one bit. All they kept on about was *my* quarrel with her.'

If Inspector Ridley wasn't interested, Flora was. Basil had become a strong suspect and, after their visit to Thelma Easterhouse today, the words she'd used about her brother had lodged deep. He's determined, she'd said, and when he wants something, he doesn't let anything get in his way. Had he wanted the Dickens? More than likely since it would have solved all his problems. It wouldn't have mattered then whether the conference was a success or not and, more importantly, it would have saved his sister from eviction and possibly a life-changing divorce. If Basil had wanted to steal the book, though, he hadn't succeeded. The Dickens was still missing.

'What was the quarrel about?' she asked, trying to sound as if it didn't matter. 'I thought Basil was a champion of the mobile library. That he was the one keen to have it on site.'

'He was. It was his idea, not Maud's. She wasn't at all happy, put up quite a fight against getting involved. It was Basil Webb who negotiated with the library service, phone calls to County Hall, et cetera. It was he who got them to agree that we'd abandon our usual route for the conference week.'

'Did he ever say why he was so keen?' It had been a puzzle to Jack that, having provided a bookstall for the attendees, there'd also been the need for a library.

'He didn't involve me in the plans, but I heard what he said to Maud when he was trying to persuade her it was a good thing. He was insistent that not everyone could afford a new book – ones they'd buy from your stall – but they could browse our stock in the mobile van, then borrow from their local library. Authors would get some payment even if they didn't get sales.'

'It sounds reasonable, so why the quarrel?' Flora got up to refill the teapot. She had a feeling that this could be a long evening.

'It was because Webb was insisting that Maud change our stock. He wanted books written by the authors who were attending the conference to be the only crime novels in the library.'

Flora turned back from the kitchen counter, her eyebrows raised.

'That's what I thought,' Lowell agreed. 'It didn't seem reasonable and Miss Frobisher refused point-blank. Even threatened to make a complaint about him to County Hall. After that, Webb said he'd compromise if his authors' books were prominently displayed and outnumbered the crime books written by others.'

'Did Maud agree to that?' Flora searched her memory, trying to remember the interior of the van, but all that came to mind was a pool of blood and Maud's lifeless body. Immediately, she shut down the picture.

'She was stubborn,' Lowell said. 'You know how she was. Didn't like to be told how to run what she saw as her territory. She told him it would be too much work and in any case it didn't properly demonstrate what the mobile library offered.'

'So, an impasse.' Flora poured two more cups of tea and brought down a box of biscuits from the top shelf.

'Pretty much. But then she died and the issue died with her.'

Flora sat down heavily. 'You can't think Basil Webb would kill a woman because she refused to prioritise his authors?'

Lowell shrugged his shoulders. 'Who knows? He seemed pretty frantic that the conference was a success. I got the feeling that any obstacle would be steamrollered out of the way. And Maud was an obstacle.'

It seemed incomprehensible to Flora that anyone would kill for such a petty reason, but she imagined there had been murders for less.

'It sounds as though they were quarrelling for weeks. Did you see Basil the morning Maud died?'

'No, but it doesn't mean he didn't come to the van. He

could have taken his chance while I was walking the playing fields. They could have quarrelled again, only this time...'

'When was it you last saw him?'

'The previous afternoon. Maud was showing Mrs Lawson the Dickens. I think they'd worked together at a publishing firm way back and Rose was keen to see the book. She knew about rare editions. Anyway, Maud was showing the book to Mrs Lawson when Basil banged up the steps and said he had some writers outside who wanted to see the book and, if she couldn't do anything else to help them, could she at least invite them into the van?'

'So Rose Lawson was in the van?' The small snippet pricked Flora's attention and for the moment she forgot Basil.

Lowell frowned. 'Is that a problem?'

'No,' she said swiftly, 'of course not.'

But it was a problem, wasn't it? Rose had been clear. *I peeked through the window! Miss Frobisher was showing some of the writers who are speaking at the conference a book she's acquired.* An obvious lie. But why? Flora had been right in her speculation that Rose knew a great deal more about the book than she pretended. Had she also been right about the parcel in Rose's basket?

She debated whether she should ring Jack and tell him. Tell him, too, what Lowell had said of Basil. The man was already high on Jack's list of suspects and maybe this was the lead they needed. But Jack was not a happy man and had left her in a very bad mood.

She would let him ring her, Flora decided.

~

When the telephone rang at Overlay House on Wednesday morning, Jack rushed to answer. It would be Flora. They hadn't spoken since Monday evening and he missed her sorely. But she was here now, he was sure, happy to speak and ready to tell him that Lowell Gracey had gone.

But it was the voice of his agent, Arthur Bellaby, that came down the line. Jack liked Arthur, enjoyed their conversations, and was always ready to hear good news of his latest book, but this morning he felt a fierce disappointment.

'How are you, Jack?'

Was Arthur sounding hopeful? 'Fine, fine,' he murmured, distracted by the question that hung in the air of why exactly his agent was making this unexpected contact.

'The new book progressing?'

'Sort of,' he extemporised. It wasn't like Arthur to check up on him. What was behind this call?

'Good. You've a fair few months ahead to get it sorted, I know. But I was wondering...'

Here it comes, Jack thought.

'... how you'd feel about working in a college?'

It was so unforeseen that Jack sat down hard on the hall bench and stared at the receiver.

'Jack? Are you there?'

'Yes,' he said faintly. 'You're suggesting I become a teacher?'

'Not a teacher, more a mentor. There's a college near you, well, not too far away, one that specialises in arts subjects. Cleve, it's called. Cleve College. They like to have a published author on their staff, to help students with their work. You wouldn't be involved in examinations, that kind of thing. It would be more advice and discussion. To show them how it's done.'

'How what's done?'

'Writing a novel, of course. A lot of the students write in their spare time.'

'What if they want to write poetry or plays?'

There was a short silence. 'General advice should cover that,' Arthur said briskly.

'Is this a new venture?' Jack was cautious. It sounded like nothing he'd heard of before.

'Not entirely new.' Arthur seemed reluctant to go into details. 'I believe there was another writer employed but... but he left.'

'Left, as in being dismissed?'

'I imagine so. The college principal didn't say much. And he *is* talking to other agents and other writers. I mentioned your name when he telephoned me. You're an experienced writer and you live locally.'

'I'm surprised you suggested me.' It was genuine surprise that Jack felt. 'Any job is bound to lessen the time I have to write.'

'There'd be a trial period of six months, Professor Dalloway said. After that, you or whoever they appoint could dip out, or *they* could say no thank you. And the job is only for two or three days a week. I reckon you could manage it – you sound as though you're well ahead in meeting the next deadline. Anyway, something to think about,' Arthur said breezily, 'particularly as you'll soon be a married man. More cash in the pocket.'

'OK... well... I'll think about it.' It was all he could say, bemused by an opportunity that had arrived out of nowhere.

'I'll be in touch with Dalloway next week. If you can let me know by then... oh, and Jack, I remembered the other day what it was I heard about Felix Wingrave. Do you recall, we were talking about collectors of rare books and I said that something rang a bell?'

'Yes?'

'About a year ago, I was at a dinner given by an editor I'm friendly with and a rumour was going around the table. It was just a rumour, of course, and an unfortunate one, but I thought as you were interested, I'd mention it.'

'Very interested.' Jack sprang up from the bench, his uncertainty gone.

'What was said at the dinner was that Wingrave was at an auction, bidding for a first edition of a George Eliot novel, but lost out to a higher bidder. Later, though, a journalist wrote an article saying he'd seen the book in Wingrave's collection and how had that happened? Felix Wingrave took him to court for libel and won the case. The legal fees and the fallout to his reputation ruined that particular journalist, but interestingly, the book wasn't in Wingrave's library when, after the court case, he invited the great and the good to an event there. And it was never seen again.'

'And your take on that, Arthur?'

'Either the journalist was mistaken or—'

'Or Wingrave keeps the George Eliot in a bank deposit box!'

'Something like that,' Arthur agreed equably.

19

Jack pushed from his mind Arthur's talk of the job at a local college. His agent appeared keen that he give it consideration, but right now he had too much else to worry about. An investigation that was barely stuttering forward, for instance. Solving the mystery of Maud's death was key to a less complicated life, Jack was certain. Once her killer was revealed, Lowell Gracey, whether he were innocent or guilty, could disappear. And disappearing with him would be any trouble the man had sown between himself and Flora. Life would return to an even tenor, in time for their wedding, now only weeks away.

With the investigation dominating his thoughts, he walked to the Cross Keys for his meeting with Alan Ridley. He had little more to offer the inspector today than the rumour he'd heard surrounding Wingrave's collection and, of course, the news of the man's attempt to break into Flora's cottage and his willingness to use violence.

Basil Webb, too. He should mention him. Perhaps not the description Thelma Easterhouse had given them of her brother's ruthlessness – their visit to Crawley might be seen as pre-empting the police enquiry – but certainly the conversation he'd had with Basil at the conference. At the time, it had made Jack wonder what was behind Basil's seeming willingness to break the law. Now he knew that his brother-in-law had lost his job and the Easterhouse family were in trouble, but was there more to it than that? Why was the man finding it so difficult to get another job when alternative work was plentiful?

The last few days had been overcast and humid, the inn sign as he approached the pub hanging listlessly in the windless air. It seemed that its pair of crossed keys had recently been repainted, and their newly bright gold cast a splash of brilliance in an otherwise dull day. Walking through the entrance, Jack felt the pub humming, despite the food on offer being some of the worst he had ever tasted. He guessed the beer must make up for it. As if to prove him right, customers were three deep at the bar and having to shout their orders over the loud chatter filling the low-ceilinged room. Ridley, he saw, had made it to the front and would be ordering his customary glutinous pie, along with a pint.

The inspector, his business concluded, turned from the bar, two full glasses of beer clasped between his hands, and spied Jack over the heads of the queue. 'Jack, old man, how are you?' was his greeting. 'Got our drinks, but anything to eat for you?'

'A bag of crisps will do, thanks.'

The crisps ordered, they weaved a path together through the noisy crowd, finding a reasonably quiet table at the far end of the saloon.

'Phew!' Ridley plumped himself down on the wooden settle. 'Quite a crush today.' He took a long draught of beer, then whisked a plain linen handkerchief from a pocket and patted his damp forehead.

It was several minutes and a good half a glass later before he said, 'Right, Jack, got anything for me? Or do I continue with our man?'

'Our man being Lowell Gracey?'

'The very one. I know Miss Steele will argue otherwise, but I'm convinced he's the killer we're after. What's more, so is my team. We've done a lot of digging and what we've found does not look good for him.'

'But you let him go.' Jack stared at his beer. Gracey's release continued to rankle.

'I had to but it doesn't mean I'm not still after him. Did you know he owed money?'

He nodded. 'Flora said something about it.'

'Did she say how much?'

Jack shook his head and took up his glass.

'Well, we've found that out and it's a pretty big sum. Did she mention who the money's owed to?'

'Only that they weren't exactly upright citizens.'

Ridley pursed his lips. 'She wouldn't know the details, but we do. Some pretty bad people, it turns out; people who'd have no compunction in tightening the screws, shall we say. If that doesn't give Gracey a motive, I don't know what does. He's had the job he expected snatched from beneath his nose, the money he expected suddenly disappear into thin air, and all the time he's got the hounds braying for his blood.'

'That's very poetic, Alan.'

'Don't they say everyone can be a writer?' The inspector beamed.

Jack tried not to show the pain that gave him. 'You've a strong case but you'll never convince Flora. Gracey is an old friend who deserves her loyalty, and she'll give it. Along with her spare room, I imagine.'

The inspector stopped eating and waved his fork, a section of pie halfway to his mouth. 'Gracey is staying with Miss Steele?'

Jack nodded, gloom filling his face.

'I can't think that's very wise. What if those blokes come calling? The hounds? You should warn her.'

'I can't warn her. Flora knows her own mind and she'll know the risks involved. We're at odds over Gracey and anything I say will simply add fuel to the fire. Hopefully, if they do go looking for him, they won't think to find him in Abbeymead. Or you'll have re-arrested him by then.'

'Any reason for me not to?' the inspector asked. 'Have you found me another suspect?'

'There are a fair few and they all have strong motives, though perhaps not as strong as Gracey's. Basil Webb is desperate for money and the book, if he has it, will make sure he can pay for the conference.'

'Is he likely to be out of pocket?'

'He might be lucky and break even, but he needs money for his sister. She's threatened with losing her home. And maybe worse. There's trouble between her and her husband though how bad, I don't know.'

Alan Ridley took a final gulp of his beer. 'I agree, it's a solid motive, but no evidence?'

Jack shook his head. 'And no real evidence on Felix Wingrave either. He has a dodgy past when it comes to rare books and he tried to break in to Flora's cottage. He seems to have got the idea that she might have the missing Dickens.'

For a moment, the inspector look fazed. 'What! He broke in to Miss Steele's cottage? Is there something wrong with him?'

'Plenty.' But before Jack could enumerate on Wingrave's many faults, Ridley pointed to the window.

'Isn't that your girlfriend?'

Jack looked where he was pointing. It *was* Flora and she was coming out of the front entrance of the Cross Keys accompanied by a tall man dressed in a three-piece suit of grey-striped flannel. A deep blue silk tie against a crisp white shirt was just visible.

The inspector grinned. 'You better watch your step, Jack. He looks quite the business.'

Jack didn't answer. He was too busy watching as the pair shook hands and Flora turned to walk in the direction of the All's Well, while the man – Jack had seen him before, but where? – made for the inn's car park. Then he remembered. Another car park. The school playground. That's where he'd seen him.

Charlie's words came bouncing back to him. Flora had talked to this man before and he'd left her, according to Charlie, looking shocked, as though she'd heard something she hadn't wanted to. And here he was again. Their meetings were evidently important, yet Flora had said nothing of them. Why ever not? They were to marry soon. Surely, she should have told him what was happening, confided in him if she was in trouble.

'Yes, that's Flora,' he responded after long minutes had passed, forcing himself to smile. 'On another of her missions!'

A mission he had no idea of. Flora wasn't telling him the truth or she was deliberately withholding it. Jack stood up, eager to be out of the pub and walking.

'Sorry, Alan. I must go. I'll keep in touch and, if anything interesting turns up, I'll let you know.'

The inspector stared at him, evidently confused by this sudden turn of events, but Jack wasn't about to explain. Betrayal, and it felt a betrayal, was a private matter and he'd had more than enough in his life. He strode from the pub, making for the spinney and a long walk.

He wouldn't be the one to pick up the telephone, he decided.

20

The following day, Flora was about to lock the All's Well's front door when Sally Jenner, looking flushed and out of breath, rushed into the shop.

'Sorry, Flora. I know you're about to close for lunch but I've only just managed to escape the Priory. Telephones, staff queries, food deliveries – it's endless and I need that book.'

Flora was forced to search her mind before it came to her. 'The one with recipes for cocktail snacks? *Good Housekeeping's Appetizer Book*, wasn't it?'

'I've no idea,' Sally confessed. 'It was Auntie who wanted it. She's in militant mood at the moment – we have a whole raft of cocktail parties coming up and she hasn't a clue what to serve.'

'That title came in a while ago,' Flora remarked mildly.

'I know you phoned to tell me, but to be honest I forgot, life's been so busy. I am *not* in Auntie's good books!'

'I'll get it for you. It will be with my other orders in the cellar.'

It took Flora only seconds to locate the recipe book vital to Alice and she was soon emerging at the top of the cellar stairs and waving it at a relieved Sally.

'I'll wrap it, shall I?'

'No need, but thanks. I should scoot and so must you, I guess.'

'Is the hotel that frantic? What does Dominic do these days?' Flora was curious as to how what must be an awkward partnership was now faring.

The pink in Sally's cheeks deepened further. 'To be honest, I can't rely on him. He seems to have lost interest in the hotel ever since...'

'Ever since you decided your relationship was business only,' she finished for her.

Sally nodded, her blonde curls bobbing energetically. 'I'm not sorry I made the decision, Flora. I know I did the right thing, but Dominic has never really accepted it. He's ridiculously jealous – can't stand it if another man dares to look at me. Hector, for instance. I mean... my sous chef. As though I would!'

'Well?'

Sally took a sudden interest in her handbag, rifling through its contents. 'I like him,' she said, her head bent. 'He's a nice chap, interesting, too, but I'm his boss, not his girlfriend.' She looked up. 'Dominic is always finding fault with him and I wish he wouldn't – Hector is a good chef. But I've made Dom angry and this is how he reacts.'

'You dipped out of the relationship before Hector ever came to the Priory,' Flora pointed out.

'I know, but I've made him even angrier since. Last month I found the ring he'd given me – a dress ring, but a gorgeous emerald – and gave it back. Now I've sold the bicycle he bought. A beautiful one, bright red and very sleek, but I never rode the damn thing! I'm sure Rose will get more use from it.'

'Rose? Rose Lawson?'

Sally looked surprised. 'Yes, I met her a few days ago. She said she was looking for a new bike – hers had just gone to the scrap heap. It seemed a perfect opportunity to get rid of something that was going to waste, though Dominic hasn't seen it that way.'

'Was the bike expensive, do you know?' Flora ventured.

Sally threw back her head in genuine laughter. 'Of course it was! It was Dominic who bought it! I didn't charge Rose anything like I imagine he paid, but I still got a good price.'

'Do you remember when exactly she agreed to buy it?'

'Tuesday, I think. Anyway, must buzz. And thanks for the book – you've saved me from another torrent of complaints!'

Tuesday, Flora thought. Several days after Rose had gone to London to see her husband, carrying a basket that held a suspicious-looking parcel. Basil Webb, she supposed, must still be their main suspect, but Rose was beginning to come a close second and she wished with all her heart that it wasn't so.

Flora's lunchtimes were rarely used for eating – a sandwich at her desk usually sufficed – it was rather a time to shop for food or finish any small task she hadn't managed at the weekend. Today, though, small tasks were not going to satisfy her. Particularly after what she had learned of Rose. Depressed, she gathered up her bag and jacket and locked the All's Well door.

Despite being desperate to see Jack, clear the air, and recount her latest news, Flora was adamant that she wouldn't make the first move. As long as Lowell remained her lodger, Jack would be prickly and unreasonable, she argued, and since her old friend seemed in no hurry to leave the cottage, it was best for the time being to keep away from Overlay House. For the moment, she'd put him out of her mind, Rose Lawson alongside, and set about the task she'd promised herself: a visit to the mobile library, one she'd been meaning to make for days.

As far as she knew, the van was still parked in the school playground and, with it, the present that Maud had never received. The rosewood casket had been a much loved item of her aunt's and Flora was eager to retrieve it and bring it home where it belonged. She still possessed the spare key Maud had given her and, though she imagined the library van might be roped off by a police cordon, she thought it worth the effort to cajole Betty into an additional journey on what was another very humid day. Cycling hard beneath an oppressively low sky, she arrived in the school grounds sticky and uncomfortable, but was rewarded by the sight of the mobile library still in place. A police cordon was visible but thankfully a policeman was not.

Taking care to check that no one else had decided to visit the school playground this afternoon – there were so many unanswered questions hanging in the air, so many likely suspects, it wouldn't have surprised her to find she was not alone – she ducked beneath the cordon of rope, walked up the metal steps and slipped her key into the lock. Success!

Maud's desk was exactly as she'd last seen it and the present she'd left, the half-written note alongside, sat exactly where she'd placed it. She looked up from the desk along the narrow aisle between the walls of books and saw the door of the small safe hanging wide open. Now she knew it was there, it was obvious, but to anyone simply passing through the van, it would have been almost invisible. Her gaze carried on towards the rear and stopped at the point where she'd seen Maud's body. The remembered image of that poor battered woman had Flora thrust the present and card into her handbag and make for the door again.

Something, however, made her pause. Had the police gone through Maud's desk? They were bound to have, she decided, and presumably found nothing, unless the inspector had spoken to Jack in the meantime and there was news she hadn't been told. On impulse, she pulled out the top right-hand drawer. A set of pens and pencils, a ruler, rubber, and a spare scribble pad were its entire contents. The bottom drawer revealed a scarf and a carrier bag and it wasn't until she turned to the drawers on the left that anything approaching interesting appeared.

The deeper of the two drawers held notebooks, piled neatly together and, flicking quickly through the stack, she could see that they were organised in strict date order, the most recent at the top. No wonder Maud and her aunt had been fellow spirits. Meticulous, organised, in charge of their worlds, they were so much alike. Both had lost fiancés in the First War and never married. Both had worked all their lives and been highly competent at the jobs they'd taken on. And both had shown immense kindness to others, offering help to any who'd needed it.

Flora reached down into the drawer and tipped the pile of notebooks onto the desk top. The first contained a list of book titles, seemingly stock that Maud would like to acquire for the library van. Flipping to the back of the book, Flora read down another list of titles, many she recognised as old and out-of-date. These must be books that Maud had wanted to offload and return to the main library stock.

Putting the notebook aside, Flora picked up a slimmer pad filled with the same neat handwriting. This one contained the names of many of Maud's readers, listed beneath their various villages, and with a note of the kind of books they preferred to read. The bulk of the notebooks, though, were ledgers filled with figures and at first glance seemed less interesting: essentially records of the money coming into the mobile library service and the money going out.

There were figures noting every year's council grant and, against this credit balance, the actual sums Maud had expended on new purchases. A final column showed how much money had been left at the end of the year – the reserve held at the bank. A quick trawl through several of the notebooks revealed that every six months the books were audited by a local accountant – the same professional stamp, a signature scrawled across it, appeared in the books twice a year. Maud's figures, it seemed, were then approved by the head of accounts at County Hall, and once again signed off.

The format remained true throughout a dozen ledgers except for the most recent which had virtually no entries. The first column recorded the yearly grant awarded by the council but the second column, which should have registered expenditure, was empty – presumably Maud had made no purchases during this half year – and the final column, where what remained of the grant should appear, contained only several heavily scored question marks. There was a scribbled note beside it, so faint that Flora had to walk to the open door to read it in daylight. *Where is the reserve?* Maud had written. £100 *but bank account empty*.

Flora took the notebook back to the desk and sat down. The message was clear. Maud had been given money by the council to buy new books for this financial year, but for one reason or another had made no purchases. Yet the one-hundred-pound council grant, which should have remained intact, had disappeared. She sat back in Maud's chair, thinking hard, disturbed by her find.

Had the police gone through these books? It looked very much as if they hadn't. But if they had, surely they would have seen the message, faint though it was. A serious oversight then. Perhaps they'd been in a hurry, perhaps the officer deputed to search the desk had been sloppy at the job, his mind elsewhere? Whatever the case, the notebook was something that Alan Ridley should see. Though maybe not just yet! It offered a pathway to the truth – the first real evidence to support any of the motives she and Jack had come up with – and she wanted them to be the ones to follow it.

Looking back at the earlier ledgers, she could see that this was the time of year the accounts were audited. Had Maud begun to prepare her notebook accordingly and it was then that she'd found this devastating loss? Had she raised the issue at County Hall? And if so, to whom would she have spoken? The accounts department would be large, Flora reckoned – it was responsible for so many county services – and would employ a correspondingly large number of people.

She searched through the remaining ledgers once more, the accounts going back at least five years, looking for a name. All except the most recent set of accounts had been audited and stamped as correct, but nowhere in all the paperwork was there mention of any member of staff at County Hall.

The only way of finding out the employee responsible for overseeing the library accounts would be to ring the council – except that Flora was certain they would be reluctant to divulge a name, if not refuse outright. But the matter was too important to ignore. Maud had discovered a huge discrepancy and the missing money could well prove the motive behind her killing.

Not just too important to ignore, but too important to maintain a petty silence. Locking the van door, she tucked her bag into Betty's wicker basket and set off for Overlay House. There was a hatchet to be buried.

21

Flora arrived at Jack's front door just as he was making an early afternoon cup of tea.

'No Lowell Gracey with you?' he was surprised into asking, her appearance so unexpected. She looked flushed and uncomfortable and Jack immediately felt mean.

'Come on in. I've just made tea.' His tone was apologetic. 'Actually... I've just made a cake. For you.'

Her eyes widened. 'You made a cake?'

'I can't guarantee what it tastes like,' he said awkwardly, while Flora continued to stare. She seemed too surprised to speak. 'I just wanted to say sorry and...' He tailed off.

Before he could say any more, she was by his side and grabbing him by the waist. 'You are the most beautiful man, Jack! What did you make me?' She was half laughing.

'Your favourite. Pineapple upside-down cake. It's just... the pineapple got a bit singed.'

'There's nothing better than singed pineapple.'

Jack grinned. 'In that case, let's take it into the garden. The terrace should be cool enough.'

Once they were seated at the wicker table, each with a mug

of tea and a slice of upside-down cake, he asked what had been in his mind from the moment he'd opened the front door. 'You've come with news?'

Flora nodded and, with barely a pause, spilled out all she had learned in the last few days: the fact that Rose had lied about seeing the Dickens novel, that Basil had quarrelled with Maud and continued to quarrel with her right up to the start of the conference, and that this afternoon she had discovered Maud's accounts showed a discrepancy of a hundred pounds, a situation that had clearly worried the librarian a great deal.

'Maud's question marks suggest she took the matter further,' he said, as Flora finished her recital.

'I'm sure she did. It would have been out of character if she hadn't. This cake is scrumptious, by the way.'

'I had a bit of a problem with the layers,' he confessed. 'I couldn't do the cream bit so I sandwiched them with jam instead.'

'Still scrumptious!'

Relieved, Jack leant back in his chair. 'So... Maud would have gone to County Hall and told someone she was missing the money? Who, I wonder, and when?'

'It must have been recently, or she would have amended the account book. It was still an open question when she died.'

'The accounts department must know something. I think we should ring them.'

'Now?'

'Why not? It's the most significant clue we've unearthed so far. The fact that Rose lied to you isn't proof she stole the book, any more than the suspicious-looking package in her basket was the Dickens in disguise. And as for Basil, all we really have are words, opinions: his sister's, Lowell Gracey's, my own impressions. But the account book is solid and definitely worth pursuing.'

Draining his mug, he jumped up and walked back into the

sitting room while Flora cleared the table. His search for the telephone directory was prolonged and, washing up in the kitchen, she heard several thumps, several rude words, before Jack appeared in the doorway with a hefty volume.

'I was so long getting a phone connected that when this arrived, I hadn't the energy to look at it,' he explained. 'I stuffed it at the back of the sideboard under a pile of books I don't want to read. Anyway... to work.'

He was soon through to County Hall and asking for the accounts department, specifically the section that dealt with the library service. The request seemed to confuse whoever was on the other end of the line and Jack was redirected several times before finally reaching his destination.

'The mobile library, you say?' the unknown voice asked. He felt Flora at his shoulder and shared the receiver.

'Yes, the service run by Maud Frobisher until a few weeks ago.'

'Let's see. That would be – ah – no, we don't have anyone in post at the moment. Our head accountant, Mr Little, is in his office but unless it's important... he's very busy. Otherwise, Mr Brownlow will be here next week. He's our new recruit. Yes, it's best to phone back next week.'

A shuffling came down the line, their respondent about to put down the phone, when Jack intervened. 'Presumably, there was somebody looking after the mobile library accounts before Mr Brownlow?'

'Yes,' his respondent said tersely, 'he left.'

'Can I ask why?' He exchanged a look with Flora.

'I'm afraid I can't divulge that information.'

'He was dismissed?'

'Yes,' the voice said even more tersely.

'Was his name Derek Easterhouse by any chance?' Flora gave a thumbs up.

The response was a loud clunk at the other end of the line.

He turned to Flora and gave her a quick hug. 'I think that was a yes.'

'Easterhouse is a thief,' she said, walking back into the sitting room and plumping herself down on the lumpy sofa. 'He lost his job because of it and it's why he's finding it impossible to get another. The council must have refused him a reference.'

'And it's why his wife doesn't know the true reason for his dismissal, and why Basil does and is extremely tight-lipped.' Jack dropped into the chair opposite.

'If he was dismissed, it means that Maud went ahead and reported the discrepancy. Do you think it was Easterhouse that she contacted?'

'Maybe, but if she did, she didn't get anywhere. And the money is probably still missing.'

'Easterhouse might not have had the funds to repay the money, even if he wanted to.' Flora frowned. 'Perhaps he promised he would and then didn't. If I think how Maud would react, I'm fairly certain she would have given him the chance before she took it further.'

'Easterhouse lost his job, we know, but was it Maud who went to the head of accounts? She must have known what would happen.'

'I think,' Flora said slowly, 'that she would feel she'd given him the opportunity to do the right thing and he'd let her down. That she was ultimately responsible for the mobile library and its finances and had no option but to make a report to the chief accountant.'

'Which means that she was to blame – at least in Easterhouse's mind – for his losing his job.'

They sat thinking for several minutes.

'Revenge?' Flora asked.

'It has to be. Easterhouse is our killer! But how to prove it? How to prove he embezzled the money? It won't still be in his bank account, if it ever was.'

'False invoices,' she said succinctly. 'That's the way he could have embezzled the funds without anyone in his department suspecting, and we should be able to prove he was behind them.'

'False invoices?' His mind was busy with how that might work.

'I've heard of it happening,' Flora said, her eyes bright. 'Aunt Violet told me of a large bookshop in Oxford where one of the assistants got away with hundreds of pounds before she was found out. She did it by creating invoices for books that had never actually been bought. If we can check the invoices that were supposedly raised by the mobile library this year, we've got him.'

'There is a major problem – we'll never get hold of them. The council will close ranks and refuse outright to let us see them. You saw their response just now.'

'They can refuse us but not the police. Talk to the inspector, Jack. Tell him what we've discovered and get him to insist the council hand over Easterhouse's records. Tell him we can save the police hours of work!'

'Alan will need some persuading. He seems fixated on nobbling Gracey.'

She jumped up and walked over to him, taking his hands in hers. 'If anyone can persuade him, it's you. But I must go. I have a shop to open and by now poor Betty will be near to melting in this humidity.'

He jumped up to follow her out of the room, catching hold of her arm at the front door. 'Flora, who was that man with you at the Cross Keys?' He hadn't meant to ask but the question escaped despite his best intentions.

She let out a little gasp. 'You've been spying on me!'

'Believe me, I haven't. And never would. I was having lunch with Alan at the pub and he was the one who saw you.'

She took a step back. 'I can't say. Not at the moment. Well, I can but I want to wait until I'm sure, then you'll know everything.'

He felt disheartened. Why make a mystery of it, why not confide in him? And what exactly was she keeping secret?

She reached up and kissed him on the lips. 'You need to trust me, Jack. Otherwise, why are we getting married?'

22

Jack stood on his front path, watching Flora as she rode down the lane towards the high street. They were mixed emotions that he felt: happy, very happy, that they had rebuilt their bridges and were once more together, but stupidly fretful that whatever role the mystery man was playing in her life would stay a mystery until she chose otherwise. He would have to be patient, he told himself. Trust her, as she'd commanded.

It was trust he found difficult. After the debacle of his wedding that never was, it had returned only slowly and was still fragile. This new development in Flora's life was a test, if anything was. But she was her own woman, he'd always known that, and if he didn't like it, he should never have fallen in love with her. As though he'd had any choice, he thought mockingly.

As for the investigation, Easterhouse as the villain they sought seemed almost too good to be true. On the surface, he was a perfect fit: he appeared to have motive, it was likely he'd had the opportunity and, if Ridley could be persuaded to intercede, there was a good chance he'd provide them with the proof they needed to bring him to justice. But was it too perfect? Had they galloped ahead too quickly, jumped on Easterhouse as an easy win?

The only way to be sure was to obtain the man's ledgers, the records he'd kept of the movement of cash in and out of the library's account. Proving him an embezzler would unravel his tangle with Maud and establish revenge as an indisputable motive for her killing. He'd be under arrest, interrogated by Ridley's team, and the gaps filled. Those records were paramount. He'd do his utmost to persuade Alan to breach the barriers of County Hall, but it was clear the inspector was still gunning for Lowell Gracey and was bound to be reluctant to take on a distraction he'd consider unhelpful.

There was a small part of Jack – a part he didn't want to think too deeply about – that hoped the inspector would be proved right about Gracey – though a far stronger wish that for Flora's sake her friend wasn't the killer Ridley believed him. A guilty Lowell Gracey would hurt Flora badly and over the last few years Jack's goal in life had been to protect her from hurt at all costs.

The telephone call to Ridley would be tough and, before he made it, Jack needed to ensure their case against Easterhouse was clear and comprehensive. He had to be certain that their other suspects could be discounted, or at least put to one side. Rose Lawson was easy enough to suspend from the list. Jack had never seen her as a killer – but then who had seen a puny weed like Easterhouse as a killer? He wouldn't disregard her entirely, he concluded, but leave it to Flora to decide whether or not to pursue their questioning. By now, she knew the woman reasonably well, had employed her at the bookshop and might do so again. He would go with Flora's instinct.

As for Basil Webb, they had already looked at him closely, decided he had ample motive and opportunity, but found no concrete proof of his guilt. The publicity posters they assumed were his, forecasting a real-life murder at his crime conference, were damning, as were Basil's quarrels with Maud – at least according to Gracey – but ultimately they amounted to nothing that would stand up in a court of law. In other words, when it came to accusing Basil, they were stumped.

That left only Felix Wingrave and, thinking back, Jack realised that he'd never followed up the snippet of news his agent had divulged. Over their lunch, Jack had certainly mentioned it to Ridley, but the inspector hadn't been impressed and perhaps because of that he'd allowed it to drop from his calculations. Now, though, before they went hammer and tongs for Easterhouse, it might be the moment to dig more thoroughly. Or ask someone else to. Ross Sadler, a journalist at the *Daily Mercury* was an old friend and most often willing to help.

His call to the *Mercury* was brief. Ross had been about to cover his typewriter and make for home. 'Good job I was trying for an early getaway.' He sounded cheerful. 'You have my full attention.'

'Only if you can spare the time to talk.' Jack crossed his fingers.

'More than happy to pack up and switch focus. But tell me, Jack, how does someone living in deepest Sussex get involved in so many spicy cases?'

It was a question Jack had asked himself on numerous occasions, but had never managed an answer. 'It's an old friend of Flora's who's involved. She's keen to see him exonerated and I'm simply casting around for likely information.'

Briefly, he outlined his suspicions of Felix Wingrave.

'Casting around could be fun,' Ross said, a laugh in his voice. 'Wingrave is quite the man of the moment, isn't he? In literary circles, anyway. Could this be his nemesis? Who knows, I might get a story out of it! I'll call you back this evening with anything I find.'

'Thanks, Ross, but don't waste too much of your time on it.'

Replacing the receiver, Jack wandered into the kitchen and

was about to make himself a ham sandwich – a favourite and one, he decided, he deserved this afternoon – when a loud bang on the front door heralded his second caller of the day.

Charlie Teague stood on the threshold, his bicycle strewn untidily across Jack's front path. 'I've come to do the plantin',' the boy announced.

Jack looked at his watch. 'It's a bit late in the day. And I thought you said you weren't coming until Sunday.'

'Things have kinda changed. I got the time and... I need some money.'

'That's honest, at least. Is your need for money so urgent it can't wait a few days?'

Charlie nodded, his face serious. 'It's Mum. It's her birthday Saturday.' He pointed at the loaf and plate of ham. 'You makin' more o' those, Mr C?'

Resignedly, Jack took up the knife and cut several more slices from the loaf, layering each with a thick chunk of ham. 'Mustard?' Charlie shook his head vigorously. 'Lemonade, then?'

'Please.'

'You didn't think about your mother's birthday earlier?'

Charlie kicked the kitchen table leg. 'I did but... then I forgot. And now she's havin' this party with her friends and—'

'And you'll be the only one without a present?'

Charlie nodded again. 'So can we plant somethin'?'

'We can, Charlie.' Jack relinquished any idea of returning to his typewriter that day. 'The lettuce, I think.'

Out in the garden, they stood together eyeing Jack's large vegetable patch. 'Not much room,' he commented, 'and I guess lettuce will need some space.'

'Them marrow will soon be finished. We can do a coupla rows beside them.'

'OK, Chief. Let's earn you some money. If I remember rightly, you've been promised a present if the headmaster gives you an excellent reference, so probably sensible planning to get something for your mum.'

Charlie screwed up his nose. 'It's not goin' to be anythin' decent when I get the present,' he said gloomily. 'Probably some borin' book. I arsked for a new bike. I mean it's a big thing leavin' school, but Mum says there's nothin' wrong with the old one and they're too expensive.'

'I can't say I blame her, seeing the way you treat the bike you have. She won't think it worth buying anything too smart.'

'I'd look after it,' he protested. 'If it was new. Like Alf's. My best mate's got a Dawes Domino – his uncle just bought it for him. It's not fair, he's not leavin' school till Easter and it wasn't even his birthday. Everyone gets new bikes.' He kicked at a stone, sending it flying through the air to nestle in a row of beetroot. 'Even Mrs Lawson. I don' wanna bike like hers, not ezactly, that's kind of girly, but I like the colour – it's scarlitt and very shiny – I like that.'

'Mrs Lawson has a new bike?'

'Yeah, why?'

'No reason.' Something to tell Flora, he thought, fetching tools from the garden shed. How could a woman reduced to sleeping on friends' sofas afford a shiny new bike? Just as earlier how could she have afforded the trip to London?

After weeding the patch they'd chosen, he'd just opened the first seed packet when, through the open French doors, Jack heard the telephone ringing.

He scrambled to his feet. 'I'll be back,' he told his helper and sped through the sitting room and into the hall, reaching the receiver on its dying ring.

'Did I make you run, Jack, or are you into heavy breathing?'

'Ross, hello! I wasn't expecting your call until this evening.'

'I've been lucky. Discovered some very interesting stuff and thought you should hear it straight away.'

'Go on.' He tried not to sound too eager.

'I found the court case you were talking about. Actually, while I was reading it up, I realised that I knew the journalist who got stung. Only vaguely, but he was a decent bloke and if he says he saw the missing book in Wingrave's house, I believe him. Particularly when I found with a bit more digging that it wasn't the first time there's been questions over Wingrave's collection.'

'The same thing has happened before?'

'Not precisely the same thing,' Ross said carefully, 'but very close. A few years before he took the journalist to court, and incidentally ruined him, Wingrave bought a first edition of *Animal Farm* from some upmarket bookseller in London. But, because he was staying in town for a few days, he asked the chap to send the book to his home address – through the mail but insured for quite a large sum. The book was published in 1945 and by the early fifties had been reprinted several times so first editions were becoming much rarer.'

'Don't tell me! The book never arrived!'

'Correct. When Wingrave returned to his mansion and discovered the book hadn't been delivered, he rang the shop to query it. The bookseller swore he'd sent it off the same day Wingrave bought it, and it was the post office that must be to blame for the delay. But the mail bigwigs were having none of it. They swore their postie had left the book in the personal post box that Wingrave has at the end of his ridiculously long drive – can you imagine, your own little post box!'

'So who triumphed? As if I didn't know.'

'You might well. Wingrave said their employee must be mistaken and that the postman had obviously left the parcel at the wrong address. Pretty weak, I thought, and so did the bookseller. By this time, he'd claimed on the insurance and had the money for the book, but he was refusing to repay Wingrave.'

'What did Wingrave do?

'This is where it becomes really interesting in the light of what you told me. He went up to London and paid the book-shop another visit. Physically threatened the owner, roughed him up quite badly, according to the report I read.'

'Really? Charges could never have been brought or I'm sure the book world would have got to know.'

'The bookseller reported the assault to the police, which is why the incident got into the local paper – I found the article in the archives at Colindale, by the way – but after that, nothing happened. For some reason, charges were dropped. Maybe Wingrave paid off the shopkeeper when he realised the chap was going to expose him and ruin his reputation. Who knows?'

Jack began to mutter something about money always talking when Ross interrupted him. 'I haven't told you everything. We're getting to the really juicy bit now. Quite by chance, I looked at some of the society magazines around that time, thinking Wingrave's name might have popped up here and there. He courts publicity, doesn't he?'

Jack nodded to himself.

'Well, *The Tatler* was a revelation. A year after the fracas, a photograph of Wingrave's study and his collection appeared in the magazine. It was one of those "puff" jobs. Meet the rich and famous, et cetera. I had a thought the photograph might be useful and got our library to make a copy – luckily, they've got a Thermo-Fax on site – brought the photograph home and found my old magnifying glass. It made the image blurry but not so blurry I couldn't see with a pair of reading specs some of the titles on Wingrave's shelves. And guess what?'

'*Animal Farm* was there.'

'Right first time.'

'It could have been a recent edition,' Jack demurred.

'It could, but then why house the volume in your collection of rare books? The whole focus of the article was exclusiveness and that's what the *Tatler* photograph was about – having the money to own something unique.'

'More skulduggery, deception and violence,' Jack said slowly.

'Seems that way.'

'Thank you, Ross. That's quite some information.' Jack's thanks were heartfelt.

Promising Sadler he'd come up to London soon for a Fleet Street supper, he rejoined Charlie in the garden. Wingrave, it seemed, was back in the frame but first, he needed to tackle the Easterhouse problem. Prove one way or another the man was guilty – at least of theft. He would ring Alan Ridley tomorrow, ask, beg, plead, that he get copies of the man's last set of accounts at County Hall, together with any invoices he'd filed.

'I finished 'em while you were talkin' all that time.' Charlie looked up accusingly, the last packet of lettuce seeds in his hand.

'Sorry, old chap – you've done a great job. Another ham sandwich maybe?'

23

It was Flora's turn to host the traditional Friday evening supper, but with Lowell Gracey still lodged in her spare room, the situation was difficult. Lowell would need to eat that evening, which meant that either he'd be joining her friends at the dining table or sitting on his bed with a tray on his knees, both options equally uncomfortable. To spare everyone's awkward feelings, she'd asked Kate if she could use the Nook after hours. Dear Kate had immediately offered her own cottage and to do the cooking as well, but Flora had been adamant. It was her turn to act as hostess.

Congratulating herself on having navigated a tricky evening, she was disappointed when Alice's first words were a grumble.

'I dunno why we have to meet in the café. It's not as if I haven't seen enough of it.'

Despite her job as head chef at the hotel, Alice had frequently helped Kate in the months the girl had been forced to run the Nook more or less single-handedly. Married now to Tony Farraday, Kate's permanent staff had doubled, and Alice had been happy to retire back into her own domain, the Priory kitchen.

'It's always pleasant to eat here,' Flora said, determined to be cheerful. 'It's such a bright, comfortable space.' And it was, particularly as this year Kate had bought soft-cushioned seats to replace the old wooden chairs and ordered brand new blue-checked cloths for each table, along with matching napkins.

'And we get a view of the high street,' Kate put in, 'which we wouldn't at Flora's cottage!'

'Not that anyone's around at this time of the day,' Alice continued to grumble.

Flora and Kate exchanged a look but made no comment. It was better when Alice was in this kind of humour to say nothing and let the moment pass. But Alice wasn't in a forgiving mood and, as soon as they had sat down to bowls of creamy mushroom soup, her grievance became obvious.

'I can't believe you've still got that man staying with you, Flora.'

'That man has a name,' she said, more sharply than she'd meant to. 'It's Lowell and I've known him for years.'

There was a loud sniff from across the table. 'That's as mebbe, but I wonder what Jack thinks about it?'

'Jack?' she asked innocently.

'The man you're supposed to be marrying.'

'I'm not supposed to be marrying, Alice. I *am* marrying.' Cudgels were being taken up.

'A single man,' her old friend said, 'moving in with you! Jack can't be happy.'

'He's not expressed an opinion,' Flora lied.

'I'm surprised, I must say. I'd think it was the last thing he'd want. But there, you young 'uns, what do I know? Just don't come cryin' to me when the weddin's cancelled. It's a good a way as any to lose a man.' Alice dropped her spoon loudly into the empty soup bowl.

'If Jack was so shallow as to cancel our wedding over something as trivial, I'd be happy to lose him,' Flora said fiercely.

What did Alice know about it? she seethed inwardly. A woman who had never married, never, as far as Flora was aware, come close to the altar. But she was being crabby, she realised, and she shouldn't succumb. Maud's murder seemed to have turned her into an irritable bear. First, angry with Lowell at his foolish gambling, then with Jack and his jealousy, and now at Alice's pinched view of love.

'Let me help you,' Kate said gently, collecting spoons and bowls. 'I'll bring in the veg, if you like.'

'Thanks, Katie.' Grateful for the reprieve, she made for the kitchen to rescue the fish pie from the Nook's oven.

Once the pie and various vegetables were on the table, it was Kate who kept the conversation going. While Flora served, her friend made a determined effort to introduce a topic that was unlikely to prove controversial.

'You know last week we were talking about Thelma Bolding?'

'Easterhouse,' Alice corrected.

'Yes, Thelma Easterhouse. It was really strange because days later I saw her here.'

'In the village?' Alice appeared to shed her grumpiness with this new interest.

'Not just in the village but actually here. In the Nook. She was meeting someone, her cousin, I think.'

'That gawky red-haired woman who lives past the Barnes' palace?' Pelham Lodge, the massive architectural disaster belonging to the wealthiest couple in Abbeymead, would always be 'the palace'. 'Why was Thelma meeting her? It's the first time she's been back to the village, I reckon, since she got married, and that was years ago.'

'I've no idea what prompted her to come, but the two of

them sat over a pot of tea for at least an hour. It seemed as though they were having a really serious conversation.'

'It will be about the husband,' Alice decided. 'Bound to be. Another divorce, I'll wager.'

Not necessarily, Flora thought, but was asking herself the same question. What *was* Thelma doing in the village, and why return to Abbeymead, now, of all times? Was it possible she'd got wind of their investigation into Derek's activities? Flora couldn't see how that could be. Jack had promised to telephone Alan Ridley at the earliest opportunity and hopefully badger him into forcing County Hall to release Derek's ledgers and any invoices supporting his figures. But Thelma could have no notion of that call.

A thought flashed into Flora's mind, sudden and worrying. What if, after Jack had persuaded the inspector to use his authority with the accounts department, there turned out to be nothing to see? No false invoices and Derek's records a spotless copy of Maud's, showing no purchases of books and nothing in the bank. The one hundred pounds would still be missing but would have to be searched for elsewhere, leaving an inspector deeply unhappy that he'd wasted time and effort, maybe compromised his authority, to follow what was nothing but a stupid distraction. It wouldn't be too good for Jack, either.

Flora's skin burst into a light sweat as her thoughts took a downward dive and she was only recalled to the present by Alice asking her somewhat plaintively, 'Is there a puddin', Flora?'

'Yes, of course.' She jumped up from her seat, realising that Kate had once more cleared the table, and rushed into the kitchen to collect the special trifle she'd been so pleased with. 'It's a new recipe,' she said brightly, hoping her friend hadn't noticed her mind was elsewhere, wandering in forbidden territory.

'Looks good.' Alice helped herself to several large spoonfuls.

'Tastes good, too.' Kate beamed. A prickly relationship had been restored to normal. 'I'll have to get the recipe. The one I'm still using was from old Mrs Waterford. She had it from her ma who had it from *her* ma. It's good, but it's always canny to try something a little different.'

'You can offer Mrs Waterford this one when you see her.' Flora smiled. 'Though she'll probably stick to what she knows best.'

'I might at that. I met the old dear yesterday, in fact, coming out of the baker's, and I thought as how she was doin' so well. Lookin' pretty chipper for her age.'

'The summer helps,' Kate put in.

'I s'pose, but I think she's feelin' a lot better now that she's been paid the rent she was owed. I think it was playin' on her mind.'

'Maggie owed rent?' Maggie Unwin had been a model tenant as far as Flora knew. 'Perhaps we shouldn't be surprised. She's been off work for quite a time.'

'Not Maggie.' Alice shook her head. 'It was that Rose Lawson. She was sharin' with Maggie – only temporary-like – but Mrs W moved her sewin' machine and materials out of her boxroom and let Mrs Lawson have it for her clothes and stuff – so the girls wouldn't be too crowded, she said.'

'That was kind,' Kate commented, licking her spoon clear of the cream that clung to it.

'She's a kind woman,' Alice said, 'and was worryin' somethin' fearful that she'd have to tell Rose to go. It's all extra water and electricity, you see. But now she's happy. Everythin' paid up and for three months in advance.'

'Rose must have found another job,' Kate said. 'Apart from the days she does at the post office. When I saw her there this morning, she was wearing a lovely polka dot sundress. It had to be new. She's not still working for you, is she, Flora?'

Flora felt her mouth dry and throat grow thick. Since Rose's visit to London, it was clear she had come into money. What had seemed wild speculation was turning out to be the truth. Rose must have been carrying the Dickens in her basket the day she'd called at the All's Well, a book that would solve every one of her money problems.

'She's not, is she?' Kate prompted.

'Working for me? No. But I'm glad she's found something else.'

'*If* she has,' Alice said trenchantly. 'She might have got back with that husband of hers. Except he's not her husband now. But you know, he's a man and she was his wife for years.'

Flora was puzzled and looking across at Kate, she saw that she was puzzled, too, neither of them sure what they were supposed to take from their friend's cryptic remark. It was probably best not to delve too deeply.

Kate got up, evidently meaning to do the washing up, but Flora laid a restraining hand on her arm.

'Your café, Kate, but my turn at the sink. If you could make tea?'

Walking back to her cottage – Betty had opted to stay in her shelter for the evening – Flora felt unsettled, only vaguely aware of the sounds and scents of a summer evening. Unnoticed, the air, soft and sweet-smelling, warmed her skin. Silver moths, their wings almost translucent in the shimmer of dusk, went unheeded. This evening had been difficult. Alice had been difficult. But it was the questions, first over Derek Easterhouse's guilt and then over Rose's, that tormented her. A guilty man and an innocent woman? Or was it the other way round?

24

It was Saturday and, since Flora would be at the All's Well until lunchtime, Jack schooled himself to use the rest of the morning to write – he'd already spent too much time on a leisurely walk around the Overlay back garden. The cabbage that he and Charlie had planted back in the spring appeared a little limp – in need of water, he thought – but the different types of lettuce he'd recently begun to grow were looking good and, with tomatoes and cucumbers flourishing in the greenhouse, he reckoned he'd have sufficient salad for weeks ahead.

Reluctantly, he tore himself away and walked back into the house. He'd been away from his desk far too much lately and the deadline that had been shimmering in the distance was now well and truly on the horizon. Walking through the French doors into the sitting room, he picked up a handful of notes from the coffee table, scribbled in odd moments over the last week, and made for his study.

His foot was on the first stair when there was a ring on the doorbell. Louder than a ring, a peremptory clang, more like, and when he retraced his steps to the front door, it was to be confronted by a uniformed motorcyclist, his figure large enough to fill the open doorway.

'Jack Carrington?' the man demanded.

He had barely time to acknowledge that yes, indeed, he was Jack Carrington, before the padded figure thrust two leather-covered gauntlets towards him. 'Here.' He pushed a large cardboard box into Jack's waiting arms, followed by, 'Sign on the line.' This time a scrap of paper was pushed at him.

Jack bristled. He'd no wish for the courier to engage in meaningful conversation but basic courtesy would not have gone amiss. Making no attempt to take the sheet of paper, he stared directly into his visitor's face.

The man looked away, shuffled his feet, then finally managed a 'please.'

Jack had no idea what he was signing for, but the courier's attitude hardly lent itself to argument. Tucking the box under his left arm, he scribbled a signature with his right.

'Thank you,' he muttered at the man's retreating back, still feeling ruffled and unsure exactly why he was giving thanks.

Once he'd taken the box into the kitchen and sliced it open with his best bread knife, the mystery was explained. One battered ledger and a fat bundle of invoices stared up at him from the open box. A note lay beneath the contents, brief and to the point.

Here's what you asked for, Inspector Ridley had written. *Probably a waste of time but I wish you luck!*

You and that girl of yours was the laconic addendum.

Jack took a deep breath. Alan Ridley seemed to have worked at lightning speed. It was only yesterday that he'd spoken to him and, at the time, the inspector had seemed half-hearted, less than half-hearted in Jack's estimation, and almost deafeningly uninterested in the idea of pursuing Derek Easter-house. But Ridley must straight away have phoned the head of accounts at County Hall, waved a big stick, then had one of his

constables collect the papers and pack them. He'd even gone to
the expense of hiring a courier service. Perhaps, after all, Ridley
had an inkling that he and Flora might be on to something. Or
he'd run out of ways to nab Lowell Gracey, his number one
suspect.

Jack took another deep breath. It had put paid to a morning
in his study. While this box sat on his kitchen counter, there
was no way he could concentrate on the complex plot waiting to
be untangled for the next Carrington thriller.

He needed Flora. In a few hours, she would close the All's
Well and he'd be waiting for her. An afternoon's work lay ahead
of them, maybe longer. In the meantime, he'd best get busy with
the watering can.

Flora wasn't surprised to see the Austin parked outside her shop
as she locked the wide, white-painted door.

'I had a hunch you'd be here,' were her first words, followed
by a soft kiss, one for each cheek. 'Shall we have lunch at the
Nook? I've only a single pork pie in the larder. I've never known
anyone eat as much as Lowell. Well, perhaps I have – you.
What's that?'

Her sharp eye had spotted the cardboard box sitting on the
back seat.

'"That" is why I'm here instead of wearing my fingers out
on the Remington. It's how we're going to spend the afternoon.
Alan came up trumps.'

Her eyes widened. 'Easterhouse's records? Really? I *am*
surprised. I was certain the inspector would turn you down.'

'So was I, but a very large and very rude courier arrived
with the box earlier this morning. I've had a brief look. There's
just the one ledger and the rest are invoices. Some of them have
stuff written on their reverse but, as far as I can see, the scribble

has nothing to do with any book orders. I thought we'd go some-where and trawl through the contents while we ate.'

'Go somewhere?' she echoed.

'Anywhere but Overlay. I don't have even one pork pie in the larder.'

'In that case, we'll buy sandwiches from the Nook, then go back to the cottage,' she said briskly.

'Are you sure? Shouldn't we find somewhere... more private?'

'It *is* private.'

'Your lodger?'

Flora's look was challenging. 'I'm thinking,' she said, her tone deliberate, 'that Lowell could be an asset in our search. He worked with Maud for months and will have a pretty good idea if the invoices are genuine and, if not, which ones are false.'

'But will he want to help?' Jack was unsure. The man had been in police custody, questioned over the murder of Maud Frobisher by an inspector who seemed determined to prove him guilty. At the moment, though, Gracey was a free man – would he really want to be dragged back into a case that must give him nightmares?

'Of course he'll want to help.' Flora was decided. 'If we prove Derek Easterhouse is guilty, it means Lowell isn't. He'll be safe.'

Flora's conclusion proved correct. As soon as Lowell understood what they intended, he was keen to forget the ham and lettuce sandwiches they'd bought from Tony at the Nook and make an immediate start.

'*You* might want to delay lunch, but I don't.' Flora laid out teacups and plates while Jack unpacked their purchases. 'I think we might have a long afternoon in front of us. And there's a pork pie, too, if you're hungry.'

Lowell brightened. 'Really? No one else fancy it?' He was into the larder before either of them could answer. Flora raised her eyes in a 'see what I mean?' expression.

Their meagre lunch was soon consumed, plates and cutlery cleared and teacups filled. It was Flora who reverently unpacked the box Jack had been guarding since this morning.

'What do we look at first? The ledger? The invoices?'

'Definitely the invoices,' Jack said. 'Let's see if Lowell recognises any of them.'

Flora was relieved. It seemed that Jack's attitude to her unwelcome lodger had softened considerably since the last time they'd met.

Removing the rubber band that held the bundle of papers together, Lowell slowly went through the invoices, sounding out their dates as he went and stopping when he'd reached the previous half year. 'The accounts were audited up to here.' He tapped the last invoice he'd uncovered. If we're searching for false invoices, we won't find them after this.'

'How about the ones you've extracted? They're the most recent, aren't they?'

He picked up the papers he'd put to one side and began very slowly to read through them page by page, shaking his head as he did. 'I recognise a couple of these orders but most of them I don't.'

'None of the books listed ever found their way to the library?'

He went through the sheets once more, this time more quickly. 'The van didn't carry any of these titles, I'm certain. Let's see...'

Lowell grabbed hold of the ledger that had hitherto sat at the bottom of the box unopened and flicked through the pages until he came to the date that signalled the beginning of the unaudited period.

'Plenty of entries in the ledger,' he said, 'and I reckon they'll match the invoices. But only a couple of the books ever made it to our shelves.'

'Was it usual for Maud to buy so little? Do you know why she held off purchasing new stock?'

He nodded. 'Actually, I do. She was planning to go to the big book fair in London – the one that was held last week. She'd decided she'd take a short holiday, stay in town for a few days and have the opportunity to wander round the fair. I think she wanted to get a sense of all the new stuff coming out, wanted to bolster our stock. She was really fed up with having to take cast-offs from the local libraries. And it was a bigger grant than usual – that's why she was husbanding it.'

There was a long silence while everyone sitting around the table recognised how sad that now sounded, until Jack came back to life, rattling his cup into its saucer and taking charge of the meeting.

'We've established there are invoices here – most of them – that Lowell doesn't recognise and therefore were never genuine. But the big question is how on earth were they produced?'

'They certainly look authentic. Every one of them has a firm's heading.' Flora shuffled through the top layer. 'Are all these real firms, Lowell? I recognise a few names, but not every one.'

'They're real all right,' he confirmed. 'There are one or two independent bookshops here, but most of the names are book distributors, ones the library service deals with. They all exist.'

He took one of the invoices that Flora was holding, bringing it up to his eyes to look more closely, then feeling the paper between his fingers.

'It doesn't look quite right, though. And it doesn't feel right,' he said.

Flora leaned forward. 'In what way?'

'I'm not sure but... see the date, it's been changed, I reckon. It's an old invoice that's been changed!'

'As a matter of interest, what's the invoice for?' Jack asked.

'Six hardbacked copies of *Room at the Top* and another six of *Dead Man's Folly*. The Christies are borrowed a lot and Maud always said it was worth splashing out on a hard cover because the paperbacks were likely to fall to pieces in a year.'

'If this is an invoice from, who is it...?'

'Hardings. Maud often ordered from them.'

'OK. Hardings. Let's find an invoice from them that has been audited as correct and see how it compares.'

Lowell went back to the pile of papers he had abandoned, and within seconds had located a Hardings invoice. 'This is one but... I reckon it's a copy done with a Thermo-Fax. The paper is thinner for one thing, and the text is slightly fainter.'

Flora jumped up. 'That's it!' She bounced excitedly around the table. 'Easterhouse copied an original invoice, one that had been passed by the auditors, slipped it into the records where it should be – presumably in case anyone wanted to check when that particular book was ordered – then set out to alter the existing invoice to read what he wanted it to read. A different date, and an order for books that the library never saw. And in the unlikely event that anyone did check back to the original, it wouldn't have been immediately obvious that it was a copy and not the real thing.'

'Phew.' Lowell stood up, too, as agitated as Flora. 'That's exactly what he did.'

'Hang on a minute.' Jack's tone stopped their celebration. 'He's taken the original invoice and altered it, but how?'

'All he had to do was blank out the date of the original order, then add in a date from the most recent half year and list an order that was four times the size and four times as expensive.'

'I get that, Flora, but the question is *how* did he do it?'

She sank back into her chair, Lowell following.

There was a long pause before Lowell said, 'It's possible he made up a liquid to blot out the information he didn't want. You could do that, just about, by mixing stuff.'

'What stuff?' She was puzzled.

'Stuff he could find in the kitchen, I guess. Starch, water, calcium carbonate. Maybe cellulose.'

'Slow down, Lowell. I know you're a chemist but you need to explain.'

'You can get calcium carbonate from a type of baking soda—'

'And cellulose from grinding down white cardboard perhaps,' Jack added thoughtfully.

'That's right! Once he got the mix right, Easterhouse could add a colour to match the paper – it would have to be a water-based tempera paint, I guess. He could use a watercolour brush to eradicate the old typing, then, when the sheet was dry, he could type the new details onto headed paper, making it seem a bona fide invoice!' Lowell looked triumphant.

'Extraordinary.' Jack collected their cups. 'More tea?'

There was a shaking of heads. 'Could he really do that?' Flora asked.

Lowell pointed to the bundle of unaudited invoices. 'It must have taken him an age, but he could and did.'

'And having proved the council's grant had been spent on books, he transferred the money from Maud's mobile library account into his own, I'm guessing.' Jack came back to the table. 'The man had nerve, I'll give him that.'

Lowell was thoughtful. 'He probably withdrew the money in cash. That wouldn't have made the bank suspicious. We've a system by which people who look after an account at County Hall can do that. They can withdraw a small amount of cash from the bank if a library needs it – if it's an emergency.'

'The emergency being Derek's future,' Jack remarked caustically. 'And small amounts can add up over a period. Mr Easterhouse has certainly been busy. But why would he do it? The life he leads is modest. Or it certainly seems so. The house when we visited – there was no sign of extravagant spending. And he was playing with fire. His dishonesty has lost him a permanent job and made sure he'd find it darn difficult to get another.'

'I don't know why he stole, but I do know his stealing is behind Maud's murder.' Flora rested her elbows on the table and frowned. 'I'm certain she would have asked him what was going on, given him the chance to explain and maybe put it right if he still had the money. She wouldn't have gone straight to this Mr Little. He's the chief, isn't he? It must have ended with him, though, because he sacked Easterhouse.'

'Whatever happened, we'll probably never know.'

'What we do know, Jack, is that he was out for revenge and poor Maud paid the price. But it's been a brilliant afternoon. We have him, folks!'

'Before we gallop to the obvious conclusion... yes, I know' – he held up his hand – 'Ridley won't accept this evidence unless it's as right and tight as we can make it.'

'Because he wants to pin it on me,' Gracey burst out. 'And a policeman can never be wrong.'

'I think you'll find Inspector Ridley will accept his mistakes,' Jack said quietly, 'but let's make it easy for him. The distributors are too far away to visit, but there are several invoices here – doctored ones – that come from local book-shops. We can pay them a call, ask them to check their records and bring back the proof. As long as the shops deny ever receiving the order or issuing the invoice, we're home and dry.'

'I agree, but it's too late to go today,' Flora said practically. 'And tomorrow is Sunday.'

'Then we'll make it Monday.' She could feel him looking at her hopefully. 'Is there any way you can spare the time? But if you really can't close the shop, I'll do the rounds.'

'I can help,' Lowell chirped up. 'I don't have a job at the moment. I'm hanging around doing nothing.'

'It's a nice offer, but I don't think you should.' Flora patted him on the shoulder. 'You're Ridley's number one suspect. What would it look like if it was you who found the conclusive proof against Easterhouse? The inspector might smell a conspiracy that doesn't exist. Better let Jack do it. He won't mind taking another day away from his book, will you, Jack?' She gave him her sunniest smile.

When he grimaced, she said, 'It's frustrating, I know, but tomorrow you'll have the whole day to sit at your typewriter.'

25

The morning was bright, the sun floating lazily between innocent-looking clouds, and the air markedly fresher than it had been for days. Standing at his kitchen window, Jack made a vow. Today he would get down to work in earnest. It was a Sunday and how many interruptions were likely on the day of rest? There would be no telephone calls, no couriers at the door, no dashes to see Flora. In a short while, he would wedge himself into his office chair and only move from it to make a sandwich for lunch.

It had been a foolish vow – he realised that immediately he'd made it – and sure enough had barely washed up his breakfast plates when the telephone summoned him to the hall.

'Jack! Glad to find you up.'

Up and just about to start work was what he wanted to say. But Alan Ridley had sounded impatient and Jack silently resigned himself to another day of distraction.

'I've got another body,' the inspector said baldly.

He was stunned. It was the last thing he'd expected and, in response, stood motionless, grasping the receiver so tightly that his knuckles turned white. Hearing Ridley on the line, he'd been about to launch into his tale of financial dark deeds, ready to argue that tomorrow he'd attempt to make the case water-tight, but the inspector's shocking news had pushed it firmly aside.

'A body,' Ridley repeated, in case he hadn't been heard. 'In Abbeymead.'

'Where?' was all Jack could think to say.

'At the Cross Keys. The chambermaid found the man this morning when she went to clean the room and Timpson, he's the new landlord but you know that, rang the police house. That was after he'd revived the maid. Tring is at the pub right now standing guard.'

'Waiting for you?' he asked mechanically.

'I've told the team to get there as soon as possible and Norris is on his way with a detective constable and forensics. But it's your village, and another murder on top of Miss Frobisher's. I thought you'd be interested.'

'Yes. Yes, I am.' Jack was trying to gather wits that had temporarily fled. Was this new death linked to Maud's? But how could it be? Easterhouse was their villain and he'd had his revenge.

'Do you have any identification?' He asked the question with little expectation that Ridley would know.

'Not at the moment.' He could hear the inspector puffing slightly down the line. 'The landlord said he'd never seen his guest before yesterday. The bloke signed in for just the one night, apparently. I suppose the village grapevine hasn't reported seeing a stranger?'

'Not that I know of, but I'm the wrong person to ask. I'm still a stranger myself.'

'Ah well, Timpson will have a register – haven't had a chance to look yet, but we should get a name from there. If you fancy walking along, I'll be in the pub. On a Sunday, too! At least I'll get a pint when the landlord opens up.'

'I'll be there in ten minutes,' Jack promised, though unsure of why exactly he was going.

They had their villain, he muttered to himself, casting around for shoes, jacket and watch, then dashing back for his wallet. Easterhouse could have nothing to do with an unknown man who had taken a bed for the night at the local pub.

To save time, he drove to the Cross Keys rather than walk, and found Ridley waiting in what must be the reception area for the rooms above. Jack had never visited this part of the inn before, having confined himself to beer and a plate of unspeakable food in the saloon bar, and was surprised at how small and stuffy it was. Really, little more than a dark panelled corridor. A pair of upright chairs, their cushioned seats gently sagging, sat either side of the narrow room while an oversized desk straddled its far end. Walking towards the wooden sign that announced Reception, he was aware of a pair of mournful eyes – the head of a long-dead stag – looking down on him from the oak-covered wall.

The inspector had his own head down, studying what Jack saw was the pub register. 'Our victim is a Mr Blessed or Bless*ed*. No first name. I don't suppose you know him?'

Jack shook his head.

'Like I said, poor devil only signed in for a night. It turned out to be one he wasn't expecting, by the look of it.'

'Was it a robbery?'

'Nothing's been taken from the pub, Timpson said. Not that there'd be much to take.' Ridley glanced around, his expression dissatisfied. 'But I haven't checked the room yet. I've told Tring to go home – he'll only get in the way – but we can take a look before my team get here.'

While they had been talking, Jack had sensed the landlord

hovering in the shadow of the staircase and, on hearing this, Timpson leapt forward, a bunch of keys in his hand, singling one out before handing the whole bundle to the inspector.

'A pass key to number three,' he explained. 'Constable Tring locked the door when he went to phone for help.'

'Where's the guest's key?'

'I couldn't see it. It might still be there... I didn't really look. There was Ruby screaming and fainting all over the place. I had to get her out of the room. Had to get my cook to look after her and give her a pint of strong tea.'

It was news to Jack that the Cross Keys boasted a cook. Maybe a few lessons from Alice?

'I can understand that, Mr Timpson,' the inspector said calmly. 'Not exactly what you hope to find on a Sunday morning. I'll need to talk to you later and also to the chambermaid. Miss Hargraves?'

'Ruby Hargraves. She's in the kitchen still. In a bit of a state.'

'I imagine so, but I'll still have to have a word.' Ridley jangled the bunch of pass keys. 'Perhaps you can warn her.'

'Yes, yes, of course.'

'We're well rid of him,' the inspector said quietly, giving a tired smile as he turned towards the staircase. 'One of those nervous blokes, all twitches and trembling.'

It was hardly surprising, Jack thought. Finding a dead body in his pub was probably not something the landlord was accustomed to.

'Could the man have died naturally?' he asked. It was probably a stupid question.

Ridley's pursed lips told him it was. 'I wouldn't be here if he'd popped off naturally. Tring was adamant when he phoned. The man had been killed. Said it looked as though he'd been suffocated.'

Jack was not about to try the inspector's patience further, but he did wonder how the policeman was able to diagnose suffocation, unless Mr Blessed had been found with a pillow over his head. Perhaps he had. He would soon find out.

Following Alan up the staircase, its old wood creaking beneath their weight, he came to an unexpectedly spacious landing, with just three doors leading off it.

'Not too much accommodation,' Ridley remarked. 'There's a couple of attic rooms on the top floor and two others on this one, but all of them empty last night.'

'So, an intruder?'

'Seems like it. Unless Timpson has gone in for murder. He sleeps in the annexe apparently and heard nothing untoward.'

Ridley fitted the key in the lock and, with some difficulty, opened the door. Jack blinked. The room ahead had filled with sudden bright light. The inspector strode to the window. 'The chambermaid must have come in, walked over here to pull the blinds, and only when she turned, saw that.'

He pointed to the bed where a body lay in the middle of the quilted eiderdown, rigid and perfectly positioned.

Jack stared, unsure of what he was seeing. 'Are they... are they pieces of sheet?'

The inspector walked over to the bed and looked down at the dead man. 'Unusual,' he remarked. 'It certainly looks like sheeting, torn into large strips and wrapped around the body. Tightly. Very tightly.'

Jack continued to gaze at the dead form, trying to make sense of what looked to be a gruesome death. 'This was how he was killed?'

'Tring reckoned he was suffocated and, for once, I don't think he was far wrong. Sheeting would suffocate if you muffled a person in it from top to bottom. I can't be completely sure until the forensic chaps get here.'

Jack felt slightly sick at the thought and could only hope the poor man had been unconscious before he was 'muffled', as Ridley put it.

'Not a robbery, though,' he said. 'See – his wallet and his watch, it looks expensive, have been left where he put them, on the bedside table.'

Ridley scratched his head. 'If it's not robbery, what on earth is it?'

It was a question neither could answer. Jack tried frantically to penetrate the mist befogging his brain. The watch was somehow familiar, a will-o'-the-wisp memory that, try as he might, he couldn't grasp hold of.

'Let's see what else Mr Blessed brought with him, apart from a wallet and watch.' Flinging the wardrobe doors wide, the inspector peered inside. 'No clothes.'

'He was only here for one night,' Jack pointed out.

'True, but he'd need night things, a change of underwear. Where's his luggage?'

Together, they glanced around the room, Jack walking over to look behind the single other piece of furniture, a chest of drawers, while Ridley got down on his knees and searched under the bed in case the man had brought nothing more than a bag that he'd pushed out of sight.

'Nothing,' he announced, getting to his feet. 'Not even a toothbrush. Why would you sign in to a hotel room without a spot of luggage?'

'You didn't intend to stay?'

'Exactly. Our Mr Blessed didn't come to Abbeymead for fun. I reckon he came to meet someone.'

'And likely did,' Jack remarked drily.

A noise on the staircase announced the arrival of the forensic team.

'We'll let you get on with it,' the inspector said to the man in charge. 'Call me when you get to unwrap him. I'll be downstairs in the saloon talking to the landlord.'

The talk with the landlord proved little help. Timpson confirmed that he had booked Mr Blessed in at seven the previous evening, shown him to his room and then gone down to help at the bar. It was a Saturday evening and very busy.

'Pretty raucous, it was. That lad, Hughie Walker, it was his birthday and his mates on the farm decided to pile in here to celebrate.'

'Were you in the bar the entire evening?'

'When I wasn't in the cellar bringing up more drink.'

'And you didn't see your guest again, after you'd shown him to his room?'

Timpson shook his head. 'I told him he could eat in the pub but he said he wasn't hungry.' He must have seen the menu, Jack thought irreverently. 'Said he was tired and was going to bed early.'

'And you saw no one else that evening – apart from those drinking in the bar? No strangers?'

There was a second shake of the head. 'I've not been landlord here that long, but I recognised all of 'em in the bar. Some of these chaps, well, you know, they're pretty reg'lar with the drinking.'

'Let's see if Ruby saw anyone this morning. Can you fetch her?'

Ruby was duly fetched, appearing white-faced and tear-stained a few minutes later.

'Can you tell me what happened this morning?' the inspector said gently, while Jack watched the girl's face. No more than sixteen, he thought. What a dreadful thing to happen to her.

Ruby began pleating an already sodden handkerchief before she could speak. 'I went up to number three to clean. I came in specially. Mr Timpson asked me to.' She sounded accusing.

'When did he ask you?'

'Last night. He telephoned my mum. We'd just finished watching *Dixon of Dock Green*. Mr Timpson said he had a guest at the Cross Keys and could I do an extra few hours next morning. I needed the money so I said yes.'

'You must have got here fairly early. Did you see anyone?'

'Just Mr Timpson and Dave. He's the pot man. He won a lot of money,' she said wistfully.

The inspector looked confused and Ruby said, 'He was tellin' me. He won a lot of money last night at the greyhounds. That's in Hove,' she said proudly.

Jack could see that Alan was mentally factoring in the pot man and deciding to check on whether he actually went to the dog racing.

'When you arrived...'

'I got my cleanin' stuff from the cupboard and went up to the room.'

'Was it locked?'

'No.' Ruby looked uncertain. 'No, it wasn't. I'd got the pass key with me but I didn't have to use it.'

'Are bedrooms usually locked when you go to clean?'

'I always knock,' she said. 'I did this time but no one answered.'

'And the door?' Jack asked intently.

'It was open. I thought the chap had gone down to breakfast and forgot to lock the door. Not wide open, just a few inches.'

'As though someone was in a hurry to leave and didn't pull the door fast behind them,' the inspector said, after Ruby had left them for more tea in the kitchen. 'He or she – best to keep an open mind – would want to get away as soon as possible. There was a racket going on in the bar which would have provided good cover.'

'The guest key seems to be missing and the door left open for poor Ruby to walk into this morning,' Jack said. 'Hopefully, Timpson will send her home soon.'

'He should pay her a bonus,' Ridley remarked, 'faced with that on a Sunday morning.'

'Ready for you now, chief.' One of his white-suited colleagues appeared in the doorway.

'Then let's go and unwrap our mummy!'

Back in the bedroom of number three, the two men from forensics began very slowly to unwind the strips of sheeting, one lifting the inert body as the other pulled the bandage from beneath, rolling it into a thick wodge of cotton. The operation was lengthy, but before the body had been revealed in its entirety, a chin made an appearance, then a small square of forehead and finally a pair of staring eyes.

'Good morning,' the inspector said to the dead man. 'Sorry for this indignity, old boy, but at least you're fully dressed, hey, Jack?'

The inspector spoke lightly but Jack felt himself freeze, unable to respond. He was staring at the face, his mouth slightly open.

'What's the matter?' Ridley demanded. 'You've seen a dead body before. Plenty in the war, I reckon.'

'Not this dead body, I haven't,' he croaked. 'This isn't Mr Blessed, no first name. It's Felix Wingrave.' No wonder the watch had seemed familiar.

'Wingrave? The author chappie?'

'The author chappie,' Jack confirmed.

'What the hell is he doing here and why the false name?'

Jack had no idea why Wingrave had ended up dead in an Abbeymead pub, but he could enlighten Alan on the name.

'It's a play on words.' He hadn't quite got his voice back and was still croaking. 'Felix is Latin for happy, contented – thus Blessed.'

The inspector looked annoyed. 'Very clever. I could do without those kind of games.'

And we could do without the dead man being Wingrave, Jack thought. It had taken him only seconds to work out just what this meant. In death, his old nemesis had struck again – and smashed his and Flora's impeccable theory into fragments.

26

Leaving Alan Ridley at the crime scene, Jack walked slowly back to his car. He should return home, he knew, continue with the day he'd planned, but the thought of buckling down to serious writing after such a blow was impossible. And it was a blow. The more he thought of it, the more right he'd been in realising that Wingrave's death drove a coach and horses through their brilliant deductions. By the time he slipped into the Austin's driving seat, the excitement of yesterday's discoveries was no more and, instead of driving straight to Overlay House, he stopped halfway along Greenway Lane and knocked at Flora's cottage.

She came to the door, tea towel in hand.

'Jack! What are you doing here? You're supposed to be writing. What was it you said, you'd be "slaving over a hot typewriter all day"?'

The mocking was gentle but he didn't respond. 'Can I come in?'

The tone of his voice had Flora step back and wave him into the hall. 'Of course you can. You don't need to ask. There's no food, I'm afraid. I've just finished lunch.'

'Really not a problem. I'm not hungry.' He paused. 'I could murder a beer, though.'

He could have stopped for one at the Cross Keys, he supposed, Alan was almost certainly on his first pint by now, but somehow he'd needed to put distance between himself and the dead man lying in the bedroom above.

'Beer? No, sorry. It's not a favourite, you know that. And I'm out of elderflower wine. I can do a sloe gin, if that's any use.'

He held up his hands, warding off the suggestion. 'Not after the last glass, thanks. I didn't even make the stairs before falling flat on my face.' He broke into a grin and saw the relief in Flora's expression. He must be looking particularly joyless.

'It will have to be a good old cuppa then. I've been eating in the garden, the weather is so balmy. Find a seat and I'll bring it out.'

Flora's back garden had a slightly tired look, the sun having parched the grass quite badly over the last few months, and the occasional summer storm battering the flower borders. But the bees were busy at their work and the roses, still in full flower, filled the air with their heady scent. A drowsy place to wile away the hours and Jack found himself falling into a doze.

He woke, though, as soon as Flora appeared with the tea tray. 'Where's Lowell today?' he asked, realising the question had been playing on his mind.

'Out walking. He's taken a picnic – well, his idea of a picnic. Sausage rolls, sausage rolls and sausage rolls. Oh, and a bottle of pop. He's gone for a hike over the Downs. Why? Are you hoping to avoid him? And there's me thinking that yesterday you behaved beautifully!'

'And I'll carry on behaving beautifully. I'm not at all jealous.'

When she smiled knowingly at him, he jumped up from his chair and grabbed hold of her, kissing her neck, her cheeks, her hair. 'Not. At. All. Jealous.'

She laughed, the tray wobbling dangerously in her hands. 'OK, message received. But, what about Lowell?'

'I think what I have to tell him will disappoint him hugely, and I'm not sure how to tackle it. I'm hoping perhaps that you'll be the one to break the news.'

'Why disappointed? Lowell is bouncing. And what news?'

'A few words that will almost certainly deflate his bounce.'

'You're being cryptic again, Jack. What's going on? You intended to spend the day writing, but instead you come to the door looking as though you've been to a funeral or you're just going to one. Now you're suggesting something really bad has happened.'

'It has. Easterhouse can't be our murderer.'

'Of course he can.' Balancing the tray on the small wicker table, she reached for the teapot to pour. 'Tomorrow, remember, you're off to gather the evidence that's sure to convict him.'

He shook his head while accepting the cup she handed him. 'There's little point in my going now. Not with Wingrave dead.'

'Wingrave! Dead?' Flora plumped herself down in a second deckchair. 'I think you should begin at the beginning.'

So he did and, when he'd finished describing the scene at the Cross Keys and what the writer's death must mean for their investigation, she sat silent for a while, hands clasped around her knees.

'I don't follow your logic,' she said at length. 'I don't see why Wingrave being murdered prevents Easterhouse being the villain who killed Maud. He embezzled money and she reported him. Those invoices don't lie.'

'It's obvious, Flora! You must see that – except you probably don't want to. It's almost impossible that we have two murderers within the same group of people. A quite distinct group, too: the writers and readers who attended the Abbeymead crime conference. If Easterhouse killed Maud, he must have killed

Wingrave. But why? He has an iron-clad motive for Maud but Felix...'

'There *could* be more than one murderer, or Wingrave's killer might be someone outside the group.' She was desperate to cling to what they had, Jack thought. Desperate to protect her friend. 'Or Easterhouse might have killed Wingrave after all,' she went on. 'You can't dismiss the possibility.'

'But why? What possible reason could he have? Easterhouse was a huge fan of Wingrave's books. According to Basil, he idolised the writer. Remember how he made a beeline for the chap as soon as he had an opportunity to talk to him.'

'I remember, but I also remember that Wingrave brushed him off. Putting someone on a pedestal can prove as dangerous as hating them.'

'Felix gave everyone the brush-off – he was unbelievably arrogant – and Easterhouse wasn't unique in getting a rough response. But a rough response doesn't immediately turn a huge fan into an enemy, does it? Why on earth would he kill a man he admires? Where's the reason?'

'There might be one we've no knowledge of,' she said stubbornly.

'Might be? Too vague, too uncertain. We need to be honest and admit that Felix's death has sent us back to square one. No matter how angry Easterhouse was with Maud, how much he must have wanted to take revenge on her, it seems to me now that it's unlikely he killed her. Someone else did, though, and we're as far away as ever of finding out who.'

Jack leant over and poured himself a second cup of tea before continuing. 'Once Lowell gets back from playing the jolly wanderer, you'll have to break it to him that he's still very much a suspect for the inspector.'

She gave a glum nod, absently spilling her own tea on the patch of grass beside her chair. 'I guess then that we start to look for Wingrave's killer. He must have gained a fair few enemies during his career and it won't be easy.'

'More than a few. And not just disgruntled fellow writers. From what I've learned recently, he's guilty of worse than sarcastic reviews. According to Arthur, it seems the man is in the habit of acquiring valuable books in an underhand way. To put it bluntly, stealing them.'

Flora's gaze became alert. 'The Dickens? The book is still missing.'

'Or maybe not. Maybe it found its way to Felix's mansion, but that's something we won't know for a while. Not until probate is granted and whoever is lucky enough to inherit his estate sells off his trophies.'

'They might not sell. They might enjoy the spoils for them-selves. The point, surely, is that Felix had enemies, lots of them, and they were widespread. He was horribly critical of other writers and now you say he acquired books by deceit. Anyone he cheated could be responsible for his death. When did Arthur tell you this?'

'Last week. Arthur was phoning me about something else and remembered a rumour he'd heard a while ago. I asked Ross Sadler to check and sure enough Wingrave was involved in a court case involving another first edition. He won, of course.'

'I knew none of this.' Flora sounded piqued and he accepted she had a right to feel annoyed. But then she was keeping secrets from him, determined to stay silent until she decided otherwise.

'I didn't tell you at the time – things got in the way,' he said a trifle weakly. 'In fact' – his voice strengthened – 'there was something else from Arthur that I didn't mention. Something I need to talk to you about.'

'Is it serious?' She leant over and touched his arm.

'I think so, if I agree to his proposal.'

'Is he sending you to Mongolia to research your next thriller?' she joked.

'Not quite as far. Lewes is a few miles closer. There's an independent arts college there.'

'I know it. Cleve. It has a good reputation.'

'It also has need of a writer.'

Flora managed to look surprised and anxious at the same time. 'A writer, not a teacher?'

'A writer who could be a teacher. Apparently, students there are encouraged to pursue their own work, separately from the exam curriculum – painting, writing, designing, whatever they're studying. In terms of writing, the college likes to employ a professional author who'll guide students through whatever independent project they have up their sleeves. Creative stuff they might work on once they graduate.'

'And they've asked you?'

Jack tried but failed to read her face. 'They've asked Arthur and, I think, one or two other agents if they have a writer on their books who lives locally and might be suitable. They're particularly keen on having a crime writer.'

'Are you going to take the job?'

'I haven't been offered it. In fact, I haven't agreed to put my name forward. Not yet. Yesterday, I had a letter from Arthur with full details of the job and an ultimatum – more or less. Do I want to go for it or not?'

'And do you?'

'It would mean a regular income.'

'You have a regular income,' she pointed out. 'Well, not exactly regular but an income.'

'It's that uncertainty that's making me wonder if I should go for the job.'

'Because we're getting married,' she said shrewdly. 'You shouldn't feel constrained to do it. The bookshop brings in a profit.'

He gave her a steady look.

'OK,' she said, 'a small profit but we can manage. We don't exactly live riotously.'

'I'd like us to do more than manage. The occasional treat, the occasional holiday. And I want you to have more free time. Time away from the shop, and that means employing someone else. Have you asked Rose, by the way?'

'No. I'm still wavering. I like her and I'm sure she'd do a good job, but she hasn't been honest with me and it's making me hesitate. I don't want to mention the All's Well until I'm certain – until we've found Maud's killer.'

'Which means finding Wingrave's. You know it's impossible to imagine Rose murdering Wingrave?'

'I don't see why. We have no idea of a motive – it could be anyone. Rose is part of the same group you mentioned, so why not her?'

Flora got to her feet, collecting their teacups to take back to the kitchen. 'Why was Wingrave at the Cross Keys anyway?' She looked thoughtful. 'He must have gone there to meet someone – and Rose is a very attractive woman. She could have enticed him there for a reason we don't know, and despatched him for another reason we don't know. How was he murdered? You didn't say.'

'Suffocated in bedsheets.'

Flora pulled a face. 'It's imaginative. The sort of thing you get in books.'

'And that makes Rose our murderer?'

She leaned over and gave his hand a light smack. 'I'm not saying that, but the case is wide open and until I can be sure... Rose supposedly has no money but, according to Kate, she's buying new clothes.'

'And according to Charlie, a new bike.'

'Sally told me. It was her bicycle, an expensive present from Dominic. Like I say, the case is as wide as the English Channel.'

She settled back into her chair. 'We should talk about the job. You're tempted, I can see, but reluctant, too. Why haven't you given Arthur an answer?'

'I was unsure how you'd react. It would mean a different life to the one we planned. I'd be away from Abbeymead for three days a week and though Lewes isn't Mongolia, it's a fair journey there and back.'

'Would the college expect you to live in?'

'I don't think so. As long as I put in the hours, I can live where I like. But it's not just the journey. If I'm away for three days, I'll have to double down on my writing the rest of the week. I won't be around much. I won't be able to help here or at the shop.'

'Do you now?'

'Well no, but—'

'Jack' – she put her arms around him – 'I've been running the bookshop single-handed ever since Aunt Violet died – in fact, for several years before when she was too ill to manage much. And the same can be said about the cottage and my garden. Marriage won't change that.'

'You think I should go for it?'

'I think you should do what feels right for you.'

He pulled her onto his lap, the deckchair creaking ominously beneath them. 'I could give it a go,' he said, burying his face in her hair.

'You could. And knowing you, you'll succeed.'

Jack went to bed that night, relieved that he'd told Flora of the college job and had her blessing if he chose to apply. And he rather thought he would. There was the offer of a new challenge – you could go stale doing the same thing over and over – and being in daily contact with young, creative minds could only be invigorating. He hoped they would feel the same. But he was getting ahead of himself. He might not even get the job; he'd been so dilatory it could well have gone to someone else by now. He would telephone Arthur first thing tomorrow morning.

For five blissful hours he slept soundly but, around dawn, a bad dream had him tossing and twitching, the bedsheets soon awry, one pillow landing on the floor. Then, quite suddenly, he was wide awake. A thin stream of light crept between gaps in the curtain, but it was too early. He needed to sleep again, then found that he couldn't. Something had woken him and whatever it was continued to irritate. A sound? A smell? No, it was a thought. One that was exciting and terrifying at the same time.

He needed to go back to those invoices. The false papers Easterhouse had manufactured. He still had them, piled in a corner of his writing room. Padding barefoot along the thin strip of carpet that lined the upstairs corridor, he pushed his office door open and looked hopefully around for his spectacles. The glimpse of tortoiseshell rims beneath a scattering of papers had him hook them out, then lump the invoices on to his desk.

Taking his time, he carefully examined each sheet of paper, looking for whatever it was that had danced through his dream. Not figures, he thought, trying to call back the moment. Not figures... he was struggling with the impossibility of remembering... but words, he decided. Words other than book orders and, for some reason, important.

Halfway through the stash of paper, he found what he only half knew he was looking for. Writing on the reverse side of an invoice. The back of the sheet was covered in doodles but then, at the bottom, a paragraph, words rather than scribble. And words that were familiar.

Reaching up to the shelf above the desk, he brought down Wingrave's latest book, the novel that Jack had finished last week, and skimmed the pages so closely that his eyes were soon red and sore. Doggedly, he carried on to win his reward. He'd found it! A passage that was a replica, or almost a replica, of the writing on the back of the invoice.

Methodically, Jack combed through the remainder of the invoices, extracting three more sheets in all, each with written passages on their reverse. Some were only a few lines long while others constituted a good chunk of text. For each, he was able to find the exact same passage in the novel he'd read. The author of *The Sphinx Murders* was Derek Easterhouse, not Felix Wingrave!

No wonder the novel had read differently to any other Wingrave that Jack had read. He'd imagined the writer making a new beginning, proud of a book that was superior to anything he'd written before. But that hadn't been the truth. It was someone else who should have been proud. A vivid image of Easterhouse at the conference, angry and dejected after Wingrave had turned his back and refused to talk, sprang into life.

Plagiarism – there was a motive, if ever there was.

27

Taking little heed of the clothes he pulled from his wardrobe, Jack washed, shaved and was dressed in minutes. He was a man in a hurry. He needed to see Flora before she left for the All's Well, needed to apprise her of his magnificent discovery – she would be bubbling – but make sure, too, that she knew what he was about to do. Not the planned visit to the shops that had supposedly supplied books to the mobile library, but one to Thelma Easterhouse. He had petrol in the car and could be in Crawley before ten o'clock, in the hope that it was a day she was spending at home. The whereabouts of her husband worried Jack slightly, but he would trust to luck that the man was out and about, still on the hunt for a job.

He caught up with Flora wheeling Betty down her front path.

'Another surprise!' She was laughing. 'You just can't keep away, can you?'

Reaching up, she kissed him good morning and once Jack had returned the kiss, he wasted no time. 'I'm on my way to Crawley. To Thelma Easterhouse.'

She looked bemused. 'Crawley, but why? And you do know you've buttoned your shirt askew?'

'Have I?' he asked distractedly. 'It doesn't matter. I'm going because I know it was Easterhouse who killed Felix Wingrave. And I know why.'

She stared at him. 'He did kill Felix, after all? I told you there might be a motive we didn't know about.'

'OK, you were right. But I found the motive. Plagiarism,' he announced proudly. 'The book we've both been reading is East-erhouse's work, not Wingrave's.'

Flora was quick to understand. 'That was the reason you thought it so different from all the others. *The Sphinx Murders*... is that why Wingrave was wrapped like a mummy?'

'It has to be.' Jack hadn't thought of it before, but the manner in which Felix had died fitted perfectly. 'A gruesome response, but very effective.'

Flora leant against her handlebars, steadying the wide wicker basket. 'I don't follow, though. Why are you going to Crawley? Shouldn't it be Alan Ridley and his men buzzing up the Brighton Road to arrest Easterhouse?'

'I'm keen to find the original manuscript. That will be proof positive. Otherwise, all I have to give Alan are scraps of writing on a bunch of false invoices.'

'What if Easterhouse is at home? And if he isn't, what if Thelma won't let you in, or says she doesn't know where her husband keeps his manuscripts, or pretends she doesn't know?'

'I've been wondering whether she might actually help me with the search – if I couch it right. The book Basil's supposed to be writing, for instance. I could suggest he use the manuscript of an aspiring writer to prove how useful his conference has been. As for Easterhouse, I'm hoping he's elsewhere, job hunting for the day.'

'Thelma might be willing to help without the need to tie yourself in knots,' Flora said thoughtfully. 'She came back to the village last week, for the first time in years, and spent hours talking to her cousin. Something is obviously disturbing her.'

Pushing through the garden gate, she manoeuvred Betty into the side of the road. 'It's a brilliant discovery, Jack, and you must tell me every detail – maybe tonight – but right now I'm going to be late opening the shop. Just be careful!'

'Forget the shop. Come with me,' Jack urged. 'It's your investigation, too. Let's catch our killer together.'

'How can I—'

'Ring Rose Lawson. If it's not her day at the post office, she'll be glad to look after the All's Well.'

Flora shook her head. 'I told you, I'm still unsure about Rose.'

'Then ask Charlie. He can stand guard for a few hours. In fact, take Betty back to her shelter and I'll drive you to the Teagues and you can give him your spare key to the shop. By now, he'll be out of bed – just.'

'Can I come, too?'

Deep in conversation, neither of them had realised that Lowell Gracey, slightly tousled from sleep, had walked down the front path and heard enough of Jack's plans to want to join in.

'I'm not sure that would help,' Jack prevaricated. 'The less obvious we make our visit, the better.'

'I'll keep out of sight. Just be there, hanging around if you need assistance.'

'It's a good idea,' Flora agreed, turning to her lodger, while Jack allowed himself a silent sigh. He'd hoped to do the thing quietly.

'Can you wheel Betty to her shelter, Lowell?' Flora asked. 'And I'll go back and lock the front door.'

～

Ten minutes later, they had collected Charlie, delighted to be in sole charge of the All's Well, and dropped him at the bookshop, having seen him settled behind Flora's desk.

She was uneasy about leaving the boy in charge. He'd done it before, but there'd always been an adult or two loitering in the wings, ready to help at a moment's notice. This time, Charlie really was on his own. But he was fifteen now and knew the workings of the All's Well almost as well as Flora, having delivered books for her every week for a number of years, as well as helping with sundry jobs in the shop. She must stop worrying about Charlie, she told herself, and start worrying about the visit to Crawley.

Jack had found evidence on the invoices that Easterhouse was the author of Wingrave's latest book, but he could only have turned up short extracts, sentences, phrases, and to prove that an entire book had been plagiarised was a whole different undertaking. To knock on Thelma's front door and demand she help them look for a manuscript that would see her husband convicted of murder was on another level of madness. And danger, too – there was always Derek, lurking in the background, and Derek had killed twice already.

They turned in to Willow Walk as Flora's watch showed ten o'clock. Ahead of them, an older woman, laden with bags, was returning from her morning's shopping, but other than her figure in the distance, the street was deathly quiet. Front doors were firmly shut, windows heavily curtained, and the neat handkerchiefs of newly mown lawn rested undisturbed beneath a cloud-strewn sky.

They sat looking at the scene for a while before Lowell said, 'I'll lose myself, like I promised,' and clambered from the back seat, poking his nose through the open passenger window to say, 'But I'll be around.'

Flora wasn't sure if that was a comfort or not, though she

noticed that Jack looked relieved. Lowell was an addition he hadn't bargained for.

Their first piece of good fortune, perhaps their only one, was to find Thelma Easterhouse at home. The woman's smile was uncertain as she took in who was standing on her threshold.

'We're glad to find you home,' Flora said cheerfully, trying for some normality in a situation that was anything but.

'I'm not working until this afternoon.' Thelma dragged a hand through her tight brown curls. The tortoiseshell clips were missing today, Flora noticed. 'My brother isn't around, if you've come to see him.'

Jack had suggested they use Basil as an excuse for calling – he'd been the focus of their attention the last time they'd visited the house in Willow Walk – but that now seemed a world away. Quite suddenly, the investigation appeared to have grown legs of its own, galloping ahead to take an entirely different direction.

'Is your husband here, by any chance?' Flora asked, pushing the subject of Basil to one side. Jack's face, she saw, was intent. It was a crucial question.

'He's off shopping. Was it him you wanted to see?'

'It was you we really wanted to talk to, Mrs Easterhouse,' Jack said smoothly.

She looked surprised but stood back from the door. 'You better come in then.'

In the hall, she seemed nonplussed as to what to do with her uninvited visitors. 'Tea?' she suggested hopefully.

'No, but thank you. We were wondering if we might see Derek's study?' Flora's tone was tentative.

'His study?' Creases in her forehead told of Thelma's puzzlement.

'Or the room where he writes.'

'That's the boxroom. There's not much to see. It's not much of a room.'

'But he keeps his manuscripts there?' Flora pursued.

'Well, yes, but... what's this about?'

Flora turned to Jack and a look passed between them, a mutual agreement to come clean with Thelma.

'We think your husband wrote a book that was published under another name,' Jack explained. 'We thought we should check.'

Thelma was thinking, her slim figure quite still. Then she nodded. 'Felix Wingrave, that's the man. Derek did a course with him and afterwards sent him the book he'd written. He wanted to know how good it was. Or how bad.'

'My guess is that Felix never replied,' Jack said.

'He didn't and Derek was that disappointed. He thought the story was really good. The best he'd written, he said. He'd only sent it to Wingrave because it was something he'd started while he was on the man's writing course.'

'And because he admired Wingrave?' Jack suggested.

'That's right. He bought all his books. I couldn't see anything in them myself, but Derek lapped them up. But then earlier this year he went mad and threw them out of the house. Every one of them. He said he'd been cheated. He never told me why he thought that. Never told me what it was about. But he said he'd never write another book.'

'Does Derek still have a copy of the manuscript?' Flora could feel the urgent need to get down to business. If Easterhouse had gone shopping, he was unlikely to be away for long and it would take time to search through what was bound to be a copious amount of writing. They needed to get to *The Sphinx Murders* before Derek arrived back on the doorstep.

'I imagine he must,' Thelma said indifferently. 'I'll take you upstairs and you can have a look through his files.'

The boxroom was well described, a small square of a room in which you'd be hard pressed to fit even a cot. Derek's desk was pushed up against the window, with just enough space for a chair and a tall cabinet. It was the cabinet, standing on a square of rough sisal carpeting, that she and Jack fixed their eyes on.

'It will be in there, I guess.' Jack's manner was easy but Flora knew that inside he would be fizzing. They were so close to cracking this case.

'I expect so.' There was another tugging at the curls. 'Has Derek done something wrong, do you know?'

'We're not sure,' Flora lied, abandoning an earlier frankness.

'If he has, I'm not surprised. He's been impossible to live with these last few months,' she confided. 'More than impossible. To be honest, I've wanted to get away, move out completely.'

'Back to Abbeymead?' It was a good guess.

'My cousin has a room for me. She'd like me to live with her permanently. A bit lonely, you know. And we only rent here so giving up the house isn't a problem.'

Out of the corner of her eye, Flora saw Jack at the cabinet, a sheaf of handwritten pages between his hands.

'It's a very big decision to make,' she said to Thelma, hoping to keep the woman distracted, but feeling sad for her, too.

'It is big, but I don't think I'll be sorry. I've never really settled here. Always had my heart back in the village. And Derek – well, I suppose you could say he was a bit of an escape. At the time.'

'And there's no longer a need for escape,' Flora said shrewdly.

Thelma's face lit from within. 'Mum passed away two years ago.' She had no need to say more.

It was then that Jack looked up from the papers he'd been quietly sorting. 'This is the book. *An Egyptian Murder* was Derek's title.' Pulling a sheet of scrap paper from his pocket, he began to check the page numbers he'd noted down. They would be different between book and manuscript but not that different, Flora thought.

'Here.' Jack stabbed his finger at a passage halfway down the page he was looking at. 'The same paragraph, word for word. And here.' He'd found a second page. 'I'm sure if we compared the entire manuscript with *The Sphinx Murders*, we'd prove beyond doubt that Derek wrote the original. Wingrave lifted the lot.'

'That's right, clever dick. He did.'

Derek Easterhouse stood in the doorway, thumping a shopping bag down at his feet. 'And what are you planning to do about it?' He advanced aggressively towards Jack.

'Derek! Stop! Don't be rash,' his wife said in a voice that wasn't quite hers.

He swung round to face her. 'You can keep quiet, you stupid woman. Letting these nosy parkers into the house, bringing them into my sanctuary. Letting them touch my papers. How dare you! And how dare they!'

Jack tapped the manuscript he'd been studying. 'This is evidence, Mr Easterhouse, and I think you know that. It should go to Inspector Ridley.'

'Over my dead body. Or rather yours.'

Thelma put her hand to her mouth. 'What's happened to you? What have you done, Derek?'

'Murder, Mrs Easterhouse,' Jack said calmly.

'So, another one isn't going to hurt, is it?'

And suddenly there was a sharp glint of a knife, caught in a lone beam as sunshine inched its way through the window.

Jack took a step back, holding out his arm to protect Flora standing close to him.

'Thought I'd come up here unarmed? More fool you. I knew you were trouble, the minute I saw you at the conference. And her, too. Miss Poke-Nose. Questioning Basil, sneaking in here when I'm not around, messing in what doesn't concern you. Believe me, it's the last time you ever do.'

Clearly maddened, he ran towards Jack, his arm raised and

ready to kill. Flora was stupefied, seemingly anchored to the floor, but before she could force herself to move, there was a loud thumping on the staircase and Lowell Gracey burst through the doorway and dived for Easterhouse's legs, bringing him crashing to the floor.

As Easterhouse fell, he tried and failed to stab Jack in the chest, but the force of his lunge had his prey stagger back and topple to the floor. There was a tangle of limbs, a wild thrashing of legs and arms and feet, and somewhere in the middle, a knife.

Flora danced around the swirling mass of men, trying to locate the weapon before Easterhouse did, unaware that Thelma had run onto the landing and grabbed an enormous ceramic vase. In a second, she was back beside Flora and bringing the ornament down with an almighty thud on her husband's head.

Easterhouse lay sprawled unconscious while Jack and Lowell scrambled hastily to their feet and Flora grabbed the handbag she'd left beside the desk. 'I have a scarf. I thought it might rain.'

Still breathing heavily, Jack took the long ribbon of material and, together with Lowell, made a businesslike job of trussing Easterhouse tight. Not quite as tight as Wingrave must have been trussed, Flora observed, but it would do.

Turning to Thelma, standing white-faced and clutching at her skirt with hands that trembled, Jack asked, 'May I use your telephone, Mrs Easterhouse?' A quaint courtesy amid a scene of devastation. 'We should call Brighton. Inspector Ridley will be keen to get here. The police will have some tidying up to do.'

Jack was always good at understatement, was Flora's thought.

28

Flora woke the next morning with a feeling of well-being. Of freedom, maybe. They were safe, the murder was solved and Maud would receive justice. In her imaginary conversations with Aunt Violet, she no longer need feel ashamed. Violet's friend had been avenged.

She turned towards the window, her eyes still only half open. The curtains were barely moving and patched with bright light, the sun already riding high. The promise of a beautiful summer's day! Shaking off the night's slumber, she stretched her limbs wide and, with new energy, threw back the covers.

There would be freedom, too, from secrets, she decided. She would talk to Jack of Mr Mulholland, tell him of a possible legacy – in all probability not enough to change their lives for ever, but sufficient to provide a comfortable cushion when the All's Well was doing poorly or Jack's latest sales weren't as good as he'd hoped. Sufficient maybe for him to relinquish the idea of Cleve College before he accepted any offer?

The job at the college bothered her and was the one single cloud she saw ahead. Jack had appeared willing, in fact happy, to take on the new challenge if it were offered, and she was equally happy to accept whatever decision he made. But there was a disquiet she couldn't lose. Jack was someone who enjoyed solitude. She'd come to appreciate that early in their friendship – all those years living as a virtual recluse in Abbeymead was ample evidence – and it had been only gradually that she'd managed to tease him out into the world. His natural instinct was to live in his mind rather than in company with others, and a college environment would certainly include others. A good many of them.

The hustle of society would never be for Jack, which was strange when you considered that for years he had been a journalist before turning soldier. His five or six years in the military had not been a choice, of course, but a newspaper man? Possibly it had been a career to placate his parents, or at least his father. For Ralph Carrington, novels were fluff and a life spent writing them was a wasted one. Jack had probably always been an author, but had dressed himself in journalist's clothes to keep the peace.

Shuffling on slippers and dressing gown, she made her way to the bathroom, noticing immediately that Lowell's toothbrush and toilet bag were missing. For the first time that morning, Flora realised how quiet the cottage had become. Running the hot tap until the water was piping, she turned over in her mind where Lowell could have got to. Her guess was that he was on his way first to County Hall and then, toothbrush in hand, to his old address.

Last night, Lowell had made it clear that he'd soon be leaving the cottage – it was possible he'd moved out already. A further cause for celebration? Not that she didn't like Lowell, but they had never truly recovered their old camaraderie, vanished with the years, and the delight of having her home back to herself – herself and Jack – was strong.

Before she and Lowell had said their goodnights, they had talked over his future together. He would go to County Hall, he'd said, and demand an immediate appointment with the officer in charge of Sussex libraries. He'd been adamant that he expected to be reinstated, and not just reinstated but promoted to Maud's old job with a salary to match. Once money was flowing again, there'd be no problem in paying the rent for the flat he'd shared in Brighton. He'd heard from his former flat-mates that the newcomer who'd replaced him hadn't settled at all well and he was sure to be welcomed back. He'd promised, too, Flora remembered, that he'd repay his debts, slowly, month by month, and he wouldn't be gambling again. His life was too full now to need that kind of distraction.

Lowell, she thought, deserved whatever luck was going. Despite being wrongly accused of murder and his livelihood taken from him, he'd been key to apprehending the real killer. Yesterday, events had moved fast. There had been an uneasy wait in the Crawley house while they listened out for the arrival of Ridley and his team. Jack and Lowell had appointed them-selves guards, Lowell at one point sitting on Derek Easterhouse when the man came round and began struggling. Flora's job had been to make continuous cups of strong tea, sitting with Thelma in her kitchen and trying hard to be of some comfort to the woman. Once Easterhouse had been arrested – Ridley appeared to have taken no chances, bringing with him a posse of burly police from the local station – and bundled into the back of a police van, she had helped Thelma pack a small bag. All four of them then had crammed into the Austin for the drive back to Abbeymead.

Thelma's cousin was a full-time housewife and likely to be at home during the day, and so it proved. She must have been watching from her kitchen window because the minute Jack pulled up at the house in Church Row, she came running out of the front door and down the path. The cousin had said nothing, simply looked at Thelma's face, then put her arms around her and, without another word, led her relative back into the house.

Yesterday's excitement was over now and another day at the shop lay ahead. One, Flora hoped, without murder on the agenda. Feeling an old lightness in her heart, she washed and dressed, choosing a thin cotton frock in response to a temperature that had risen steeply. In the kitchen, she found the bread bin looking sad, its only offering a small knob of stale bread. It would have to be cereal again, not her favourite, and it was a modest helping that she poured into one of the flowered bowls she'd recently discovered tucked away in a top cupboard. The vintage china had stayed hidden from the day Violet had brought it home from Abbeymead's summer fair, the year before she fell ill. If nothing else, the bowl did a solid job in cheering up the cornflakes.

Flora had taken only a spoonful before the telephone rang. The wonderful feeling of lightness drained away. This morning had been altogether too comfortable. Something had happened. Something was wrong. But hearing Mr Mulholland's voice coming down the line, her shoulders loosened. The investigation was finished, she told herself, the villain caught and any threat well and truly over. It was time to relax, time to remember she had a wedding close at hand.

'Can we meet today, Miss Steele?' he asked. 'I have something to give to you and I'd prefer to do it personally. Say, lunchtime when you close the shop?'

She thought quickly. 'I can do that, Mr Mulholland. Thank you. But can we meet on the village green? The weather looks to be settled and I'd rather we talk where we can't be overheard.'

Whatever the solicitor had to tell her, Flora didn't want the whole village to know – at least, not yet – and that would certainly be the case if they took a table at the Nook or a seat in the pub.

'I understand. I'm happy to drive to the green. One o'clock then?'

'Yes. I'll be on the first bench you come to.'

There was a murmur of agreement and Mulholland had gone.

Flora went back into the kitchen and sat, her cereal bowl untouched, looking into space. This was an opportunity to make things right, she decided. To feel completely at ease. She wasn't entirely convinced that it was the challenge of the new that had persuaded Jack to consider the job at Cleve College. Rather, she suspected that, with their wedding imminent, he was allowing financial reasons to steer him towards it. If the solicitor's cheque was as substantial as she hoped – and Flora guessed that was what he was to hand her – there might be no need for Jack to contemplate the move. Either way, he should be involved in the discussion and she'd been wrong to keep him in ignorance until now.

Jumping up, she left the despised bowl of cornflakes on the kitchen counter and walked back into the hall. Jack was a long time coming to the phone and for a few seconds a frisson of panic took hold. What had happened to him? Why hadn't he answered? But, finally, after a prolonged ring, he picked up the receiver. Mentally, she shook herself. Really, she must stop this. Wasn't her name Steele? She should live up to it!

'Been hanging on long?' he asked, sounding slightly out of breath. 'Sorry, I was in the garden. What a glorious day!'

'It is,' Flora said, recovering a little. 'Do you fancy enjoying it on the village green?'

'Come again?'

'The green at lunchtime. Can you be there at one? I've someone I'd like you to meet.'

'Yes,' he said uncertainly, 'but what—'

'Be patient. All will be revealed.'

'More mysteries, I suppose,' he grumbled.

But no more secrets, she thought, replacing the receiver and racing upstairs for her handbag. Betty would be getting impatient. Their usual time for leaving was well overdue.

Flora had already arrived on the green when Jack brought the Austin to a halt. Extricating himself from the driver's seat, he saw her straight away, sitting on a nearby bench and not alone. A man was with her. That man, Jack thought, the one he'd seen her with before. Dressed in a three-piece suit, shirt closely buttoned and with polished leather shoes on his feet, the chap looked ready to conduct a board meeting. If there were any justice, he should be sprinkled in sweat – a heat haze was already forming over the grass – but instead appeared cucumber-cool. Feeling unreasonably annoyed, Jack made his way over to the bench where the two of them were chatting together like old friends.

Flora caught sight of him when he was only feet away. 'Jack!' she called out, jumping up from her seat. 'Let me introduce Mr Mulholland. He's a solicitor.'

'James Mulholland,' he said, rising as he spoke and offering his hand.

'This is Jack, my fiancé,' she said simply.

'I'm delighted to meet you, Mr Carrington, and have you here to share the good news.'

'Really? What good news is that?'

'Sit down, Jack, and he'll tell you.'

Mulholland beamed, making space on the bench for a third person. 'I've already explained to Miss Steele that for many years Mulholland and Mulholland have been holding funds from the sale of her family home, unable to contact the beneficiary, namely Miss Steele. She will enlighten you, I'm sure, as to how I finally found her.'

He turned to Flora. 'I have your birth certificate to return, Miss Steele, and your aunt's letter which I imagine is very precious to you. Both are ample proof of your identity as

Christopher and Sarah Steele's daughter. And, as such, I'm delighted to present you with this.'

He fished in his inside pocket and brought out an envelope which, with great solemnity, he handed to Flora.

'The house?' Jack was trying to catch up. 'Your childhood home?'

'Yes,' she said, her happiness palpable. 'It was in Hampstead and sold after my parents died. This is the money from it.'

James Mulholland gave a delicate cough. 'Relatively little, I'm afraid. Debts,' he explained apologetically. 'But the sum has accrued interest over the years and I venture to hope it will provide a comfortable addition to your income. You are getting married soon, I understand, Mr Carrington. This may have come at just the right time.'

'It would seem so,' Jack said dazedly.

'You will have much to talk over.' The solicitor rose smoothly to his feet, brushing invisible specks of dust from his trousers. 'I will leave you now. Business calls. But if you have any questions, Miss Steele, you can always reach me on the telephone. You have my card still?'

'I do. And thank you for your kindness.'

She jumped up to join him and, resting her arms on his shoulders, kissed him on the cheek.

'Goodness. Hardly deserved, but thank you.'

A gentle incline of his head and, turning, he strode towards the road. The very smart car that Jack had seen in the school playground was no doubt waiting.

'So, that was the mystery. A solicitor! Why didn't you tell me?'

'I wasn't sure I could prove it was me that Mr Mulholland should pass the money to. And even if I were able, I wasn't sure how much it would amount to. He warned me it was very little in relation to how much the house was worth. It's hard to accept but my father had large debts when he died and his creditors had to be paid before either Aunt Violet or myself inherited.'

'And Violet never did.'

Flora sank back onto the bench. 'She disappeared before the solicitors could contact her with the news that there was a little money after all. I think maybe she was ashamed of the way her brother had managed things. Not that he could have known he was going to die and leave a six-year-old orphan.'

'But the money for the All's Well?'

'Violet's godfather died about the same time and bequeathed her his estate. That's how she was able to buy the bookshop and the cottage. I think she just blanked off what had happened in London. Losing her brother and sister-in-law, losing the family home, the financial mess it left. It was the need to rescue me that was most important.'

'She did a good job. Are you going to open it?' He pointed to the envelope lying between them on the bench.

Flora pulled a face. 'It could be our honeymoon money.'

'To Cornwall again?'

'Maybe.'

Very carefully, she opened the envelope and drew out the flimsy oblong of paper. Jack said nothing but watched her face. First incomprehension, then shock, and finally a bright red flush.

'Five hundred pounds!' she announced. 'How can he say that's a modest sum?'

'Because he deals with very rich people every day?' he suggested wryly.

'But it's—'

'Amazing.'

'Huge. I've never had so much money.'

Neither had he, but Jack was Ralph Carrington's son and had seen not dissimilar sums pass across a gaming table on several interesting evenings. Money was relative, he thought.

'I guess with this we could venture further afield than Cornwall. What do you think?'

She grabbed hold of his hands. 'You know what I'd love, Jack? To go to Egypt. That book...'

'And find another murderer?'

She shook her head. 'To see those wonderful monuments in Wingrave's book... sorry, Easterhouse's. But I think the trip might take too long,' she finished mournfully.

'Far too long. Ten days to Port Said and ten days back, before you add in the time you'd want to spend in the country. Think nearer home. Maybe Paris again but for longer? Or Rome? Or Athens? There's some fairly amazing monuments there, too.'

'Paris?' she murmured. 'The city was wonderful. But... There's a picture. I was going to ask you to help me hang it. In the sitting room, I think. The buildings it depicts are wonderful and the sun and the water and all those boats... Venice,' she decided, 'that's where. It has to be Venice.'

29

Two days later, a letter arrived at Overlay House, offering Jack the position at Cleve College. He was sceptical. He'd probably been the only writer who fitted their requirements; the one local crime writer, in fact. But the offer of a job at what was a well-known and respected arts college was a welcome boost and a tribute, he imagined, to Arthur's powers of persuasion. His only decision now was whether or not to accept.

The choice had become more complicated after what he'd learned at Tuesday's meeting on the green. Five hundred pounds was a very large sum of money, a satisfying nest egg for any married couple. But it was Flora's money. Money she deserved after the heartbreak of her childhood. He was delighted for her, not only for the security it offered but for the questions it answered from the past, questions she'd never had answers to.

Her aunt had made the decision not to tell the young Flora the truth surrounding her parents' tragic death, nor anything of their life before she was orphaned. But even Violet, so close to her brother and sister-in-law, would not have known everything.

There were bound to remain gaps in Flora's history that she would never fill. Gaps she would have to learn to live with – but wasn't that so for everyone? Jack felt satisfied that, for the most part, the woman he loved had discovered what was most important to her: the graves in a cemetery in southern France, the knowledge that she had once belonged to a happy family, and now the fate of her childhood home, built by her grandfather and passed to her father.

Flora was eager to share her good fortune. Already, she was planning their honeymoon and Jack was happy to accept the gift. He wasn't a man given to control, but his determination to contribute as much as she, was unaltered. He could write books and earn a decent income, but books took time to write and time to produce and there were large sections of the year when his income plummeted worryingly. The college job meant a steady salary, a comfortable if modest sum in the bank each month. He would go for it, he decided. And work out later the logistics of travelling in winter with a less than reliable car and when bad weather could lead to treacherous roads.

Before he had time to telephone Flora, however, and tell her his news, Alan Ridley was on his doorstep.

'Good! You're home! Not that I thought you wouldn't be,' the inspector said. 'You writer chappies have it easy. No battling the world for you.'

Jack forbore to answer. It was hardly worth the effort. 'I'm about to make lunch,' he said. 'Can I get you a sandwich?' Anything, rather than a Cross Keys pork pie.

'That would be good.' Ridley stepped inside and made his way into the kitchen. He'd been to Overlay House before, Jack remembered.

'I've asked Miss Steele to come along,' the inspector said, surprising Jack. 'Called in at the shop on my way here. She said she'd cycle along as soon as she closed for lunch. Something about Betty.'

'The bike.'

'Ah, yes. The bike.'

'Cheese and pickle OK for you?' Jack opened the bread bin, grateful he'd bought a fresh loaf yesterday.

'Fine, but before you start with the butter knife, can you find those invoices? The ones Easterhouse faked. I've collected what's left of the paperwork from County Hall, any stuff dealing with the mobile library, but I need the invoices back.'

'They're upstairs. I'll get them. Won't you want Maud Frobisher's accounts, too?'

'Miss Steele is bringing those. She took them from the van – when she shouldn't, I might add. Apparently, she was after a present, but she saw Miss Frobisher's records in the desk and thought she'd safeguard them.'

'Then she did the right thing.'

He sounded a trifle snappy, he knew, but Alan Ridley had never come to terms with Flora in her sleuthing role, and at times it rankled. She was a woman – young, pretty, and clever – and for Ridley, that was an uncomfortable mix.

When Jack returned with the invoices he'd kept stacked in his office, the inspector began immediately to leaf through the pages, his smile growing broader with each sheet. 'This little lot should cook Derek's goose as far as theft is concerned. As well as being a first-class motive for Miss Frobisher's death.'

'And Wingrave?'

'No problem. He's already admitted to killing Wingrave. Told us the whole story and seemed pleased to get it off his chest. He tried to decapitate him at the conference but it didn't quite work.'

'The safety curtain,' Jack muttered. 'It was meant for Wingrave?'

'Seems so. Easterhouse was annoyed – still is – that his timing was a bit off and he bagged you instead. But Maud

Frobisher – I can't break him on that, but I will. And these little darlings will make sure I do.'

Jack had only just finished preparing the plate of sandwiches and put the kettle to boil, when a bang on the front door announced Flora and Betty had arrived. It was the inspector who let her in.

'Here,' she said. 'You'd better take these,' and handed Ridley the three notebooks she'd found in Maud's desk. 'I've not been happy having them in my cottage.'

'You should have handed them over before,' he said disapprovingly.

'You weren't interested, were you?' There was a challenge in her voice. 'It was only Jack and I who were prepared to look beyond the obvious, to look beyond Lowell Gracey.' She went over and kissed Jack on the cheek, then turned to face the inspector, hazel eyes shooting fire. 'That's true, isn't it?'

Alan Ridley flushed. 'I may have got it wrong.'

'May have!'

'Shall we take the food into the sitting room? There's not much space in here.' Jack smiled encouragingly at his antagonistic guests.

It took a few minutes for the inspector and Flora to resume friendly conversation, but the cheese and pickle sandwiches appeared to have a calming effect. They were good for that, Jack reflected. The spicy tang of pickle, the mellow taste of cheddar. A brilliant combination.

'You say Easterhouse has confessed to killing Wingrave?' he said to the inspector, as he returned from the kitchen with a tray of tea. He was hoping they could avoid any further mention of Lowell Gracey for as long as possible.

'The evidence was piling up against him even without a confession. His wife couldn't confirm his whereabouts the evening Wingrave was murdered – he wasn't at home and it was unusual for Derek to go out at night – and when we showed his photograph at the Cross Keys, Timpson recognised him straight away. He'd seen Easterhouse talking to the girl behind the reception desk, and when we asked her what was said, she told us the chap had been after a room number. Number three. Wingrave's room – whose missing key has since turned up in a jacket pocket in Willow Way. Once we had a clear motive, thanks to you, Jack, and it's a pretty powerful one, he didn't have a leg to stand on.'

'What happened the night Wingrave died?' Flora asked, and Jack was glad to see she had lost the angry flush.

'Put simply, Easterhouse lured his victim to the pub. At the crime conference, he overheard Wingrave talking to a fellow author – a Clive Slattery? – about a rare book that Miss Frobisher had in her possession. Wingrave was saying how much he'd love to have it for his own collection of first editions and arguing passionately that the book should be on the shelves of someone who'd value it properly – he hated the idea of it ending up as a showpiece in the library of some wealthy philistine. It was the bait Easterhouse used.'

Jack stood up, offering round what was left of the sandwiches. 'He must have been calculating how to use the information from the moment he heard it. It looks as though he contacted Wingrave very soon after the conference.'

The inspector nodded. 'He telephoned Wingrave to apologise for harassing him. Apparently, he'd badgered the writer during the conference. Tried to force him to talk.'

'I saw him,' Jack said. 'At the time, I thought he was an over-enthusiastic fan who'd made a beeline for his favourite author, but presumably he was haranguing Wingrave for stealing his book!'

'Derek wanted reparation. Still wants it, he told us. He writes in a very similar style to Wingrave, not so much imitating but influenced by it. When he bought Wingrave's latest book, he was astonished, then furious, to find the plot was one he'd come up with earlier – on the writing course he did with the bloke. Not just the plot either. Wingrave had stolen his words. He'd been written out of the script, as it were, and it was plagiarism pure and simple. The book should have *his* name on it, he told Wingrave. Even then, he said, he was prepared to be magnanimous and share the honours.'

'But Wingrave refused? I saw him shrug Easterhouse off and, when I spoke to him later, he was dismissive. There were always people like Derek at conferences or in workshops, he said. They were a menace and, for your own peace of mind, it was best to ignore them. You simply batted them away.'

'He was dismissive all right. It seems he told Easterhouse that there were only seven plots in the world – are there, Jack? – so there was bound to be overlap and, as for the actual text, who was imitating who? He had no intention of compensating Easterhouse, and refused point-blank to include in the book any kind of acknowledgement that the original story was another writer's.'

'No wonder Derek set out to punish him.' Jack grimaced. 'Not only had he bought every book Wingrave published, but paid money to do the man's writing course. Then, in good faith, sent him his own manuscript keen, I imagine, to have the opinion of a writer he admired, only to discover months later that he's been thoroughly cheated.'

'Wingrave wasn't very clever, was he?' Flora bit her lip. 'After what he'd done to Easterhouse, you would think he'd make sure he kept his distance. Instead, he goes to meet the man in a hotel room!'

'Perhaps it's just that Easterhouse was that little bit cleverer,' the inspector said, a smirk beginning to dawn. 'He pretended in that phone call that he wanted to make up for any annoyance he'd caused Wingrave, using the excuse that things had been going badly for him lately, personal things he didn't specify, and that he hadn't been himself. He was still a fan, though, he said, and would like to make amends. Said that he worked with Maud Frobisher, which in a way was true, and that before she'd died she had told him a secret.'

Flora snorted. 'How likely is that!'

'She'd taken the book from the safe, he said, and hidden it.' Ridley continued his story, unperturbed by Flora's outburst. 'We still haven't found the blessed book – it was nowhere to be seen when we searched Wingrave's pile – but in his phone call Easterhouse claimed he knew where it was and knew that Maud would want the book to go to a true collector. He'd heard that Wingrave had an interest in first editions – would he be interested in buying *A Christmas Carol*?'

'You bet he would!' Jack exclaimed.

'Surely Wingrave would have thought it odd that Maud had confided such a huge secret to someone with whom she barely worked and who wasn't even a friend? Again, not very clever,' Flora objected.

Ridley gave a slight shrug. 'He probably didn't question it too much. He was an avid collector after a rare item. He wouldn't know how close or otherwise Easterhouse was with Maud. Anyway, whatever reasoning he went through, Felix Wingrave bought the story. Easterhouse said he'd meet him back in Abbeymead, that he'd book a room for him at the Cross Keys under a false name – the sale would have to be kept secret and as its buyer Felix would need to stay anonymous – but Easterhouse would come to the pub to meet him that evening.'

'All very cloak and dagger. Or should it be Dirk and Dagger?' Flora pulled a small face at the feeble joke.

'Easterhouse didn't have the book, so how did he gain access to Wingrave's room?' Jack wanted to know more. 'Without the prize in his hands, he must have doubted if Felix would have even let him through the door.'

'He made up a parcel – a pretence – tucked it under his arm and handed it to Wingrave at the door. Once the chap had trotted back inside the room and was eagerly unwrapping it, Easterhouse followed and struck. As you know, Jack, when the chambermaid went in to clean the next morning, she found Wingrave's body trussed in bedsheets. Well and truly suffocated.'

'Like an Egyptian mummy, we reckoned. Horribly appropriate!' Jack picked up the teapot to refill.

While he was in the kitchen, Flora turned to the inspector. 'I don't understand why Easterhouse has confessed to Wingrave's murder, but not Maud's. He was clearly her killer.'

'He doesn't yet know the evidence we've collected and it may be that he thinks he can get away with Maud's death,' Ridley said calmly. 'He'd be up for just one murder then, not a double. And because of the motive in that case – the man had been badly cheated – Easterhouse could be calculating that the jury will be merciful. But there won't be much mercy for the murder of an elderly woman simply doing her job.'

'When are you going to show him the evidence? It's damning, isn't it?' She pointed to the stack of invoices and the notebooks sitting in a neat pile.

'It will nail him,' Ridley said confidently. 'Though why he chose to scribble on the back of the invoices he faked is a mystery,'

'Grinding them out must have been hugely boring,' Jack said, catching the end of the conversation as he came back into the room with a fresh pot of tea. 'Maybe Easterhouse relieved the tedium by writing sentences in his head – as you do – and was daft enough actually to write some of them down.'

'Do you?' The inspector looked interested. 'Write sentences in your head? Well, I never. But however those scribbles got there, they're incriminating. They give Derek Easterhouse a rock-solid motive. Only he could have made them. He had sole responsibility for the section of the accounts department that deals with the mobile library. He came to see it as a way of putting his hand in the till by falsifying figures and siphoning off the money into his own bank account. We've checked and found the money there. This lady, Maud, kept meticulous accounts and once she'd checked the County Hall version and found she'd ordered books she hadn't, she went to Easterhouse for an explanation.'

'I don't imagine he gave it.' Idly, Flora brushed the crumbs from the coffee table.

The inspector sighed. 'Unfortunately not. According to Mr Little, whom she went to next, Miss Frobisher offered Easterhouse the chance to make reparations and it was only when he refused, saying her accusations were ridiculous, that she went to the chief accountant. Inevitably, that led to his sacking. And his fury. How could he tell his wife? Where was the money coming from to continue living in the house he thought she loved? Easterhouse knew it was Maud who'd blown the whistle and, from that moment, he was out for revenge.'

'It's possible he didn't mean to kill Maud, I suppose.'

'More than likely. He could have gone to the van to scare her, maybe even hoping to steal the rare book he'd heard about. That would have landed her in trouble and, if he was able to sell it, get *him* out of trouble. Whatever the reason, we'll find out.'

'Being Maud, she would have fought back.'

'If so, it's a great shame she did. She'd be no match for a much younger man and, when she fell, it proved deadly.'

There was silence in the room, an almost tangible sadness touching all three of them, the remaining sandwiches forgotten and a second cup of tea left unheeded.

'Well, folks.' Ridley jumped up. 'I'd best be off. Thanks for these.' He picked up the bundle of papers and waved it in the air. 'I'll need statements from you both, naturally. Norris will be round in the next day or so, but it shouldn't take long. Not a lot for you to report. Apart from the faulty curtain and the incident in Crawley, you've not had too much involvement. Stayed on the margins this time, as it were.'

'On the margins and solving the case for you, Inspector,' Flora said.

There was a tight little smile on her face.

30

'That man!' Flora fumed, once Jack had seen Alan Ridley to the door.

'He's harmless enough, just clumsy in his approach.'

'Jack! He never misses an opportunity to undermine – usually it's me, he has a real problem with women – but today it was both of us being dismissed.'

'It must be galling to have amateurs forging ahead and getting it right,' Jack said mildly, 'and there have been times when we've been grateful to see him and his men. Very grateful.'

'I suppose.' It was a grudging admission. 'But we *had* forged ahead and he was unwilling to give us any thanks, any credit, for what we discovered. *And* he hasn't solved the case completely. The book is still missing.'

'We might have to accept that as far as Ridley is concerned, it will stay missing. He's got his murderer and that's his primary concern. The Dickens is bound to turn up eventually. Probably in the most unexpected place.'

'I should be turning up – and not in an unexpected place. Right now at the All's Well.' She tapped her watch.

'Before you go... I've news. I've been offered the Cleve job and decided to accept. I'll write to the college today, as long as it still makes sense to you.'

'Of course it does. If it makes sense to you, it will to me. Congratulations, Jack!' She stood on tiptoe to give him an enthusiastic kiss. 'Lewes is an interesting place and once you're established, I might find my way over from time to time. There are several antiquarian bookshops in the town – I could go hunting and who knows, I might even spot *A Christmas Carol*!'

Holding the front door open for her, he saw Betty parked neatly against his front wall.

Flora turned to say goodbye. 'Will I see you this evening? I've made a fish pie.'

'Fish?'

'It's healthy.'

Jack schooled his face.

'And delicious,' she added.

'Ah well then...'

~

Turning into the high street from Greenway Lane, Flora was aware of a figure outside the All's Well, waiting, it seemed, for the bookshop to open. Not Elsie, she thought, her customer who was always either too early or too late. The figure wasn't short or stout enough. Who else could be loitering, though? Pushing Betty the last few yards, she saw with surprise that her visitor was Rose Lawson, noticing as she did that Rose was wearing what appeared to be another new outfit, a beautifully tailored pale blue linen dress and jacket with a white Peter Pan collar and cuffs.

'I'll just wheel Betty into the courtyard,' she said, her depression returning at the thought of what Rose might have done. Not murder now, that was clear, but the book, after all, was still missing. 'Two seconds and I'll be with you.'

It was a little over the two seconds before she was ushering Rose into the shop and taking a deep breath of the much loved smell – vanilla and smoky wood – an aroma she'd missed so much when away in France.

Rose had stopped by the front display table and was smoothing first one cover and then another of the books Flora thought likely to prove the most popular. She waited in silence. It was clear that her visitor wanted to say something, but was finding it difficult to begin.

'Do you have a book you're after?' she asked at last, hoping it might prompt a response.

'No, not really... Flora...' she said in a sudden burst, 'I saw that you had that boy, Charlie Teague, running the shop the other day. He seemed very young to be your new assistant.'

'That's because he isn't. He does my deliveries on a Friday evening, as you know. He's been doing them for several years and very efficiently, too. But Monday was an emergency. Charlie is on his summer holiday until he starts work so I asked him to stand in for me for a couple of hours.'

She saw what she thought was relief in Rose's face.

'If you have another emergency, you can always ask me, you know. I have the time spare. Dilys has kept me on for a day even though Maggie is back at work, but that leaves the rest of the week free, and I really liked my time here.'

'I can see why.' Flora fixed her with a steady gaze. 'You know your way around bookshops. Actually owned one, I've heard. Is that true? Why did you never mention it?'

Rose didn't meet her eyes. 'I suppose because it was part of my old life. I wanted to forget what had happened. It's not easy being a divorced woman. Gossip can be cruel and I'm often made to feel embarrassed at the way my life has turned out.'

Flora felt an immediate sympathy but continued to hold

back from the offer she'd wanted to make. There were questions still needing answers. 'I did think that maybe you wouldn't be interested any longer in working at the All's Well,' she said carefully. 'Now that you're more comfortable, I mean.' How else to phrase it, she was unsure, her gaze fixed on the smart tailoring and shiny sandals that Rose was wearing.

Her companion saw the glance. 'I've come to an agreement with my husband,' she said diffidently. 'Sort of an agreement. He's admitted that he treated me unfairly and because of that, he's willing to help me out. A little.'

'That's really good news!' And it was.

'I was on my way to London to see him when I saw you last,' Rose confided. 'In fact,' she said with a sudden burst of confidence, 'I was returning jewellery to him.'

'Is that why he changed his mind?'

Rose nodded. 'A diamond necklace that belonged to my mother-in-law. I wore it very occasionally when we went to posh events.'

Flora did a quick reckoning. 'That was the parcel?'

Her visitor looked confused.

'In your basket. I saw a parcel tucked into your basket when you called that morning.'

'Ah, yes. That's right.' She looked down at the display table and began tapping her fingers across the upturned book covers. 'I took the necklace when I left. I shouldn't have done that.' She lifted her head and looked directly into Flora's eyes. 'The necklace wasn't mine, but I took it as a safeguard. If things got really desperate, I thought that at least I'd have a very expensive piece of jewellery to sell. But it's been bothering me ever since. Even when my life did turn really bad, I couldn't bring myself to sell it.' She paused and looked fixedly at the floor. 'I haven't been able to sleep easily for months, Flora,' she blurted out. 'I knew I had to return the darn thing.'

'You did what was right. In more ways than one, perhaps.

Taking the necklace was a pretty desperate act and it must have made your husband realise how badly he's treated you.'

'Something like that, I guess. He could see that I'd been driven to do something quite out of character and he's made sure now that I have enough to live on. But it's not a king's ransom and I could still do with some work if...'

'Could you come to the shop, say, twice a week?'

Rose clasped her by the hand. 'Truly?'

'I've been thinking about it for some time and now with our wedding so close and Jack – well, Jack's life is about to change a little – I've decided it might be the time to have a permanent assistant. How about Mondays and Fridays? Would that suit you?'

That would give her nearly four clear days, Flora thought, to enjoy her garden, read more books, be with Jack. Saturdays would be a half day and a time to bring herself up to date with what had been happening at the All's Well in her absence.

'I'd love it!' Rose reached out again to clasp Flora's hands. 'Can I start next Monday?'

'Why not? I'll be here for the day to ease you in. Ten minutes before opening time, mind – and that's nine o'clock sharp!'

31

It was Jack's suggestion that they hold a lunch party on Sunday in the Overlay garden, with Alice, Sally, Kate and Tony as their guests. It was the right time for a small celebration, he'd said to Flora. The crime conference was done and dusted and the murders it had spawned brought to a satisfying conclusion. He'd just found himself a new job and they were weeks away from getting married. There was plenty to celebrate.

Strolling through the French doors, he felt pride at the picture his garden presented: a trim lawn, colourful pyramids of sweet peas, and flower beds filled to bursting with phlox and hollyhocks and the deep blue of iris. On the paved terrace, pots of geraniums blazed red. A perfect backdrop for the forthcoming party, he reckoned, and felt slightly smug.

Flora's arrival at the front door put an end to any gloating.

'I know Alice is bringing those lovely little cheese pies she makes and Kate has baked a mountain of cakes – including your favourites, fondant fancies,' she said over her shoulder, bustling past him into the kitchen and carrying two overflowing baskets. 'So, I've stuck with sandwiches and a few bags of crisps. And, before you ask, ham features heavily in the selection. Oh, and I've bought some extra china, too.'

Jack followed her into the kitchen and peered hopefully into a basket. 'They look great. Just the job.' He gave a regretful sigh. 'I can't match everyone's culinary efforts, I'm afraid. I did pick strawberries, though – the last of the crop, I think – and this morning I whizzed to the grocer's for a tin of Carnation.'

'It should be a good lunch,' she said, and sounded satisfied.

Brushing her lips against his cheek, she was about to unpack the baskets she'd brought, when he reached out and caught hold of her, proceeding to kiss her very thoroughly. 'For the next few hours, I won't have a chance to do that,' he said, when at last he let her go. 'And today is special. We're embarking on a new life, you and me, and it's going to feel strange. But I've a feeling it will be fine.'

'It will be what we make it, I guess.' And ever practical, she added, 'Now, help me arrange the sandwiches. And have you washed the strawberries?'

'I have, maestro. In the big glass bowl over there.' He pointed to an enormous container sitting on the counter. 'And I've decanted the cream into an ancient jug I found – and don't ask, I did wash it first.'

Her hazel eyes were alight. 'As if I would! But seriously, Jack, I wanted to thank you for inviting Lowell today. I know he couldn't make it, but it was a nice gesture.'

'I thought he should be here, seeing how central he's been to both our lives these last few weeks.'

'He would have been but he wanted to see his folks in Bath – before he started Maud's old job. But he'll be back soon and no doubt raring to go.' She tilted her head. 'Was that the front door?'

It was, the knock heralding Alice, on foot and weighed down by another two baskets. Minutes later, Kate and Tony trundled up the lane in Tony's van, with Sally the last to join them in the garden, where Jack had arranged a circle of deckchairs and a foldaway table already groaning with food.

Sally hung her head. 'Sorry I'm late and I'm afraid I've just brought drink. No time to do anything else, the Priory is so busy. But it *is* champagne.'

'In that case, you can "just" bring drink any time,' Jack said. 'We've saved a deckchair for you.'

'The hotel is some busy,' Alice confirmed. 'I've been fair run off my feet these last couple of weeks. I'm thinkin', Sal, I'm goin' to need more help in the kitchen if it carries on like this.'

'Don't you have, who is it, Hector?' Flora arrived at the table with several more plates of sandwiches.

'Hector is Tony's replacement, so he's not extra,' Alice pointed out. 'He's a nice enough lad and good company when he's not talkin' about battles and all. Can't stop him chunterin' about them.'

'The lad is at least thirty years old,' Sally said.

'He's a lad to me. And he's doin' OK, but he'd do even better if he wasn't always away with the fairies thinkin' about what shield he'll carry, or what helmet will suit him.'

'What!' Flora gave a giggle.

'Those historical things, you know, where they all dress up and prance around pretendin' to be cavaliers and roundheads.'

'He'd make a very good cavalier,' Sally mused. 'Think of those wonderful hats!'

Alice gave a small snort. 'It's the cookin' I'm thinkin' of. He doesn't have your touch with the desserts,' she said to Tony, 'but he's got a light hand for soufflés, I will give him that. No, I'm thinkin' I should train a youngster up, permanent like, someone willin' to learn, not like that Joan, though she's a better kitchen maid than Ivy ever was. But learnin' to do more than peel veg is beyond her.'

'You've already got someone in mind, haven't you?' Sally took a sandwich from the plate Flora was offering and fixed her aunt with a severe look, while Jack opened the champagne with a loud bang. 'What are you plotting?'

'Not plottin', just thinkin' of the future. Charlie. I've got Charlie Teague in mind.'

'But he's a schoolboy,' her niece protested.

'Not any more, he isn't. He left school this summer and he's been helpin' me off and on for a while now. He's a good lad. He's interested in food.'

Jack and Flora grinned at each other. 'That's for sure,' Jack said.

'Not just eatin' either. He's shown a real flair in the kitchen.'

'And he can train at the Nook, too,' Kate put in. 'The boy was very good when we were catering for the conference.'

'He paid up, by the way,' Tony said suddenly. 'That Basil Webb. I thought we were going to have a problem there but his cheque went through last Friday.'

Jack was relieved. As one of the organisers of the event, he'd felt responsible for the Nook's plight, and had been crossing his fingers that Basil would pay what was owing as soon as he could.

'Charlie seems a good boy,' Sally conceded, 'and it's a probably sensible idea. Maybe I should consider taking on more staff generally. I'm going to need several more waiters and certainly more chambermaids. After the rocky start the Priory had, I've been cautious. I hadn't expected the hotel to take off with such a bang.'

'We'll see an even bigger bang when Dominic up and goes,' Alice said.

'Dominic is going?' This was news to Jack and, judging by her face, news to Flora, too.

'We've come to an arrangement,' Sally said primly. 'Neither of us think the partnership is working as it should. It hasn't been working well for some time. And Dominic is keen to do other things with his life.'

'Like loafin' around,' her aunt said caustically.

'The hotel is making sufficient for me to buy Dominic out,' Sally went on, ignoring the comment.

Flora's eyebrows shot up. 'You must have made an amazing profit!'

'Not that amazing.' Sally was quick to dampen any excitement. 'I'm taking on the loan that Dominic negotiated to pay his share of the hotel, that's what it amounts to. The bank thinks I'm now credit-worthy enough to manage it.'

'And no doubt Dominic will be walking away with a nice sum for himself.' Kate's usually mild tone held disapproval.

'Actually, no. I think he's just relieved to be free of the loan and now that he and I... well, you know... he doesn't really have a reason for staying around.'

'Amen to that,' Alice said. 'Make sure you don't make the same mistake again, my girl. Hector Lansdale is a good-looking chap, but Dominic is a warning if ever there was not to mix business with pleasure.'

'Let's drink to Sally's new venture – as sole proprietor of the Priory!' Jack said swiftly, raising his glass, and followed by a general clinking around the circle of chairs.

'We've heard there's a new venture for you, Jack. A new job!' Kate's pale blue eyes held a mischievous sparkle.

'There is,' he agreed. By now, most of Abbeymead would know, he thought resignedly. There was no chance of keeping the news to themselves. 'I drove over to Lewes yesterday, in fact, and met the principal. I was telling Flora about him. Professor Dalloway. He comes over as a bit of a martinet, but he seemed pleased I was joining the staff and obviously knew a fair amount about me and the books I've written.'

'I've heard it's a big place, that college,' Alice said. 'Here, eat up. I don't want to take any of them cheese pies back with me.'

'A big place that looks to be very well run. The grounds are stunning. I'll be working in the main building, a Queen Anne mansion no less, and with an office of my own.'

'Sounds lovely,' Sally said, 'but how will it work with your books? Will you still have time to write?'

'Three days a week was what the professor and I decided on, but I'm free to choose which days I work. I imagine it will depend for a large part on the students themselves – how they're progressing or not with whatever writing project they're engaged on. I'm also encouraged to offer lectures, workshops, on particular topics, if I think they'd be helpful.'

'An ideal job.' Tony took a swig of champagne. 'Working when you want, doing what you want, and getting paid for it!'

'Put like that, it sounds near to perfect.'

Jack heard himself sounding not quite so certain. On the surface, the job was the dream Tony suggested: to choose his own days of work, to decide exactly what he wanted to teach, if anything, and otherwise simply be there as a resource for students. But Cleve as a college hadn't felt that relaxed. He was remembering the stiffly aligned chairs in the staffroom and the grounds manicured to an inch. The few other teachers he'd met had seemed friendly enough, but also slightly wary. They probably *were* wary – of a new member of staff who'd negotiated such a cushy position. Another creative type with no idea of teaching, he could almost hear them mutter.

Alice held the teapot aloft, ready to pour everyone a second cup. 'Perfect or not, it's a long way to travel. That car of yours – it's not exactly reliable.'

'The Austin will do me proud,' he said stoutly, and saw Flora's amused expression. He knew what she was thinking. The car was his second love, his third after his books, and he was always ready to spring to its defence.

'And it will take you away from the village for days. How's that goin' to work when you're married?' Alice persisted.

'The job is term time only,' he batted back.

'We'll still see each other!' Flora added, laughingly 'We'll be living together. In my cottage.'

'And Overlay House?' Sally took a third slice of Battenberg. 'This is scrumptious, Kate.'

'The lease runs out at the end of October and I won't be renewing,' Jack said easily.

'I don't see why you'd need to take the job.' Alice was unconvinced. 'Flora's got this new money comin' – she's told us all about it. My goodness, what a sum! And you've got your books to write. Why complicate life with somethin' extra?'

'It will be a new challenge and we all need those from time to time.' It was Flora who answered. Jumping up from her chair, she said, 'I'll fetch the strawberries and cream. Best I dish them up in the kitchen or it will be too messy.'

Flora would defend his decision, he knew, even though she might share many of Alice's concerns.

'I'll go and help,' Kate offered, joining her friend on her way through the sitting room.

When the two were back again and bowls of strawberries and cream were in everyone's hands, Jack returned to the subject of his job. Flora had attempted to close the discussion down, but Alice still looked worried and he wanted to reassure her.

'Having a job with a salary will make writing less pressured. Needing to come up with a new book every year and ensure that it's a success is quite a burden.'

'I can see that, but Flora's goin' to be lookin' after the shop and lookin' after you and you won't be there to help her.'

'Jack can make a ham sandwich as well as I can!' Flora said briskly. 'And Rose Lawson will be working at the All's Well for two days a week. She starts tomorrow. It means I'll have time to do other things.'

'Not more snoopin', I hope.' Alice put down her empty bowl. 'My, those strawberries were some good.'

'More time to spend with Jack,' Flora remonstrated.

'If you've got Rose Lawson workin' for you, you'll not be needin' Charlie as much. Just as well then that I'm plannin' to take him on.'

Flora returned her empty bowl to the table, and wrapped her arms around her knees. 'With Charlie working at the Priory,' she said thoughtfully, 'I might have to find someone else to do my Friday deliveries. I can't ask Rose to cope with Betty and a heavy load. I have far more books to deliver now than I ever had.'

'It's high time you stopped deliveries.' Alice was decided. 'It was Violet's idea and she's not here any more. How many people in the village really need their books delivered? There's only a handful who aren't mobile and you could walk the books round to them.'

'I know, Alice, but—'

'It's misplaced loyalty if you think you've got to keep it goin'. You took on the All's Well when your aunt fell ill and you've done a brilliant job keepin' it as she wanted, but I don't think she'd have wanted you never to change things. Particularly if it causes problems.'

Flora said nothing, but Jack could see there was an inner tussle going on. A lull in the conversation had Tony collect up their empty bowls and carry the loaded tray back into the kitchen.

'This new job,' Alice said, when he came back. It was still on her mind, Jack could see, still bothering her. 'When does it start? It won't mess up the wedding again, I hope.'

'It won't,' he promised. 'I start next month but the principal knows I'm marrying in October and knows I'll be taking a week off.'

'Just a week?' Kate said. 'A short honeymoon then?'

'A later honeymoon,' Flora said. 'The week after our

wedding we'll be catching our breath, I think. We'll take a proper break when we've had a bit more space to plan.'

Kate brightened. 'That sounds exciting. Have you decided where?'

'Cornwall, I reckon,' Alice put in. 'You were talkin' about bringin' that Jessie up to help with the wedding.'

Flora shook her head. 'Having Jessie to help with the catering is a great idea, but I'm not sure we'd want to go back to Treleggan.'

'France then?' Tony said.

'One day. I want to return to Vaison, see my parents again, but for a honeymoon it has to be somewhere new.'

'This is getting more exciting by the minute.' Sally laughed out loud, blonde curls bouncing.

'It is exciting,' Flora replied calmly. 'We thought we'd go to Venice.'

There was a hush until broken by Alice. 'Dangerous place, Flora,' she said. 'All them canals. I shouldn't do that. Best stay home.'

Sally let out another gale of laughter, while Jack and Flora exchanged a look and together breathed a silent sigh.

32

Glancing up at Jack's kitchen clock, Flora was surprised to see that it was almost four in the afternoon. Their guests had stayed a long time talking and the subsequent clearing of dishes seemed to have gone on for ever.

Jack had just hung up the last tea towel. 'That was quite a lunch. Exhausting but delicious food and great company.'

'The food *was* delicious. I'm not sure about the company, though. Alice was in one of her twitchy moods, determined to find fault.'

'She's worried, that's all. Things are changing and she doesn't like change.'

'*Her* life isn't changing,' Flora pointed out. 'Except for the advent of Charlie. That was a surprise, wasn't it?'

'Not so much for me. He mentioned the idea of training with Alice the other week. He seems to have a real interest in cooking – and he'll need a job this autumn. But you'll miss his help at the bookshop.'

'I will, but it's his future, if training as a chef is what he wants to do. To be honest, I hadn't thought of him leaving school.'

'Fifteen in May. It's crept up, hasn't it? Apart from an inability to prop his bike against the wall, he's lost a lot of his boyishness. It's been quite noticeable this last year.' Jack picked up his house keys from the kitchen counter. 'Have you packed all the stuff you brought?'

'In my baskets.' She pointed to the heavy wicker panniers at her feet.

'I'll walk them back to the cottage with you.'

Wandering slowly along the lane towards Flora's home, he said, 'At least with all the news of Dominic leaving the Priory and Charlie starting work in the kitchens, there wasn't much time to talk weddings. No rundown from Alice on how preparations are going. We escaped unscathed!'

'Not for long, I imagine, and the Dominic thing was another surprise. Though a good one.'

'You never much liked him, did you?'

'I never trusted him. Sally will do much better on her own.'

'If she stays on her own. Did you catch the mention of Hector? Alice evidently spies trouble ahead.'

'Hopefully, he'll be too busy playing at fighting when he's not cooking.'

'Poor Alice.' He shifted the baskets into one hand. 'Did we really need this extra china? First she loses Tony to the Nook and now she's worried she could lose Hector – to a re-enactment society!'

'Who's that?' Flora peered ahead. 'Outside my front door. It can't be Lowell.'

But it was. 'Hello,' he called out cheerily as they approached. 'I thought I'd call by before I start work tomorrow. I hoped you'd be in.'

'I was imagining you still in Bath,' she said. 'When did you get back?'

'Yesterday, a day earlier than I intended, but Inspector

Ridley phoned – I didn't know he had my parents' number – and asked me to call at Brighton police station.'

'You're not in any more trouble?'

He beamed. 'Just the opposite. I'm flavour of the month! They wanted me there to identify a book.'

Flora stared, her mouth slightly open. 'Not... not...'

'*A Christmas Carol*? The very same.'

'Where was it found?' Jack intervened.

'Where I suggested in the first place.' Lowell sounded smug. 'I was right all along. Maud took the book home with her the night before she was murdered. I imagine she did it for safe keeping.'

'But the safe was wide open,' Flora protested. 'It looked as if the book had been stolen. Why didn't she lock the safe behind her?'

'Like I said before – Maud's memory was beginning to play tricks. Maybe she simply forgot to close the safe that evening and didn't notice it was still open when she walked in the next morning.'

'Was it the police who found it?' Jack asked.

Lowell shook his head. 'Maud's family. The police had searched but found nothing. When her family started clearing her house last week, they're putting it up for sale apparently, they found the book in the attic – tucked into an empty flour bin!'

'Maud *was* a keen baker.' Flora was unsure whether to laugh or shed a tear. 'Sorry, Lowell, you were saying?'

'They're not book people,' he went on, 'but they said it looked special and it was an odd place to keep a book, so they thought they should tell the police. I think the detective sergeant had mentioned earlier that an important book was missing.'

'The Dickens wasn't stolen,' Flora said softly, talking almost to herself.

'Safe and sound. Even better, the mobile library has definitely been promised the proceeds once the book is sold at auction. Anyway, folks, I won't keep you. It looks like you've had a busy day.' He gestured to the baskets that Jack had dumped on the front path. 'I just wanted to say thanks for giving me a bed, Flora. You were a pal when I needed one. And thanks to both of you for getting me off the hook.'

Flora gave him a swift kiss while Jack offered his hand. 'Make sure you enjoy Maud's job now you've got it,' she said, smilingly.

'Come and check on me. I'll be parked on the green next week.'

'I might just do that!' she threatened, and waved him goodbye.

Jack was already unpacking plates and bowls when she walked into the kitchen. He turned as she came through the door. 'And yet another surprise! It's been quite a day for them!'

'Let's hope that's the last for a while.'

'No chance. We still have Venice. Remember – all those canals! They could be the death of us.'

'Not to mention the lagoon!' Flora finished emptying the second wicker basket, returning the last few bowls to their usual cupboard.

'I think it's best we don't mention either,' he said. 'Keep our plans secret until everything's arranged.'

'For next summer maybe?' Her face brightened at the thought.

'Perfect. Something amazing to look forward to. But there are a fair few days before then. Any idea how we'll fill them?' Jack's expression was bland.

'Mmm. I might need to think about it,' she said.

'Really?'

'No, not really.' And wrapping her arms around him, Flora pulled him close.

A LETTER FROM MERRYN

Dear Reader

I want to say a huge thank you for choosing to read *The Library Murders*. If you enjoyed the book and want to keep up to date with all my latest releases, just sign up at the following link. Your email address will never be shared, and you can unsubscribe at any time.

www.bookouture.com/merryn-allingham

The 1950s is a fascinating period, outwardly conformist but beneath the surface there's rebellion brewing, even in the rural heartlands of southern England! It's a beautiful part of the world and I hope Flora's and Jack's exploits have entertained you. If so, you can follow their fortunes in the next Flora Steele Mystery or discover their earlier adventures, beginning with *The Bookshop Murder*.

If you enjoyed *The Library Murders*, I would love a short review. Getting feedback from readers is amazing and it helps new readers to discover one of my books for the first time. And do get in touch on my Facebook page, through Twitter, Goodreads or my website – I love to chat.

Thank you for reading,

Merryn x

KEEP IN TOUCH WITH MERRYN

www.merrynallingham.com

 facebook.com/MerrynWrites
x.com/merrynwrites

PUBLISHING TEAM

Turning a manuscript into a book requires the efforts of many people. The publishing team at Bookouture would like to acknowledge everyone who contributed to this publication.

Audio
Alba Proko
Sinead O'Connor
Melissa Tran

Commercial
Lauren Morrissette
Jil Thielen
Imogen Allport

Data and analysis
Mark Alder
Mohamed Bussuri

Cover design
The Brewster Project

Editorial
Jayne Osborne
Imogen Allport

9 781837 908462